I0736220

NEVER-ENDING NIGHTMARE

AMANDA BOOLOODIAN

DEDICATION

For silver, thank you for learning to format. All by yourself, with no help at all.

CONTENTS

Chapter 1	1
Chapter 2	11
Chapter 3	21
Chapter 4	30
Chapter 5	43
Chapter 6	56
Chapter 7	70
Chapter 8	82
Chapter 9	89
Chapter 10	99
Chapter 11	111
Chapter 12	124
Chapter 13	136
Chapter 14	151
Chapter 15	165
Chapter 16	179
Chapter 17	188
Chapter 18	201
Chapter 19	213
Chapter 20	220
Chapter 21	238
Chapter 22	252
Chapter 23	262
Chapter 24	270
Chapter 25	285
Complete Works	295
About the Author	297

CHAPTER
ONE

The seatbelt harness crinkled in my grip. The truck barreled down the road, swerving around everything that got in the way.

Why, why, why, did I ever let Rider drive?

"Maybe you should slow down a little," I suggested, trying to sound casual.

"The office said that it was important," Rider said.

"Which is why we should arrive alive."

Rider chuckled, but thankfully slowed down.

When it felt safe enough to let go of the death grip I had on the seatbelt, I stretched out my fingers and grabbed my phone.

Still no call.

It wasn't like I wouldn't have noticed if it rang. During the drive to the office, I probably checked to make sure the volume was up two, three... or maybe seven times.

"I am sure that he meant to call," Rider said.

"Of course," I lied, not believing it for a second.

"He will be home tomorrow."

The he, of course, was Vincent. He'd been gone for almost three weeks and had only called three times.

Correction, he'd only called *me* three times. Apparently, he called Rider several times more than that. Hell, he'd called the office more often than he called me.

"Gran said he won't make it back tomorrow," I said, my heart falling a little at the thought.

"Did she say why he would not be back?"

"No, only that she didn't see him tomorrow in any of her visions, and didn't even think he'd be around later this week."

"Maybe you should call him to make sure he is okay."

What could I say to that? I had already left two messages. Anything more would seem needy or anxious... or something. How could he kiss me and run away like that?

Okay, I get why he ran away. There wasn't much of a choice with a changeling attacking. To save us all, he had to go. But then to barely hear from him?

"It's no big deal," I said. "I'm sure he's fine."

"Friends should not lie to each other."

I sighed and stared out the window. "This lie is more for me than you."

"If you would let me tell him—"

"No." I couldn't stress the word enough. "I appreciate the gesture, but it's really not a big deal. At least it shouldn't be. His sister needs him—he doesn't need to be worried about me right now. Have you worked everything out with him?"

"I think he is upset, but it is hard to tell over the phone. Do you think that is why he is not coming back tomorrow?"

"No. If he weren't planning on coming back, he would have at least let Hank know. Maybe something popped up at the last minute."

"That is possible."

Whether intentionally or not, Rider had sped up again. I

closed my eyes when he swerved across the road and into the driveway of the Farm. I was surprised that the tires didn't squeal when he came to a stop at the first gate.

"Are you coming with us to see Essy tomorrow?" Rider asked.

"Are you taking the horses?"

"Logan said that we cannot ride the horses while the Griffin is living out there."

Logan was my usual partner. With Vincent gone, Rider was working with us.

"Makes sense. I'll let you all know in the morning." It would technically be my day off, but my mind tended to wander when I wasn't working. If I let that happen, I'd start thinking Vincent wasn't coming home because of me.

Is he not coming home because I'm here?

I shoved the thought away, not allowing it to go any further.

Would the four of us working together be awkward if Vincent and I started to see each other? It was hard to say for sure, but I was getting ahead of myself. It was possible that Vincent had changed his mind about wanting to be with me. We'd only had a few minutes together before he had to be all heroic and disappear.

And we hadn't exactly spent our short time talking.

We took the winding road within the Farm faster than anyone should until we reached the second gate in record time, which didn't seem to faze the guard.

"We could go hiking after," Rider suggested.

"It depends on the weather. It's getting really cold."

"It might give you a chance to practice Reading."

Everything in this world leaves traces. As a Reader, the Path showed me where people and even objects have moved through an area. On a good day, I could Read the past for days, and sometimes, even weeks in the past. On rare occasions, the Path pushed me into the future, which was interesting and sometimes a little scary, not that I'd ever admit it.

Now, though, I tried not to use the Path unless necessary. Over the past few weeks, things had changed. If I didn't meditate consistently to keep myself in the right state of mind, Reading was like a cold spike through my mind. Not only that, but something else had moved into the Path. Whatever it was, I'd only seen it out of the corner of my eye.

It creeped me out.

Maybe if I went far enough away from civilization, I'd be alone once again in the Path. "You're right, we should go. Count me in." One day in the cold wouldn't hurt.

The parking lot was virtually full when we arrived. A month ago, this would have been a rare occurrence. Now, we had investigators and DC staff in and out of the office constantly.

Technically, we weren't under investigation, but the first week the newcomers were town had been awful. I left the office on medical leave and went to help MyTH, but the DC folks called every day trying to reach me. Kyrian pushed back, but with a missing agent, there was only so much she could do. Once Vincent returned, the bureaucracy finally started to leave me alone.

With all the out-of-town visits still happening, we actually had someone manning the front desk. He looked flustered and only nodded when he saw us walk in.

Once we passed through the last major security checkpoint, we were able to use our keycards to enter the main control room. Desks were scattered around the room and every one was in use. The conference rooms around the edge of the room appeared to be occupied as well.

Hank wasn't manning his station in the center of the room,

his usual position. Another handler, Red, worked the big screens while scanning satellite readings.

"I think we need to find an office," Rider said.

I curled my nose up at the idea. While working in my office, I'd nearly been killed once and another time I found a fellow agent dead.

Experiences in my office had never turned out well.

"Agent Heidrich?" asked someone coming up to us.

"Yes?" I couldn't place the person. With so many new people around, I couldn't say if the person was new or if he had worked here for ages.

"The director would like to see you," he said. "She's in her office."

"Thanks." I started in that direction, but was brought up short.

"She asked to see you alone," he said, glancing nervously at Rider.

Rider can take people like that the first time they meet him. He appeared Native American and stood around six-and-a-half feet tall. Some people were intimidated by someone that towered over them.

"I'll catch up with you," I said. "Try to find a desk out here if you can."

Being asked to the director's office used to feel like being called into the principal's office. Over the past year, I had gotten to know Kyrian a little and I'd become more comfortable in my job, which made the experience not quite so bad.

At least that's what I told myself.

"Come in," Kyrian called after I knocked on the door.

"You wanted to see me?" I asked, poking my head in.

"Yes. Come in, and please close the door."

I took a seat opposite her.

"Our relations with other branches of AIR are a little

strained right now," Kyrian said. "Which can happen with situations like we had last month. Several good agents were lost, along with their families."

It was hard not to shift uncomfortably, but I managed it. We hadn't done anything wrong, but we were involved all the same.

"The branches that work closely with the military are especially estranged from us." Kyrian looked at me expectantly.

I had no idea what I could even say to that, so I just nodded and replied, "Okay."

"Over the past year, several other departments have requested temporary assistance from some of our more skilled agents."

My heart started to sink. Was she getting ready to tell me that Logan was going away or that Vincent wouldn't be coming back at all?

"I've said no to all of these. This time, however, I'm leaving the decision to you."

"To me?" *Did that come out squeaky*? I cleared my throat before continuing. "Why me?"

"There is high demand for a Reader. In this case, though, Agent Boone has requested your assistance on an upcoming assignment."

I frowned. Asking for help wasn't something I expected from Boone. "What type of assistance?"

"I'm afraid the entire assignment is classified. Even if you agree, I have very little information to give."

"How long would I be gone?"

"Unknown at this time."

"Is there anything you can tell me?"

"Only that Agent Boone has personally asked for your help."

"Is it only me he wants?"

"If you agree, your team would accompany you—if they choose."

A friend needed help, so there was only one thing I could say. "I'll do it, but I can't speak for the others."

"Very good." Kyrian took a tablet out of a drawer and slid it across the desk. "Here is the information. You'll be traveling tonight to an undisclosed military instillation. There, you will meet Agent Boone and take his lead."

I put in my password and clicked on the only file on the tablet. "A nightmare?" I asked, reading the description.

"Yes. There is almost nothing on them on file. Two cave paintings were discovered in the past, one in Africa and one in Asia. Legends and rumor say the picture is a nightmare."

I scrolled down to find the pictures. The drawings looked completely different from each other. One was barely distinguishable and might have been an animal. Then again, with the amount of detail it showed, it could have been a boat. There wasn't even enough on the page to recognize it was a drawing.

The other was more pronounced. It looked like a deer or antelope with two long tails.

"I'm not sure how long you'll be gone," Kyrian said, "but I am making it very clear to Agent Boone that you are to come back. This is a temporary transfer only."

"Of course," I said, still studying the picture.

"Your team is too valuable to let go. Once Hank is filled in, he'll have some paperwork for you to sign and he'll start the itinerary. You leave tonight. Send Logan in to me next." The dismissal was clear.

Tonight? That was fast. "Thanks. I guess I'll see you when I get back."

Kyrian was staring at something on her monitor. "Get it done quickly."

Whatever 'it' is. "We will." I turned off the tablet and left before it got awkward.

Back in control central, Rider was chatting with Logan by the desk where Hank and Red were shifting places. Hank was usually the first person to arrive and the last person to leave. Over the past few weeks, he'd been coming and going with Logan every now and again. Logan was an early morning person, but I think Logan and Hank had better ways to spend their time together than worry about work.

Other people could take over when Red and Hank weren't there, at least in theory. The fact was they both reigned over the area and their charges almost constantly. When things were slower, though, I'd caught other people sitting there, looking as though they were making the most of their time in the hot seat.

Logan tipped his hat to me, a large Stetson that he wore almost constantly. "Howdy, partner." He nodded at the hallway I had just entered through. "Everything okay?"

"Um, I'm not sure. It's a new case."

Logan raised an eyebrow and glanced at Hank, who hadn't settled in yet.

"He doesn't know," I said hurriedly. "In fact, I agreed to go, but I said I didn't speak for you all. It's up to you."

"Go?" Logan was frowning now.

"Yeah."

"Where?"

"I don't know, really."

"For how long?"

"No idea. But Kyrian said to come back quickly, so it can't be that long."

Logan nodded. "What's the assignment?"

I bit my lip, not wanting to tell him again that I had no details.

He guessed the truth. "You don't know?"

I leaned in and spoke softly, not that I needed to get closer. Rider and Logan could have heard me if I whispered across the room. "I don't know much. Something called a nightmare."

Even with the Path closed, I felt the flash of anger from Logan. "You and I are going to have a few words about this."

It was so unlike Logan that it took me off guard. "Look," I started, "Agent Boone—"

"Hank," Logan barked, "we need a conference."

Looking uneasy, Hank left Red after a few words. He grabbed his tablet and led the way to a room.

"Kyrian wants to talk to you," I said as we went down the hall.

"I'll bet she does." Logan pushed his way into a conference room. He didn't even bother to wait for the door to be closed before he turned on me. "Do you have any idea what you're doing?"

I crossed my arms and glared at him. "I'm doing my job. What's your problem?"

"You agreed for us to go after a nightmare?" Logan asked.

"I agreed that *I* would go help a friend. You and Rider can do what you want."

"I will go—"

"Of course you will," Logan cut Rider off. "Because both of you have no idea what you're doing. Hank, what is this about?"

Hank had been tapping on his tablet and scanning documents. He didn't look happy. "Honestly, there's not much here. You're being loaned out for a military operation."

"Military?" Logan asked.

"Agent Boone asked for my help," I snapped, trying to get a full sentence in.

"You don't have the slightest idea—"

"No, I don't!" I leaned over the table and glared at Logan.

"I'm not asking you to come along, but if you know what this is, you can quit complaining and make yourself useful."

It felt as though all the air had been sucked out of the room, but I wasn't about to back down. I couldn't tell if Logan was going to explode, leave, or laugh. Rider subtly adjusted his stance and Hank's eyes were glued to his tablet, but he didn't appear to be focusing.

Finally, Logan let out a deep breath of air and dropped into a seat. "You're right."

Still glaring, I slowly sat opposite him.

"Hank," Logan said, "tell us what we have."

Hank started rattling off what few details I had been given plus a few I hadn't—including the request period, which ended when the assignment was complete or in two months, whichever came first.

I tried not to cringe. Maybe Logan was right to get upset. Two months would mean two more months of waiting to see Vincent.

Crap, what have I done?

CHAPTER

TWO

"You don't have to go," I reminded Logan when Hank finished with the scarce details of the case.

"Do you want us to?" Logan asked.

The question took me off guard. I had never worked without my team for more than a few days, and even then it wasn't by choice. I had been trapped in another world.

"I don't want you to do something you don't want to." It was the best answer I had, because *of course,* I wanted them with me.

"Hank, can we have a few minutes?" Logan asked.

"I'll be at my desk," Hank said, not catching anyone's eye on the way out.

Logan didn't say anything when the door was closed, and I soon felt the need to fill the silence.

"If you want to stay, it's not a problem." The last traces of my agitation were trying to hang on, but I managed to sound sincere.

"I want you to stay," Logan said. "*That's* the problem."

"What? Why?"

"Because you shouldn't be dealing with a nightmare."

"Do you know what it is?"

"I got an idea, yeah." He took off his hat and dropped it on the table. "I wasn't sure until I saw the pictures, but that's pretty damming evidence."

"What is it?"

"No one really knows for sure," Logan said. "I've heard stories on two different worlds about them. The name says it all. They are nightmares. They don't kill, mostly because they don't have to. They make you live out your worst nightmares until you either kill yourself or those around you—friends or family, it doesn't matter."

"Have you ever seen one?"

"Never. I'd rather run into another vampire than one of them. At least with a vampire they're the ones doing the killing."

"Boone wouldn't have asked for my help unless he really needed it."

"I'm not too happy he's put you in this situation, but I understand. I shouldn't have gotten riled up over it. It sounds like we need to move quickly. I'll go see Kyrian."

"You're coming?" I asked.

"I said I didn't want *you* to go," Logan said, snatching his hat back up. "It sounds like just the tussle for me."

"What about you?" I asked Rider as Logan left the room. "Are you sure you want to go? Vincent might be back in a couple of days."

"Vincent will understand," Rider said.

"Do you want to call him and let him know?" I asked.

"You should call," Rider said. I opened my mouth to disagree, but Rider wouldn't let me. "Tell him I will be going with you." He hurried out of the room, not allowing me a chance to reply.

I pulled out my phone and stared at it. It felt as though pixies were tying knots inside my chest. There was good reason for me to call now, though. I had an excuse. I forced myself to take a deep breath and then hit his contact icon.

The phone rang several times before going to voicemail. I half expected it, but it hurt all the same.

I couldn't help but think that this was so unlike me. Sure, I liked Vincent, but I shouldn't let myself worry about what might or might not happen.

"We're going out of town for an assignment," I said to the voicemail. "I don't know where we'll be or how long we'll be gone, and you won't be able to reach me. I'll talk to you when I get back."

Short and simple. That was the way to go.

I hung up the phone and tried to rearrange my attitude. Vincent was going to do whatever it was he was going to do. If he wanted to be with me, great. If not... well, life would move on.

LOGAN BROUGHT Hank with us when we left, which came as a surprise. There was plenty of room in the truck for four, but Hank was our handler, so it seemed odd to have him in the work truck with us.

By the time we got to my house, I was starting to realize that I had no idea what I was doing. "What should I pack?" I asked as I got out of the truck.

"The usual," Logan said.

"We work for an agency that monitors other dimensions and work with races that no one even knows exist," I said. "There is no usual."

Rider chuckled.

"Layers," Hank suggested as I ushered them into the house. "Whenever you don't know where you're going, layers are good. In this case, though, Agent Boone said he'll have everything you need."

A loud screech and a thump sounded from inside the house, followed by paws scrabbling across the floor. What looked like a large house cat ran into the room, its shrill voice ready to break eardrums.

"What the hell is that?" Hank asked.

Logan stepped between Hank and the oncoming flight of fur.

"Molly, no!" I said, trying to sound stern. The truth was, she was so darn cute I had a hard time making any demands of her. Sure, she was an ichneu, a mythological animal that could slay a dragon, but it was hard to imagine her doing that. At least when she looked like this.

Molly slowed and hopped up onto the back of the couch. She hissed at Hank. Beautiful wings, which most of the time went unnoticed, slowly spread out.

"Hank, would you mind stepping carefully forward and holding out your hand for Molly to smell?" I asked.

"What the hell is that?" Hank asked.

"It's one of those off-the-record things we discussed," Logan said.

"Molly is Gran's pet," I said. "She's an ichneu."

Logan stepped aside, but Hank wasn't in a hurry to hold his hand out. Molly let out a low rumbling growl. Whenever she made that noise, I always wanted to look around for the much larger animal that must surely be making it.

"Never heard of them," Hank said.

"They're almost extinct. Think of her as a kind of a watchdog for Gran and me. Watch cat, rather."

"A winged guard cat?" Hank very slowly moved his hand out.

Molly hissed again and showed fangs.

Hank froze.

"It's okay," I said. And it was, as long as Gran or I was in the house. If it looked like someone was going to hurt one of us, however, Molly would spring into action. She was a gift from Gran's old boyfriend. It was sweet that he wanted to keep her safe. The man aggravated the hell out of me. He was crazy and I didn't trust him, but I trusted that he wanted to help Gran. It kept me safe at the same time, which was an unintentional side effect that he could live with.

For a minute, I thought I was going to have to pick up Molly to introduce the two. She didn't like to be picked up while she was meeting someone for the first time, but I knew she'd let me.

After a few moments, Hank moved closer again. Molly sniffed him, and then jumped off the back of the couch. She started circling Hank.

"Do you want anything to drink?" I asked, heading toward the kitchen.

"Am I allowed to move?" Hank asked.

"She'll be done shortly," I said.

Rider followed me into the kitchen while Logan stayed in the living room with Hank.

I stopped short. "Gran? I didn't realize you were home."

Gran stood staring into space.

"Gran?" I called again.

She didn't respond, but I wasn't going to try to interrupt her. Gran was a psychic. When she had a vision, she would sometimes stare at nothing. She usually gave some indication that she heard you, though, even mid prediction.

"Margaret?" Rider moved around the island and began to circle Gran. "She does not appear to be injured."

"How can you tell?" I believed him, but I'd been wanting to know how he could find injuries on those around him.

"Smell." Rider circled again before joining me. "Has she ever done this before?"

"Not like this." Unsure of what to do, I went to her. "Gran?" Still no response.

I picked up her hand and called to her once more.

She blinked a few times, and then focused on me. "Cassie?"

"Are you okay?" I asked. "Come sit down."

"Of course, I'm fine, sugar. When did you get home?" She sounded a little distant, as though her mind were elsewhere.

"A few minutes ago," I said.

"Everything good?" Logan asked, coming in with Hank.

Gran smiled. "Hank, it's good to see you again. You all have a seat. I've got some tea in the fridge."

"I'll get it," I said, moving to intercept her. "Have a seat, Gran."

Gran sat down with the others and started chatting, sounding like herself again. Rider seemed unfazed. Logan watched her carefully for a few minutes, but seemed satisfied that she was okay.

Everyone declined tea, but I brought Gran a glass anyway.

"Cassie never mentioned she was goin' anywhere," Gran said.

I sat down next to her. "We just found out."

"Where to?" Gran said.

I glanced at Hank, who shrugged.

"We fly out tonight, but we're shy on the details," Logan said.

"Speaking of which," I said, "any other advice on what to pack, beyond layers?"

"It's hard to say," Logan said. "Think of what you would have wanted with you on your last trip with Boone."

I frowned, not liking to remember my time in the gremlin world. "There's no way to fit a shower in my bag."

Logan chuckled. "You'd be surprised. I think Boone will take care of the big stuff. Anything personal that you want to bring along to make your life easier, pack it."

"You have a plane to catch in five hours," Hank said. "So you may want to pack fast."

"I should go," Rider said.

"We'll pick you up on the way to the airport," Logan said.

"Thank you," Rider said. "Margaret, we shall meet again when I return."

Gran smiled. "You take care of yourself and my grand-daughter. That goes for you too," she said to Logan.

For a moment, I thought I detected a trace of worry in her face, but it quickly disappeared.

"We should head out also," Logan said. "We'll be back in a few hours."

Logan and Hank slipped out the back door. A quick walk across a small field and Logan was home. Our backyards prac-tically touched.

"Do you have to leave so quickly?" Gran asked.

Little alarm bells went off in my head. Gran had never before seemed overly concerned about when I came and went.

"Agent Boone asked for our help on something," I said.

"I don't think you should go."

I bit my lip and tried to think of what to say. "Is something going to happen?"

"I'm not sure," Gran said. "I can't see it. There's something, but I just can't see it. I keep tryin', it's just not comin'."

"Trying to force it isn't going to help," I reminded her. It was a lesson that she'd taught over and over again while I was growing up. "Is that what you were doing when we got home?"

"I thought I caught the tail of somthin', but when I looked for it, there was nothin'."

"Do you want me to stay?" I asked. She was probably the only person in the world that I'd change my mind for. Well, maybe Vincent.

Maybe.

"It's probably nothin'. No, darlin'. Your friend needs your help."

"If you need me—"

"I'm fine," Gran insisted. "Besides, Dee Dee and I are plannin' a trip to the casino."

"There are no casinos around here."

"It's one of them bus trips. They put a bunch of us seniors together and take us someplace with a bit more fun. There's no use in you staying, since I'll be gone."

"Can you leave Molly alone in the house?" I asked.

"Your mother will come take care of her."

"She will?"

"Of course she will. I took care of all her dead plants the last time she went away."

I grinned. "They're fake, not dead. Besides, didn't you throw a bunch of them away?"

"I did her a favor. Those things needed to go." Gran seemed every inch her normal self.

"I'll check in with you when I can."

Upstairs, I found myself wondering what I needed to bring with me. Remembering my time in the gremlin world, my first thought was fresh socks and underwear. After that, I was at a loss. I added two pairs of jeans, some shirts—long and short sleeve—and a jacket. Toiletries took longer. A toothbrush and hairbrush were essential, but the rest I balked at.

Realizing I might be gone for as long as two months, I added a few more shirts and pants. More socks, underwear and a cardigan later. I had a large suitcase full of stuff.

I grabbed a backpack and started to pare down the heap of items into a more manageable lump.

I went from too many clothes, to too few, and then back again. At that point, I realized I was being ridiculous and went back to Logan's original advice.

When I finished packing the last time, I left the room to prevent myself from adding or taking away anything else.

Downstairs, Gran handed me a bottle of painkillers. Hoping I wouldn't actually need them, I tossed them into the bag before adding some instant coffee. I was trying to cut down on caffeine, but sometimes my powers needed the boost caffeine provided. Boone wouldn't have asked for me if it weren't important, so I snagged whatever I might be able to use to gain an edge.

"At least we don't have to worry about your mother meetin' Frank." Gran said. She never was too fond of my zombie rabbit.

"It's strange, but I miss the little fluffer, but I think his new home will be good for him and we can save Mom from pitching a fit."

"What does Vincent say about all this?" Gran asked.

"I haven't had a chance to talk with him. I left him a message, so I'm sure he'll call soon." I seriously hated that I was starting to worry once again about what Vincent would or would not do, so I shoved it out of my mind. "Do you need anything before I go?"

"I'm good. You have everything?"

"I think so."

"Socks and underclothes?"

"Yes."

"Did you bring a jacket?"

"I have one."

Did you pack your gun?"

Damn. "You know, there aren't many grandmothers that would make sure a gun is on my packing list."

"Well, not many grandmothers have a granddaughter that saves people who need savin'."

I gave her a quick hug and ran upstairs to grab my gun and a holster.

CHAPTER

THREE

"Are you *sure* we're supposed to be here?" I asked Logan for the third time.

The airstrip was small, unlit, and apparently deserted.

"This is where Hank sent us, this is where we should be," Logan said.

Rider crinkled his nose up over and over again.

"What's wrong?" I asked.

"The smells," he said.

"Is anyone around?" I asked.

"There are at least two in the hangar over yonder," Logan said.

"Three," Rider corrected.

Logan appeared to listen intently. "Is there a fourth in the plane?"

"I am not certain," Rider said.

I was standing close enough to Logan that even in the dark I could see him unfurl his ears. I couldn't tell how far away the hangar was, but it looked as though more than just a football field would fit between the building and us.

"Three outside and a fourth in the plane," Logan said. "And they're getting ready to bring out our ride."

My partners amazed me. "They didn't happen to mention where we're going, did they?"

"Only that it's a military base," Logan said. "Nothing we didn't already know."

The hangar doors opened, letting light spill out. A few minutes later, the plane had been maneuvered onto the airstrip.

Someone in a golf cart zipped over to us.

"If you would like to join me," the man said, "the pilot is almost ready to leave. Ladies in front."

I rolled my eyes, but took the seat in the cart anyway. Behind me, a quick, whispered conversation took place far too low to hear.

As we approached, I was hoping we were farther away from the machine than it appeared. The aircraft wasn't getting any larger as we approached. When I think plane, I think of large, jet-fueled flying machines.

This had propellers. At least it had two of them instead of just one, but I had never flown in something so small.

The man pulled to a stop and jumped out. "We have her fueled and ready to go."

I slung my backpack over my shoulders and gripped the straps. "How far are we going in this?"

"A little over two hundred and fifty miles," the man said. "That's where you'll meet up with your next plane."

Somehow, I managed not to sigh. "Next plane?"

"I'm afraid you'd have to make several stops in this plane to reach your final destination, so you're meeting up with another one."

"Which is where?" Logan asked.

"I'm not at liberty to say," the man said. "Now, please board and we can get you on your way."

The plane was roomier than it looked—at least until Rider got in. Sometimes, I forgot how tall he was until we get into a small space.

"It's a good thing we traveled light," I said, watching my friend twist in his seat trying to make room for his legs.

"I cannot say I've ever been in this type of vehicle," Rider said.

"But you've flown before, right?" I knew he had flown at least once, but a helicopter ride while unconscious and bleeding out probably didn't count.

"Once, but the plane was much larger," Rider said.

"Hard not to be," I said under my breath.

"Everyone ready?" the pilot asked, raising his voice to be heard from up front.

"Ready," Logan called out.

The plane wasn't quite as loud as I thought it would be, but once it was in the sky, small pockets of air made the little plane dance around. More than once, I gripped tightly onto the seat belt, which was more like the ones you see in a car rather than in commercial airliners.

I kept a close eye on Rider, just in case the experience bothered him, but once we were in the sky, he had his eyes glued to the world below, apparently fascinated by what he saw. Logan had on a headset and was chatting away with the pilot. By the time we touched down, my knuckles were white from my nervous grip and I was happy to reach the ground.

We landed at a regular-sized airport, but on a smaller runway far away from the larger aircraft. My first thought was, *Oh crap, not another toy plane.* There were plenty of them around after all. Instead, we walked across part of the airstrip to what looked like a larger private plane with all the modern systems that I expected in a plane.

There were soldiers around, including one that ushered us on board.

For some reason, I thought we'd be traveling alone or through regular airports, but inside were quite a few people. I immediately felt underdressed. There were military men and women along with other people that wore severe-looking suits. Everyone on the plane had an air of importance that made me nervous.

The looks of impatience given by some, along with the fact that the door closed directly after us, told me that the plane had been held for us, and it wasn't appreciated by the others on-board. Some of the passengers appeared curious about our arrival, which I also wasn't comfortable with. Something told me that these people knew exactly where they were going and why they were there, whereas we were still in the dark.

Which was fine, as long as they didn't ask us any probing questions.

At least Rider had more room here. Even with over a dozen people, we weren't crowded and I shouldn't have worried about awkward questions.

Mostly because Rider fell asleep when we were only a few minutes in the air and he sprawled out, taking up a lot of space. I envied his ability to sleep. Too many unanswerable questions were running through my mind. Hopefully Boone had an answer for most of them. Logan stayed alert and watchful—appearing more nervous about those around us than about what lay ahead.

Thankfully, the trip was only about two hours, but I was feeling grungy and tired by the time we landed.

This time, when we got off the plane, there were armed guards. It was a military base, so I guess it had to be expected, but considering the people on the plane, especially the generals, I wouldn't have expected the escort to be quite so large. Each one of them looked ready to fire the weapon they were holding as well, which wasn't a great comfort.

The small building they led us to had two men behind a tall desk. They checked IDs and also read from a list of people who were expected. It took more than five minutes to process each person. The new arrivals had to sign forms, and some of them were escorted down the halls or out of the building with soldiers that—even though they were armed—looked less likely to expect trouble.

Our team gravitated toward the back of the queue. I took special note of the officers that walked away without people tagging along. Logan seemed to be keeping a close eye on certain people as well. No doubt, he was hearing the low conversations held between the new arrivals and those behind the desk.

Rider was trying to look everywhere at once.

When it was our turn, we approached the desk as a group.

"IDs," the man said.

As I handed mine over, I saw that his nametag read Simms.

He studied each agency ID, front and back. "Driver's license."

We handed those over as well.

Once again, he checked front and back. He compared faces in the pictures to each other and to our faces.

"We have a few questions before you move on," Simms said. "Travers over there will take you down the hall and someone will be right with you."

A soldier stepped forward. "If you'll follow me this way." Then he left, disappearing down a hall.

"We need our IDs back," I said, feeling anxious that Travers had already walked off.

"I'll bring them to you," Simms said.

I glanced at Logan, who shrugged. It didn't seem normal being someplace like this without any form of identification, and I didn't like it.

"It might be better if we at least had one of our IDs," I said, not moving. "Just in case someone asks us along the way."

"I assure you we'll bring them back," Simms said.

I stood my ground and said nothing. My partners stuck by me.

Simms seemed to hesitate, but then he picked up one of our work IDs, which very clearly had Department of Treasury written on it, along with A.I.R. "I guess it wouldn't hurt, just in case anyone has any misunderstandings. Just a moment." He quickly put our drivers' licenses on a little scanner one at a time, then handed them back.

I frowned at my civilian form of ID. Once again, I felt uneasy. It wasn't as though I was hiding behind the AIR ID, but it held a kind of weight that a simple license didn't have.

Travers cleared his throat. I glanced at Logan once again, and he took the lead and followed the guard.

My uneasiness grew when Travers asked each one of us to step into different rooms. First Rider, then Logan, and finally I was led into a small room, where I was left alone.

I dropped my bag onto the table. At first, I couldn't sit down due to the nervous energy coursing through me. Reminding myself that this was probably normal and that I hadn't done anything wrong helped me, at least after the third or fourth time I told myself.

Not long after I sat, the door opened. Two men entered and I noticed another man outside the door. He appeared to be guarding the room, which I didn't care for.

One of the men, a soldier, stood in a corner close to the door.

The other man, dressed as a civilian, sat across from me. "You are Ms. Heidrich, correct?"

I looked from one to the other. "That's correct."

"My name is Chris Jones. I have a few questions for you."

I shrugged by way of an answer.

"Where did you get this ID?" Chris asked holding up my AIR identification.

It was hard not to roll my eyes. "The agency gave it to me."

"Which agency is this?"

"I'm pretty sure it's written on the card." When the man raised an eyebrow at me, I sighed and filed in the blanks. "The Department of the Treasury. Specifically A.I.R."

"Which stands for?"

"I'm afraid I can't help you with that." It's true I could probably get away with telling the man, but I was starting to get aggravated by this hold up. "If you don't know what it stands for, then I'm not the one that can tell you."

"Why would that be?"

"I don't know what your clearance level is. Or his," I added, nodding at the soldier.

"Anyone at this particular base has a high level of clearance."

I shrugged. "I can call my boss and have them run you through the system. My superiors will then have to approve it. That's the best I can do."

"I happen to know the different departments under the Department of the Treasury. It's my *job* to know. Your department doesn't exist."

"Then you better go talk to your superiors. Maybe they can help you out."

"I'm not sure you understand your position here, Ms. Heidrich. You are not on our list of approved visitors. Your trip here isn't logged with anyone, and the department you claim to be involved in is fictitious."

I frowned and silently vowed to give Boone a piece of my mind when I saw him. "Someone has their wires crossed somewhere. I think you better check again."

"We have. Several times. Now, once upon a time you might have received a slap on the hands for playing a prank like this and trying to get on base."

Prank! I was seriously beginning not to like Chris.

"But we no longer live in those times. Trying to get onto this base without permission equates to a prison sentence. It's as simple as that. Now, how long you go will depend on how well you cooperate with me."

If he had looked smug when he said it, I probably would have yelled at him. Instead, he just looked like someone doing his job.

"Now," Chris continued, "tell me why you're here."

"Sorry, I can't do that." I crossed my arms on the table and leaned forward. "You need to go find your superior or anyone on this base that actually knows what's going on and speak with them."

Out of the corner of my eye, it looked as the soldier was trying hard not to grin, but the look only lasted a moment.

"Why are you here today?" Chris asked.

"Can't tell you."

"Everyone in this room has a confidential clearance or higher."

"You might be right about that, but only an idiot would take someone's word for their clearance level. Besides, confidential isn't going to cut it."

"The name of your department would at least be considered Unclassified information."

"And it's listed right there on my ID."

"If you are uncooperative, Ms. Heidrich, you will start being treated as such."

The fact that he was trying to intimidate me really pissed me off. "Until you go find someone that knows what the hell they're talking about, I will continue to be uncooperative."

Chris shook his head and stood up. "Ms. Cassandra Heidrich, you are being detained for further questioning. You will be cuffed by my associate here and will be held in a cell downstairs."

My mouth dropped open. "This is crazy, just go find someone else."

"My superiors will be notified by this evening, as well as the base command."

The soldier next to the door moved forward and I tapped my fingers on the table. He pulled out a pair of handcuffs and I shook my head.

"We will be talking to your associates as well. I'm sure they understand the benefits of being more reasonable." He moved toward the door.

"Wait," I said.

Chris and the soldier stopped. There was no way they were putting those handcuffs on me, but I had to weigh my options.

"Crap. Sorry, Logan," I said quietly, hoping the elf was listening. Louder, I said. "Here's the deal. You aren't restraining me in any way."

From the look on Chris's face, that was the wrong thing to say to the man.

FOUR

I rushed on, "I'm going to sit here quietly, and you're going to go find someone who can chat with me. Preferably someone who can check with Agent Boone, who is the one that requested us to be here."

"You can wait in the cell." Chris said, cracking the door open. To the soldier, he said, "Go ahead."

Sometimes, I closed my eyes before reaching toward the Path, but that seemed like a mistake here. Within seconds, I had stretched my mind to its limits of what I knew of the world, and then made the jump beyond that to the Path.

Rushing more than I expected, I grabbed hold of the swirl of color between the soldier and me and froze it, effectively making a wall between him and me. At the same time, I grabbed the Path of the door and shut it.

I had meant to shut it anyway. It was more of a slam.

The soldier bumped into my wall of air and he was forced to stop moving. He tried a few more times, and then reached out to touch the invisible barrier.

"What the hell?" Chris turned the doorknob, then rattled it when it wouldn't work.

"Now," I said. "Anything you see or hear from this moment is confidential, and in fact, what you can't see is as well. If you take a moment to think it over, you'll understand why."

The soldier glared at me and pulled his gun.

"You really don't want to do that," I said.

"Stand down," Chris said. He appeared to be processing a lot of information all at once.

The last thing I wanted to do was push him.

After a moment, Chris moved slowly to the table. "I think it might be better if you and I talk alone for the moment. Mind if our friend here leaves?"

I shrugged. "Sure."

"You trust him not to say anything?" Chris asked, frowning at me.

"I said this is confidential. It's his job on the line if he talks, not mine." I dropped the door's Path.

The hairs on the back of my neck rose as the Path around me stirred. Trying not to move my head, I glanced around the room. There was something else here with me in the Path.

To the soldier, who still hadn't holstered his gun, Chris ordered, "Go find Captain Stone. Request that he reach out to..." Chris looked at me. "Agent Boone, was it?"

"Yes." I crossed my arms to hide the tremor in my hands. It felt as though something brushed by me and I almost jumped.

"Request he reach out to Agent Boone to obtain information about his guests," Chris said.

Once the soldier was gone, I dropped the Path and closed it off. The bright colors faded to the dull bleakness of the normal world.

When Chris sat down opposite me, I took the opportunity to do the same. Thinking about what else might have been in the Path with me made me shiver. I hoped that the movement hid the tremor.

Chris looked as though he had a million questions, but he either didn't know how to start or didn't know if he was even allowed to ask.

"You're in a specialty branch, I take it?" Chris finally asked.

"Yes. My partners and me."

"And they can do what you just did?"

"I hope no one was stupid enough to try to '*detain*' them," was my only response.

"We spoke with you first."

"Lucky for you." At this point, it was all bravado and nothing more. I knew my partners wouldn't have done anything. In fact, they probably would have been more reasonable than I had. At least it might make Chris think twice about bothering them.

The seconds seemed to click by audibly.

"I've never seen anyone... um..." Chris cleared his throat.

I raised an eyebrow at him expectantly, wondering where he was going to take that sentence.

"But I've seen other things."

"Really?" I asked, mildly interested despite my agitation.

"Around here, most people have. Sometimes that's even why they've been stationed at this base."

Curiosity overtook my mood and I leaned forward. "What type of—"

There was a knock at the door, and then it was immediately pushed open.

"I'm told we have some guests here!" The man was a bit taller than I was and had hair that was turning—what I assumed to be—prematurely gray.

The odd thing was he wasn't upset or excited, just loud. *Very* loud.

"I'm Major Buchanan! Mr. Jones, I'll take over from here!"

"It was nice to meet you," Chris said. "I'm sorry for your delay." He hurried out of the room.

Major Buchanan opened the door wider, and with a wave of his hand, invited me out of the room. "You have some friends here as well! Let's spring them and get you where you need to be!" When he said it, he motioned to a soldier.

Logan lacked his usual cheerful attitude when he joined me. I tried not to catch his eye, worried that I was the one at the root of his temper. Instead, I looked over his shoulder to see Rider approach.

"Look at that! The gang's all here! Here are your IDs! Now, let's get moving!" Major Buchanan set a quick pace, but not too quick for me to keep up.

When I stepped outside, I had to blink in the bright sun. The temperature was also heating up.

"It's going to be a scorcher of a day!" Major Buchanan said.

Rider winced.

Probably because his ears are being assaulted.

"Sorry for the mix up!" Major Buchanan said, taking off across the concreted landscape. "Sometimes it takes longer to sort out the paperwork, especially with guests that are added at the last minute!"

"I understand," I said, trying to convey that while I was forgiving, I was still aggravated.

"I've heard almost nothing about you! But what little I have heard has been good! We're going back to research hangar D-2!"

"Hangar?" Logan asked.

"Yes! Lots of coming and going! It's mostly a small hangar with a research facility built onto the side!"

"What type of research do you all do here?" I asked.

Major Buchanan's bark of laughter was just that. Short,

loud bursts. "Just about everything you can think of—and some things you can't! It makes giving tours, even rudimentary ones, impossible!"

"I can imagine so," I said, taking off my jacket. I noticed Logan twist his head, probably trying to listen into some of the buildings.

"They usually go along the lines of there's building B-5! There's A-7! There's a dining facility and there's the exit!" Agent Buchanan barked out another laugh. "We'll take this!" He pointed at a vehicle that looked almost like a golf cart, but it had some major modifications. "It takes forever to get from point A to point B here," Major Buchanan said. "And usually B isn't where you expect it!"

Once again, I sat in the front while my partners sat crowded into the back, facing the opposite way.

"Hold on!" Major Buchanan said by way of warning.

We were off like a shot. I had to grab my bag and a handle to keep from tumbling out.

Every now and again, Major Buchanan would point out a building and yell out the name. It was rare for him to say what was going on inside.

When he pulled to a stop in front of a white building sticking out of the side of a gray hangar, I was more than ready to get out of the little vehicle. Major Buchanan might have been a better driver than Rider, but they both seemed to share the idea that you should get from A to B in the fastest way possible.

"I can let you into the outer room, but that is as far as I go!" Major Buchanan slid an ID into a slot and yanked it back out. A buzzer rang somewhere inside the building and the door opened. "Good luck to you!" Once we were inside, he closed the door.

The thunk told me the door was locked securely in place, which wasn't well received after the day we'd had.

"This isn't a room so much as a box." I found that I was talking softer as a way to gain back some part of my hearing after the torment of listening to Major Buchanan.

"I am not comfortable being locked into a small place," Rider said, moving to stand so close to me that he was almost leaning on me.

"I'm sure someone will let us out soon," I said.

"I hope it's someone who knows the front end of a steer from the back." Logan looked up into a corner of the room when he said it.

When I followed his gaze, I noticed the security camera.

"I don't like being this much in the dark," Logan continued, talking to the camera.

My guilt levels grew significantly. I had agreed to help Boone. Rider and Logan may have felt the need to follow, just for my sake.

"Boone will fill us in," I said. *I hope.*

A few minutes ticked by before Logan indicated that someone was on their way.

There were a few clicks in the interior door and then it swung open.

I smiled when I saw Boone, although something seemed different about him.

"Logan, Cassie, Rider, it's good to see you all," Boone said. "Thank you for coming. We appreciate the help on this."

"It sounds like an interesting case," Logan said. "What little we know of it, anyway. Hopefully we can be of some help."

"Come back this way," Boone said. "We're in a bit of a time crunch, so forgive me for not giving you the tour. Follow me.

We can meet and debrief after I've introduced you to the team."

He hurried away before we could say anything. The hall was stark white with no windows. We passed wide metal doors that looked like they had more security than the office.

Boone stopped in front of one door that looked like all the others, where he swiped his security card.

"This is our general prep area," Boone said, pushing the door open. "In here, we have basic munitions, lockers, general supplies, and my office."

The room was large and rectangular, and unlike the hall-way, it was full of light. There were windows up near the ceil-ing. Across one wall were cages that held guns of various sizes and the far wall held a few lockers. There were benches and a conference table surrounded by chairs.

Most importantly, there were other people in the room. A woman in fatigues walked over and stood at parade rest, much like Boone himself.

It finally hit me what was different about Boone. He stood rigidly, the way he did when he didn't know someone, didn't trust them, or if they were a superior. He stood at parade rest as well, but the stiffness was something altogether different.

Boone was stressed.

"This is Davis. She is the squad lead and will assist you. Over there," Boone indicated a man cleaning a rifle by the munitions cages, "is Tolman. He is one of the best marksmen on base. Renick will also be joining us. He should currently be double checking the rest of our supplies in the hangar." Boone looked at Davis as though he had asked her a question.

Davis's eyes got a faraway look for a moment before she snapped to. "He is in the hangar and about halfway through the gear."

Boone nodded. "Davis, these are Agents Logan Seale, Rider

Wolfe, and Cassandra Heidrich. Will you take Ms. Heidrich to get ready? We'll meet back here in twenty to debrief."

That was a fast pass off.

Davis nodded curtly. "This way, Ms. Heidrich."

"You can call me Cassie." I glanced at Boone to see if he had any objection to this, but he did not appear to care one way or the other. I followed Davis out the door. It was interesting to me that she had to swipe her card to exit the room.

She said nothing as she led me down the hall, and I found that I needed to break the silence. "Where are we going?"

"Sorry, there's a women's locker room down here." Her voice was much less formal away from Boone. "The guys have one off the main room."

"That sucks," I said before I thought about what I was saying.

She smiled. "It's going to be interesting working with another woman. On general assignment there were others around, but ever since I was selected for this team, it's pretty much been just me—not that I don't love working with Tolman and Renick." She added the last part quickly.

I smiled. "I feel the same way. There are so few female field agents that I've rarely had the chance to work with any. I wouldn't give my partners up for the world, but at least having someone around the office to talk with would be nice."

"Through here," Davis said, opening another door with a swipe of her card. "During the selection process for the team there were a few other female soldiers, but I was the only one chosen."

"That's quite an accomplishment," I said.

"Boone guessed at your clothing size, but I picked up a size above and below, just in case."

"That's definitely a good idea. I can't see Boone being a good judge of women's clothing."

Davis laughed.

"Do you like working with him?" I asked.

She stopped laughing, but kept the smile. "It's not bad. We haven't been working together long, but it's going well. There are showers around the corner. You'll probably want to take one now since it'll be your last chance for a while."

"Thanks for the warning."

Since I still didn't know what Boone had in store for us, I took the advice and opportunity to shower. Then I took stock of the clothes.

"These are all uniforms, aren't they? Should I even be wearing these?" I asked.

"Don't worry, yours aren't actual uniforms. It's just in the military style."

I pulled on my underclothes and then the pants. "They don't seem very comfortable."

"Comfort isn't high on the list of considerations for these kinds of clothes."

"Is it on the list at all?"

"You'll get used to them. In a few days, you may even be thankful you put them on."

They seemed thick and far too stiff, so I couldn't imagine something like that happening, so I changed the subject. "How long have you been in the military?"

"Four years, but the past two have been training and preparing for getting on this team."

"Has this been different than the military?"

"Definitely," Davis said, "although Boone is ex-military. So when we're here it's more military, out in the field... Well, that's all different."

"How so?" I pulled on an undershirt that was lighter and felt like it was made of sweat-wicking material.

She looked uncertain. "You work for AIR, right?"

"Yeah."

"You never really know what you're going to find in the field. It makes a difference."

Since I knew almost nothing about the military, I figured I'd take her word for it.

"You can leave your clothes in the locker. You won't be able to take them with us."

"Thanks for helping me out," I said as I laced up the boots that had been given to me. They were much more comfortable than they looked and I half hoped I could take them home.

"You're welcome," Davis said. "We'll be working with each other for a while, so it's good to get to know each other some."

"Agreed," I said.

"What are your partners like?"

"They're easy to get along with. Logan likes meeting people and makes friends everywhere he goes. Rider can sometimes seem standoffish to new people since he's not completely used to the language, but he'll ask questions if something comes up."

Davis grinned broadly. "He's the tall one, right? I didn't realize he was from out of the country."

I hesitated, but being in another world was definitely out of the country, so I guess that counted. "He was born here, but left when he was young. He's only been back for a few years."

"He certainly stands out in a room, in more ways than one. Is he seeing anyone?"

"Sort of, but I get the idea that it isn't too serious."

"I imagine it's hard to meet someone. I know it is for us."

"The job isn't easy on relationships, that's for sure." Thoughts of Vincent started to flow in, so I tried to change the subject. "What are your partners like?"

"Tolman doesn't say much, but he's a great guy."

The look on Davis's face when she mentioned Tolman

reminded me of how I thought of Vincent, but since she asked about Rider, I wasn't sure what to think.

"He's an incredible shot," Davis said. "Almost inhumanly good, but don't ever tell him I said that."

"And your other partner?" I asked.

"Renick. He's actually the reason I asked about your partners."

"Is he hard to get along with?"

"He comes off as kind of a creep."

"But a nice guy underneath?" I asked when she hesitated.

"You'll probably only be here long enough to see the asshole side," Davis said. "But don't let him get to you. If he thinks he's bothering you he'll torment you even more."

"Really? Why is he even in the group?"

"He will have your back, all the time. No matter what you may think of him, he's watching over the team. He's also really good at logistics. If there's a logic to something, he'll find it."

"It almost sounds like you're describing two different people."

"He just sucks at working with people, especially women. He's not mean or cruel, just annoying as hell until he actually thinks of you as a team member. Once that happens, he's not as bad." She paused. "I don't think I'm explaining it very well."

I smiled. "I'm sure I can handle it for a few days. Although, if he bothers Logan or Rider, I make no promises about what they'll do."

"He'll probably be too intimidated to say anything to Rider. Logan, I'm not sure about."

Knowing Logan was the scarier of the two, I tried not to laugh. "I'm sure they'll work it out. If not, we'll only be gone for a short time."

"Hopefully that's all it'll take. Speaking of which, it's time to get you back for your meeting."

"You're not debriefing with us?" I asked.

"No, we already have our orders." Davis led me back out into the hall. "How are you with guns?"

"We tend to use tranq guns more than actual firearms, but I do okay with both." *At least when I don't leave my gun at home.* That last thought I'd keep to myself, though.

"Great. I'll grab your gear and get it ready."

"Thank you. Since I still have no real idea what we're doing, that'll be a huge help."

Down the hall, Davis swiped her card outside the door again. "Always make sure you're with someone that has access while you're here. You don't want to get stuck in the hallway or anything."

"I'll try to remember that," I said as we entered the room. "Thanks again for everything."

"Looks like you have a new friend, Davis," a man said as he swaggered up.

Davis turned to me and rolled her eyes, not letting the man see her. "Cassie, this is Renick. Renick, this is Agent Cassandra Heidrich."

"You look like you've been playing dress up," Renick said.

Since that was exactly how I felt, I said nothing.

"Are the kits packed?" Davis snapped the question out, showing me exactly why she was the squad leader.

"Ours are packed. Everything but the munitions, and Tolman's got that covered. The extra gear for the princess here is ready." Renick winked in my direction.

Princess? My nose curled up involuntarily.

"The rest of the AIR equipment?" Davis asked severely.

"Packed," Renick said. "And double checked."

"Where's Boone?" Davis asked.

"He's handholding the civilians in the locker room."

"I'll leave a note for him. Meet me in the hangar in ten,"

Davis said. She nodded at me before walking to other side of the room and opening a gray door, one of the first I'd seen that didn't have locks.

"So, princess, who are you gonna get to carry your bag on this trip?" Renick asked.

"I'll carry my own, thanks," I said.

"You can act all strong, but I give you an hour, tops—princess." He grinned.

The word princess was already grating against my nerves, and he knew it. It was either embrace it, or get pissed off, letting him know he won.

"If I act strong, does that mean you'll act like less of an ass?"

Renick's eyes gleamed with amusement.

The outer door opened behind me, but I didn't take my eyes off Renick, knowing our conflict wasn't done.

Tolman didn't even glance at me when he walked by, but he shot Renick a look I couldn't read.

Renick moved closer. My instinct was to step back, but I ignored that. "Tell you what, *princess*, if you wear a skirt I'll carry your bag for you." He looked over my shoulder and his attention wavered.

"I don't think your skirts would fit me," I said. "Thanks all the same."

He looked uncertain for a moment and then stepped back. "Why'd you bring *him* in here?" Renick called to Tolman, keeping his eyes on me and over my shoulder.

Tolman didn't respond.

"Maybe you should wait in Boone's office," Renick said to me, dropping the princess for once.

Frowning, I turned around, checking to see who was bothering him so much.

Five feet behind me, with eyes flat black, was Vincent.

CHAPTER
FIVE

My heart surged. After three weeks of not seeing him, this was the last place I expected him to be.

When he looked at me, the blackness swirled out of his eyes and he gave me a small smile. My heart beat faster and the only thing I wanted to do was close the space between us.

He seemed to feel the same way. We moved toward each other.

After two steps, he hesitated.

I stopped, feeling as though my heart was being squeezed. *Why did he stop?*

There was no way possible I could have read the situation wrong before he left. He didn't call me much when he got back. Three times in three weeks wasn't promising, and this was making things so much worse.

Vincent's attention focused behind me again and his eyes instantly turned black. I sighed and turned around, hating that there was an audience here.

Davis had left Boone's office and was watching Vincent

and me. Tolman was standing close by her, also facing us. Renick hadn't moved.

They were all watching us silently, but there seemed to be something passing between them. It was as though there was a current connecting one to the other. Wondering if I could see their connection from the Path, I started to reach for it.

The door to the locker room opened. I could see Boone quickly assess the situation.

"Vincent, I wasn't sure if you could make it, but I'm glad you're here. Let me introduce the team. This is Davis, Tolman, and Renick. Squad, this is the last of AIR team, Agent Vincent Pironis."

Rider appeared to be sniffing the air and didn't appear happy with what he sensed. Logan was looking cautious, but still kept his laid back manner.

"You're just in time," Logan said. "Boone was about to fill us in on what we're doing."

"You can go ahead to my office," Boone said. "I want a quick word with my team."

I smiled at Davis on my way by, trying to reassure her silently by reminding her that we were friends, or at least friendly. Her return look was tense, but there was a touch of assurance there somewhere—I was almost sure of it.

We filed into Boone's office, which barely seemed large enough for everyone.

"I didn't know you'd be here," I said, turning to Vincent once the door was closed.

"You were already gone by the time Boone reached me," Vincent said. "I tried to call."

I raised an eyebrow, wanting to be mad at him, but not quite reaching that point. "That comes as a surprise."

"Listen, Cass—"

"Stop." With one word, Rider silenced us both, but it wasn't us he was concentrating on.

If Rider wanted quiet, he probably had a good reason, so we waited and watched.

"There is a sound. Or maybe a sensation of a sound," Rider said. "Do you hear it?"

This was of course aimed at Logan. The elf concentrated for a second before he shook his head. Under his slightly too long hair, his ears twitched. Slowly, they rolled out. It always fascinated me that his ears were almost transparent at the end of their long points.

"I'm not hearing it," Logan said.

"The air is stirring where it should not be," Rider said. "It was there when we left the locker room. Now it is here."

"I sensed something like that outside," I said. "Between the others. Maybe I should look."

"Perhaps—no, it is gone now," Rider said.

"Keep your ear to the ground," Logan said. "If it comes back, let us know."

Rider blinked at him. "Do you think it affects the vibrations of the floor?"

Logan grinned. "Just an expression. It only means to stay alert in case it happens again."

The door opened and Boone came in. We parted enough for him to move to his desk. Whatever had happened in the other room, he didn't look happy.

"The squad is going to the hangar. Have a seat," Boone said. "Logan, are you sure about the boots?"

Looking down, I saw that Logan was still wearing his cowboy boots. I couldn't keep a grin off my face.

"You bet," Logan said.

"And the hat?"

Logan's Stetson was still in his hands. "Couldn't leave it behind."

Boone nodded and moved on. "Sorry we only have three chairs in here."

"We could use the conference table in the other room," I said, suggesting the obvious.

"I don't want to chance it. This may be the only time we get a chance to talk," Boone said.

"We're here for more than a nightmare, aren't we," Logan said, taking a seat across from Boone.

"Yeah, I need an outside—"

Rider held up a hand, stopping Boone.

Boone started to say something, but Rider held up a finger, asking him to wait. After a moment, Rider cocked his head, then nodded in my direction.

I closed my eyes and jumped into the Path, curious to find out if there was anything there. Seeing the bright colors swirl around the room, I tried not to concentrate on those around me. The bright glow that was Logan was distracting, as was the anxious purples rippling from Vincent.

There was something else wrapped around Vincent. A streak of olive green that he was trying to pull back. It was rude to spy, so despite wanting to Read more, I concentrated on the job at hand.

Once I could put the people behind me, a muddy brown Path caught my attention. Splashed inside was the brightest of yellow. Boone's unease tried to swamp everything else in the room, so I reached for a calming feeling and let it radiate around me. Emotions settled quickly, and then I was able to concentrate on the thin line coming into the room through the wall.

"There is something here," I said. Moving closer, I saw that the Path pulsed in both directions, as though the source was sending energy this way, but then it was feeding from the Paths in the room and pulling what it found back into itself.

"What's in that direction?" I pointed to the area where the Path came from.

"That's the hangar," Boone said.

The Path snapped back like a sprung trap.

I studied the area as best I could. "It's gone. I might be able to look back to get a better idea of what I was seeing."

"Maybe it can wait," Vincent said.

Around me, I felt something closing in and I shivered. A hand clasping my shoulder made me jump and I fell straight into Rider in my attempt to get away.

It was more than a little embarrassing that my gasp of fear turned into a high-pitched squeak.

Shaking, I pushed the Path away as fast as I could.

"It was Vincent that touched you," Rider said in a calming tone. "Nothing else."

Vincent stood there frozen, looking confused and frustrated.

"Don't do that!" My heart was racing and I felt like hiding in a hole for the rest of the day might just be enough to cover my awkwardness.

He dropped the hand that was outstretched. "What—"

"Not now," Logan said, cutting Vincent off. "Anything else, Cassie?"

"Something was coming into the room, then went back out. It's gone now, though."

"That's something, at least," Boone said.

"Do you know what it was?" Rider asked.

"Possibly." Boone shifted in his seat. "I think it was my team."

Trying to avoid Vincent's gaze, I took my seat again. "I thought they were human."

"They are not human," Rider said.

"They are," Boone said. "At least, they started that way."

Logan crossed his arms and leaned back in his seat. "I think you had better explain."

"There's not much time," Boone said before turning to me. "You remember what I said about the team? I didn't want this project to happen. I didn't like that it was happening."

"I remember," I said. "It was experimental, right?"

"Yeah. The military wanted better soldiers, and some parts of the government didn't want to rely on the Lost," Boone said.

"So they decided to take the Lost and put them into humans," Logan said, his voice full of disgust.

"The Lost weren't hurt, at least that I know of, but yeah, that's the gist of it. They studied the DNA of a bunch of species and... experimented," Boone said. It looked as though he was having a hard time looking Logan in the eye, but he was doing it all the same.

I clutched my stomach, feeling ill by what I was hearing. "How long has this been going on?"

"The study began ages ago, the experiments... a few years."

"And your team is the best of the research?" Logan asked.

"They're the only ones that survived while retaining their humanity and sanity." It appeared to be costing Boone a lot to say this.

"At least that you're sure of," Logan spat.

Looking at the elf, I noticed his face growing slightly angular.

"That's why I need your help. I need someone from the outside to watch them."

Something clicked for me. "Not just anyone. You needed *us*."

"Yes. Your skills together can help evaluate the situation."

Boone looked me in the eye. "And I can trust you. A Reader might be the best judge of character we can get."

"And the rest of us?" Vincent asked in a tight voice.

"We don't know what all they can do," Boone said. "The group studying them thinks they're aware of everything, but I've seen things that the researchers never expected and don't believe. It doesn't help that the team denies anything new I bring up."

"And if they *can* do things you don't know about?" Logan said.

"It doesn't matter what they can do," Boone said. "They can keep that to themselves, for all I care. But—"

Rider held up his hand again and cut Boone off.

"It's gone again," Rider said after a minute ticked by.

Boone turned in his seat as though he could see through the walls to the hangar. "Let's get down to business. While what we've discussed is important, what we really need to focus on is the nightmare. The most critical thing here is the nightmare."

Logan cleared his throat. When Boone turned to him, Logan tapped the points of his ears and pointed toward the wall.

Boone held up his hands, but shook his head. He didn't seem sure, but it looked like he was concerned that his team was doing something.

"Do you know what a nightmare is?" I asked.

"What we're in now," Vincent muttered.

"No one has any real information," Boone said. "We're going on theory and rumor at this point. The only recorded events that involved nightmares are cave paintings and similar. The situation we have here is that an entire village is just gone. Some disappeared, but most of them are dead. I'll save you the details, but it wasn't a pretty sight."

"What made you think it was a nightmare?" I asked.

Boone opened a drawer and grabbed a folder. He flipped through a few pages. When he found what he was looking for, he slid the photo across the desk to Logan.

I leaned in. It was a crude drawing of a four-legged creature with several long lines—tails, maybe—trailing behind it.

"This is a cave drawing?" I asked.

"Yes and no." Boone slid another picture over. "This photo is of the cave drawing found hundreds of years ago. The other one was discovered a few days ago."

"What's the story floating for the village?" Logan asked.

"The government is keeping a lid on it," Boone said.

Logan tapped his fingers on the desk and studied Boone. "We don't hear much about villages these days. Where exactly are we going?"

"We fly out in less than an hour. Our destination is in South America," Boone said.

"Awful big place," Logan said.

I could tell he was fishing for more information.

"That's true. And something they have a lot of is dense, unpopulated rainforest and jungle."

"What's the difference between rainforests and jungles?" If Boone's team had been in the room with us, I probably wouldn't have asked, but I was among friends.

"Rainforests are easier to navigate," Boone said. "Jungles usually live inside rainforests. If a tree falls or something happens to them, then more light reaches the ground. More light means denser vegetation."

I wrinkled my nose up, already knowing I wasn't going to like this mission. "So, we're trekking through the woods. Again."

Boone grinned. "We know a little more about what to expect here, and we'll have supplies."

Remembering our last time together in a forest I couldn't help but mirror his smile. "So, at least we'll have that going for us."

"Any wildlife we should know about?" Vincent asked.

"The usual," Boone said. "No known Lost in the area, but we need to keep an eye out all the same."

Asking what 'the usual' was would have been a smart move, but I decided that I really didn't want to know. At least not when there was still a chance of backing out.

"Gear?" Vincent asked.

"Once we have you outfitted, we'll go over to the hangar to review everything we'll be carrying," Boone said.

"Anything else we need to know before we head out?" Logan asked.

Boone seemed to hesitate, but then plunged forward. "This thing is dangerous. If we can capture it, we will." He looked from me to Rider. "But going in, you have to understand that might not be an option. We have to resolve this situation."

Logan looked about as pleased about 'the situation' as I did. Glancing at Rider, he seemed more confused than anything else.

"We are going to try to capture, though, right?" I said.

"If we can reasonably do so," Boone said.

The whole thing didn't sit well with me. I turned in my seat to see Vincent. His face was set in a mask of indifference, but this close, I could see from the slightest downturn of the mouth that he was concerned.

Whether the concern was about killing the creature or something else was impossible for me to know.

"We don't want to see anyone get hurt," Boone said. "That's our priority."

I gritted my teeth and didn't say anything.

"We have some clothes for you, Vincent," Boone said,

standing up. "Logan and Rider, can you show him what we have?"

We all filed out of the office and my partners disappeared into the men's locker room.

"Are you going to be okay with this?" Boone asked.

I didn't hold back. "Of course we want to keep everyone safe, but being ready to kill the nightmare seems like the wrong attitude to have going in."

"It's realistic, though. I just wanted to make sure you knew about the possibilities."

"Aren't you concerned about the others?" I asked, gesturing toward the locker room.

"Logan's been the lead enough to know it's an option. Rider is the one I'm worried about. Not only is he new to this, but he's Lost, like Logan."

I crossed my arms. "And Vincent."

"I know what his job was before he joined your team."

That took the wind out of my sails. It's true; Vincent was an agency-sanctioned assassin. He was probably often brought in on cases where there was only one way they could turn out.

"My team," Boone said. "What's happening isn't their fault. I know you've got my back and your partners have yours. The nightmare is our main objective and your partners—all of them—will greatly enhance our chances at successfully bringing it back alive."

"Will it be under military jurisdiction or AIR once we take it in?" Logan asked.

I hadn't even noticed that the elf had slipped out of the locker room.

"Both. We're working together on this," Boone said.

"Are we?" Logan leaned back against the wall and crossed his arms. "Were we working together when your team was assembled?"

Boone hesitated once again. "Not in the beginning, but I'm afraid at the end, it *was* a group effort."

"So if we capture this poor creature, is it going to be used as fodder for this perfect soldier project?" Logan asked.

"Not if I can help it," Boone said. "I've made some connections in AIR to raise concerns about this experiment."

"That's how the changeling found out about you, isn't it?" I asked.

"Seems likely," Boone said.

Rider and Vincent stepped out of the locker room. It was strange and a little surreal to see us all dressed alike.

"Let's get moving," Boone said. "We've got a plane to catch."

Boone led the way, unlocking doors at what seemed like every turn. It felt a little odd to have Vincent by my side again. He was close enough to reach out and touch, but he still seemed to be holding himself at a distance.

Why did he have to hesitate when he saw me?

It didn't help that I couldn't tell if I wanted to stay away to refrain from yelling at him—I was still pissed off he'd barely tried to reach out—or if I wanted to keep my distance so I wouldn't throw my arms around him and kiss him in front of everyone, including this bunch of new team members.

Yet, even though I thought of those as my choices, I couldn't help but walk next to him. It was a small comfort and warmed my heart.

Besides, he looked good in a uniform.

When we stepped inside the hangar our footsteps echoed in the vast space. It was also hotter. The temperature had risen and this place didn't seem to have any sort of climate control.

Then again, the next few days would be more of the same. Best to get used to it now.

The thought made me realize that I had no idea how long

we'd be gone. I picked up my pace to walk next to Boone. Even without the Path open, I could feel Vincent's frustration at the change.

"You never mentioned how long you expected this to take," I said.

"I thought your boss filled you in," Boone said.

"Yes, but she only mentioned the possibility of weeks and months."

"Yeah, I guess that's pretty standard because of the paperwork. It shouldn't take more than a week or two. At least that's the hope."

"Crap. Gran is going to kill me."

Boone grinned. "She have big plans?"

"No, but she didn't want me to come at all."

Boone slowed his pace, looking troubled. "Did she say why?"

He knew my grandmother, but he had heard even more than what he had witnessed in person and knew she was never wrong about what she said. "She didn't predict any dire catastrophes, if that's what you mean. She seemed to be having a hard time figuring out why she didn't want me here."

"We'll be on communications blackout for at least a week. Maybe you should give her a call before we leave. After we go through the supplies, that is. You'll want to know what you have."

"Thanks," I said, smiling at him. It was strange that we hadn't known each other for much longer than a month. He already knew my family and me and accepted us the way we were. It was a rare quality, even in our line of work where we dealt with the strange and unusual on a regular basis.

Boone led us to a long table where Davis stood. There was a bag laid out for each of us.

"Since we aren't strictly military, we took a note out of your team's playbook," Boone said. "Cassie mentioned the supplies you all normally carry while out in the field. Since they're lightweight and they'll work well in the environment we'll be in, we've added a few other items."

While Boone went down the list of items included, I couldn't help but notice that Davis didn't look happy. It made me wonder if she had been the one that had started the strange Path we saw in Boone's office.

Davis packed each item as Boone went over them. Food, water, first-aid kits, clothes, extra socks, toiletries, sunscreen, sunglasses, and—my favorite—the hammocks, were all reviewed and stowed.

"Let's talk weapons," Boone said. "You each have your sidearm and you'll want at least two extra magazines. If you need more, talk to Tolman. Logan's taking the lead for your team. Two of you will be carrying live rifles and two will have tranq rifles. If you get paired off, make sure there's one of each between the two of you. We expect Tolman to be our long-range man, but everyone should be prepared."

The bag looked heavy. The only positive was the fact that it should get lighter every day.

"Your knife is your last resort in combat, but you might need it in the jungle. Any questions?"

CHAPTER

SIX

Any questions? Only about a thousand. Sadly, all of my questions were things Boone couldn't answer. I glanced at Vincent. Maybe no one could answer some of them right now.

"If you need to make any last calls, make them now," Boone said. "It might be your last chance for a while. Davis will show you where the closest phone is. Everyone else, grab your gear and follow me. We'll finish loading."

Rider picked up his back and slung it over one arm, then grabbed mine and slung it over the other. Davis stared at him for a few moments before she seemed to remember herself.

"This way," she said.

Logan had pulled Vincent over to the side, but I caught Logan's attention enough so that he knew I was following Davis.

We walked quietly for a moment, and once again, I felt the need to break the silence. "Have you spent much time in the wilderness?"

"More than I cared to." She spoke rather stiffly, and I

couldn't help but think I had done something wrong. I wondered if she overheard what Boone had said about the team.

"Do you have any calls to make?" I asked.

"I made them earlier." After a few steps, she kept the conversation going. "Are you calling family?"

"My grandmother. We didn't know we'd be gone so long without a phone."

"It sounds like you're close to her." Davis's voice had lost some of the indifferent tone.

"She lives with me. I just hope I catch her before she takes off on a trip with her friend. More importantly, I hope my mother isn't at the house feeding the... cat." Molly did remind me of a cat. "She'll be ticked off."

Davis smiled. "Your mom sounds kind of like my parents. Is your dad the same?"

"Step-dad. My dad died when I was little. Bob's happy to let me do my own thing."

"Sorry to hear about your dad."

"I was too young to remember him. But I always had Gran there."

"Here's the phone," Davis said. "I'll wait for you."

"Thanks."

Gran picked up quickly, and she didn't have to wait until she heard my voice to tell her it was me. "I knew I'd hear from you."

"I'm glad I reached you before you left," I said.

"I stalled Dee Dee so I could talk with you. I'm worried about this trip you're takin'. Do you know where you're goin'?"

"Not really," I lied. "But I'm going to be out of contact for quite a while. I wanted to let you know so you wouldn't worry."

"Sugar, it's way too late for that. How do I reach you?"

"Um... you can't."

"I know they have fancy phones that can reach anywhere. I've seen movies."

"They might have one," I said, realizing that they almost had to have something. Otherwise, how could we update anyone on what we were doing? "But if there's a number that reaches it, I don't have it."

Logan approached and started chatting with Davis. It wasn't long before she was smiling. Logan had that effect on people.

"Well, I'm gonna need some way to call you," Gran said. "Your mother will pitch a fit if she knew you couldn't be reached."

"How about Hank?" I suggested. "He'll know how to get me a message."

"Are you sure?"

"He's our handler. I think that's one of his job requirements. He'll help."

"Well, if you're sure."

"I'm positive. Listen, Gran, I'm going to have to let you go. Have fun on your trip. Love you."

"Hold on! I have messages to pass on."

"Oh, I thought we'd be too far away."

"Well, it's vague, but the big visions go farther. Tell Logan there's gonna be a time where his instinct is to run to find something to fight. He'll know when it happens. Tell him in no uncertain terms that he has to stay with you."

Frowning, I looked up at Logan, who watched me curiously. Davis had disappeared.

"And I know he's listening, so I will cut off more than his sugar supply if he doesn't."

A small grin floated across Logan's face and he nodded.

"He's got the message," I said.

"Now, it doesn't take a psychic to know you and Vincent are havin' some sort of an issue."

"What's that supposed to mean?"

"I know the both of you. I've never seen two people so good at gettin' in your own way."

I shot a quick glance at Logan to see if he was listening, but if he was, then he was smart enough to pretend that he didn't hear the conversation.

"You need to make things right," Gran said. "You all have a strong connection and you're gonna need it."

"I'll talk with him," I said

"Good. You all stick together and be safe."

"Thanks, Gran."

"Everything okay?" Logan asked after I hung up.

"It's hard to say," I said. "She's not happy that she can't call me. I let her know she should call Hank if she really needs to get us a message."

"I'm hoping it's just Margaret being worried and nothing more serious," Logan said.

"Do you think that's what it is?"

Logan seemed to think that over. "No, I don't. Be careful and keep an eye out. I'll be a few minutes. Tell 'em not to leave without me."

I went back the way I came, over to the table. No one was around, which put me in mind of what Davis had said; 'stay with someone that has a key.' Well, it's not like there wasn't a big door standing open.

Our stuff was gone, so I headed outside. Someone had to be out there, right?

Renick came in before I made it outside.

"I see you got out of the heavy lifting, princess."

"Is everyone outside?" I asked.

"Yeah, I'm supposed to come and get you. Boone's worried you might stub a toe or something."

I didn't wait for him to say anything else and instead walked past him, trying to pretend he didn't annoy the crap out of me.

He grabbed my arm and I stopped.

"You know what you have on your team, don't you?" Renick asked.

"An ass? Because that's what you seem like," I said, glaring at him. "Let go."

He held up his hands in mock surrender. "Sure thing, princess. Wouldn't want to get on your bad side."

"If you grab me like that again, you better have a good reason. If not, you'll see my bad side."

He chuckled, which made me want to ball up my fists and punch him. Instead, I rolled my eyes and stalked outside. It was obvious he didn't think much of Vincent, so maybe I could take Gran's advice now and stick close to him.

But no, that seemed too much like hiding. Renick would get tired of being an ass at some point. At least I hoped he would.

Renick jogged to catch up. "Plane's over here."

Boone was loading a bag into a plane, so I made a beeline to him.

"If you need me for anything, princess, you let me know," Renick said with a wink.

Like that's going to happen. "Right."

Boone didn't say anything until Renick headed back to the hangar. "Want me to have a talk with him?"

"What? No! You can't do that."

"I don't want any trouble between your team and mine."

"What do you mean?"

"I mean that Vincent isn't allowed to kill him."

"Don't worry about Vincent. I don't think Renick is stupid enough to say much in front of him."

"You may be underestimating how far Renick is willing to push things."

"Fair enough. But I *am* allowed to hit him, right?"

Boone grinned. "If you feel the need. That's between you and him."

"They seemed pretty surprised to discover that Vincent was a Walker." I left the question unasked.

"I was kind of hoping they wouldn't find out right away. Not that I can blame Vincent for getting annoyed. Renick has that effect on just about everyone."

"And the rest of us?"

"They know you all are unique and that they should expect the unexpected. Nothing else."

"Why didn't you tell them?"

"I want to gauge their reactions. It's important to know how they'll respond in the field if faced with something they don't know about or don't like."

"What do they think about you not telling them?"

"They know that you all are out of the ordinary, and why I'm not telling them anything more about you."

"They know they're being tested."

"Of course. Listen, they're a good team and we all need to trust each other in the field."

"You do trust them, then?"

"Of course. I don't know how they'll work with others, though."

I couldn't tell if Boone was saying that because he meant it or saying it because he thought they were listening. He seemed pretty sincere.

"There's a few more things I need to take care of before we take off," Boone said.

"Where are Vincent and Rider?" I asked.

"On the plane. The rest of us will join you shortly."

I watched Boone leave, but when I noticed Renick walk out of the hangar, I casually turned around and went inside. The idea of spending a few days with that guy agitated me, so I decided to do what I did best. Ignore it.

It was significantly cooler in the little jet plane despite the door being open. This plane was altogether different from the others. It was custom made, from the look of it, and there was plenty of leg space. Even Rider would be able to stretch out.

Rider was sitting in one of the seats and Vincent was standing in the aisle—if you could call the space that. The seats were in an odd configuration. It was as though every other row had been taken out. There was even a couch toward the back, although the space was still cramped inside.

I slipped past Vincent to sit diagonally from Rider. Vincent shifted to include me in their conversation.

"Vincent was telling me what to expect in the rainforest," Rider said.

"I've never been to one," I admitted.

"My knowledge is research-based only," Vincent said. "I never made it to the forest itself."

"They have a spider—"

"Stop," I said, cutting Rider off. "I think I'd rather be surprised."

Rider grinned.

"Speaking of animals, you're going to need to make sure you're prepared out there," Vincent said to me.

"Prepared?" I asked.

"There are a lot of predators where we're going," Vincent said. "We'll keep an eye out, but you'll need to be on your toes."

"I do not think that will be an issue," Rider said.

"How is that not an issue?" Vincent asked.

"It's not important right now," I said. "But Rider doesn't seem to think it's an issue anymore."

"You two have worked everything out, right?" Vincent asked, giving Rider an uncertain look.

It took me a minute to realize that Vincent was referring to Rider's one tiny stray thought while I was trapped in another world. Due to a misunderstanding, he thought I wanted him to leave. While I was trapped away, he thought that he wouldn't have to leave if I never made it back home.

At least I hoped it was only a stray thought.

It sucked to think about, but I wanted to move past it. I hoped that Vincent was over it as well.

"Everything's good with Rider and me," I said.

Rider looked uncomfortable when Vincent still stared at him.

"Cassie will be no worse off than any one of us," Rider said.

Vincent nodded, but he didn't look entirely convinced.

"Mind if I take a seat?" Vincent asked, indicating the spot next to me.

"You can sit here," Rider said. "There is plenty of space."

Vincent looked blank faced at his partner.

I scooted over, leaving the outer seat empty. "It's okay, Rider. Vincent and I have some things to talk about."

Rider nodded.

Vincent turned his back to me. Rider looked at him, puzzled, leaving Vincent shaking his head while he took his seat. Even I had to look hard to see the smallest of smiles on Vincent's face. At least until he turned to me.

"I should have called," Vincent said.

It took everything I had not to sigh. "You did call."

"I am going to help Boone," Rider said, standing up and practically tripping over his own feet to get out of the door.

"He got your hint," I said.

Vincent did sigh.

I couldn't help but smile, though I tried to keep it to myself.

"I should have called more often," Vincent said. "Or talked more or something."

"Or talked at all."

Vincent nodded, but said nothing.

Thinking about what Gran had told me, I wanted to take back the words. My brain raced to try to think of a way to fix it.

Before the silence could get awkward, I tried to fill in the blanks. "Will you call more often next time?"

"I'm not good at this," Vincent said.

"At what?"

"You and me. I shouldn't have—" Vincent stopped.

My chest seemed to freeze and it was hard to keep my breathing steady.

"I'm making this worse," he said after a too-long pause.

"Yeah." It was all I knew I could say without letting my voice betrayed how I felt.

"I don't think we need to check again, Rider," Boone said, coming in.

Vincent moved to stand up.

"Where are you going?" I asked.

"I thought I'd give you and Boone a chance to talk on our way there." His voice was resigned.

I let out an exasperated breath. "Sit down." I tugged lightly on his shirt.

Boone stood to the side as everyone filed in.

"I don't mind," Vincent said, keeping his voice quiet.

"I do."

He didn't move.

"I'd like you to stay," I said.

He relented and sat back down. I could feel his mood shift, becoming stonier as the others sat down around us.

It was a start. Not the best one, but at least he stayed.

Davis passed us, looking unsettled, though she did return my smile.

Rider took his seat and Boone joined him once Logan settled in near Tolman.

"What do you think of the plane?" Boone asked, swiveling around to talk to us.

"It's great," I said. "Do you all go everywhere in this?"

Vincent seemed to tense next to me.

"Anywhere we can't drive," Boone said. "There's containment in the back if we need to prevent someone or something from hurting themselves or others. The whole thing is pretty roomy."

Without thinking, I put a steadying hand on Vincent's arm, trying to get him to relax. "And to think, it took me forever just to get a new phone."

It was as though Vincent's stress fractured when my energy reached out to his and mingled.

"You dropped the phone into a river," Rider said.

"To be fair, I dropped myself into the river right after it," I said.

Boone laughed and Vincent raised an eyebrow in my direction.

I smiled and let go of him, but shifted so that my arm rested against his.

"And now you've taken my phone away from me again," I said to Boone. "We *are* going to have some sort of communication on this trip, right?"

"We have a sat phone," Boone said. "Sorry to pull you all in on this, but I think we need the backup for what we're up against."

"I'm happy to help," I said.

"I'm sure there were other things you'd rather be doing," Boone said, grinning with subtlety of a sledgehammer.

"It'll be okay, but I do appreciate you bringing all four of us in on the case," I said.

"Rest up," Boone said. "In about fourteen hours, our boots are going to hit the ground in the middle of nowhere."

I nodded, and then Boone turned around. He started talking with Rider as the plane took off.

No one was paying attention, but then again, Vincent and I were within hearing range of pretty much everyone. Talking hadn't ended very well earlier, so it was probably best that we stayed silent.

Boone's whole team was asleep not long after we left. It had been a long day—actually a long two days—without sleep, so I decided to take Boone's advice to heart. The seat lay almost completely flat. Reluctantly, I reclined, losing contact with Vincent. Then low of energy between us cut off and I instantly missed the connection.

I almost sat back up again, but Vincent went to the front of the plane. When I peeked over the seat, I saw that he was chatting with Logan.

Getting comfortable in the seat wasn't easy, despite its size. Or maybe I wasn't comfortable because Vincent had walked away.

To my surprise, a few minutes later, Vincent slid back into his seat. He didn't look at me when he laid down, but after a moment, he moved his arm to lay against my own, which I had conveniently stretched in his direction when he sat back down.

I closed my eyes and felt the steady push and pull of power inside us. His soul reached out to the small part of it I had inside me, while mine reached out to the small part in him.

It was as though a circuit had been connected. One that I didn't want to break again.

I dozed off and on during our trip, making small talk when others were awake. When we arrived, Vincent was the first to pull away.

"Okay," Boone said, standing up while the plane taxied off the strip. "We have a helicopter waiting for us. Renick and Tolman, grab the equipment. There will be a loader available."

As soon as the plane came to a stop, Renick pushed open the door and Tolman followed him out.

"There is no safe place to land where we're going," Boone said. "Do you all know how to rappel?"

"What is rappel?" Rider asked.

"You hook yourself to a rope and jump, using the rope to slow yourself down," Boone said.

"I have never done that," Rider said.

"Me either." I couldn't believe that he'd waited until almost the last minute to ask if I knew how to jump out of a helicopter.

"Vincent? Logan?" Boone asked.

"I've done it a few times," Logan said.

"Same here," Vincent said.

"Good," Boone said. "Rider and Cassie, you are each going tandem with one of us. Rider, you're with me. Cassie, Davis is going to get you down."

I looked over at Davis and she gave me what she probably thought was a reassuring smile.

It didn't work.

"When we find our spot, Tolman and Renick are going to go down and evaluate the immediate area. Logan, do you want to go with them?"

"I'll join their rodeo," Logan said.

"Great. We'll send the gear down. While you work with

Tolman, Renick will secure the supplies. Once that's done, Vincent will go, and then the rest of us will follow."

It was hard to believe we were relaxing on the plane minutes ago.

"Any questions?" Boone asked.

My mind went blank. I'm sure I had many of them, but I couldn't think of even one at the moment. The idea that he was asking me to jump out of a helicopter was taking up too much of my focus.

"If it's okay with Logan, I'd like Davis to take Cassie and Rider over and get them set up."

"Vincent will go with them," Logan said. "I'll help here."

"Okay, let's get moving," Boone said.

Davis practically jumped into her gear then hustled out of the plane. Vincent, Rider, and I went at a much more sedate pace. Logan and Boone followed us out, but went to the back of the plane. Davis was waiting for the rest of us on a vehicle very similar to the one at the base.

Previous base, I corrected myself, looking around. This one was much smaller, but it was definitely a military estab-lishment.

Davis took off across the worn pavement. The sun was still hanging high, but working itself down for the day. It might have been better if it was night. The heat where we left was a dry heat, which didn't seem as bad as the thick air around us now.

"Have you been here before?" I asked as we zipped toward the helicopter.

"No," Davis said.

"But you seem to know your way around so well," I said.

"Maps," she said with a smile. "I studied lots of maps to get ready for this."

"Did you study a map of the forest as well?"

"A topographical map, yes."

"I have zero sense of direction," I admitted. "Even with a map, I'd probably get lost."

"Stick with us," Davis said. "We'll get you in and out."

"I'll try to keep up."

"From what Boone said, I figured it was going to be me trying to keep up with you."

"I can't imagine why. The only reason I'm alive is because of him."

"Whatever he saw, he was impressed by it."

CHAPTER

SEVEN

What has Boone been telling people?

I knew it probably wouldn't hurt to ask Davis, but it felt strange to ask someone I didn't know.

"It's not as hot as I expected," Davis said as she pulled to a stop well away from the helicopter.

"The rainy season is about to start," Vincent said.

Davis glanced at him with a slightly nervous look. "It definitely feels like it."

"Doesn't it rain there all time?" I asked.

"Yes," Davis said. "It just rains more during the wet season."

"You guys can get on board," Davis said to Rider and Vincent. "We'll catch up."

Vincent didn't look happy about that, but went on anyway.

I wondered what Davis wanted with me, though I didn't have to wait long.

"So," Davis said, "tell me about Vincent."

"What about him?"

"You work with him."

"Yes." I couldn't help but start to feel defensive.

"And he's a Walker."

"Yes."

"We're worried about him being on the trip."

Well, that was blunt. "Why?" I asked.

"He takes people's souls. Doesn't that bother you?"

"Just because he can, doesn't mean he will," I snapped. "You have a gun right now. You could easily pick it up and shoot me in the head. Should I be worried about that?"

Davis looked uncertain.

"Vincent's not a bad guy," I pressed. "He doesn't always give a great first impression, but I think Renick aggravated him. You don't have to worry about him."

"Renick has that effect on people," Davis said, seeming to relax.

"He *really* does."

Davis grinned, but looked as though she was trying to suppress it. "Are you sure you aren't a little biased about Vincent?"

"Why?" I asked, already feeling my face turn red.

"You two seem... close."

I looked over to the helicopter to see if Rider was listening in. If he was, he wasn't letting on.

"We're getting that way. Slowly."

"He *is* cute," Davis said.

It was impossible for me not to smile. "He is."

"Well, Boone trusts him, I guess, or he wouldn't be here. Not on this mission.

"Vincent saved our lives. He's saved mine countless times."

"Sorry if I said anything I shouldn't have."

"Sadly, it happens a lot." I watched Vincent moving around on the helicopter. "You see a lot of things in this job, but we're all just people, like any other."

"I'll remember that," Davis said.

Another vehicle was fast approaching. I could see Renick behind the wheel.

"I guess we should go," I said. "Time to wave goodbye to civilization for a while."

"Sounds good to me," Davis said, walking away.

Davis might have preferred the wilderness, but I liked my creature comforts. Maybe it was a soldier thing.

I knew I didn't have to duck my head when going toward the helicopter, but with the whirring blades not that far away, it was hard to resist the urge.

It wasn't as bad being inside, at least until Davis started strapping me into some sort of harness.

"This is awkward as hell," Davis said. "But the drop doesn't last long. You'll basically be on my back. We'll secure ourselves with a safety line, step down, and then Boone will hook us together."

"Step down on what?" I asked.

"One of the skids." Davis gestured out the door.

My stomach clenched at the thought.

"Jumping is hard and landing is difficult, but at least we're about the same height. Boone's going to have a hell of a time with Rider." She adjusted a few more straps around my legs. "I think you're set. Looks like Vincent has Rider set up. I'll go check on him."

In a few moments, Vincent joined me. He started testing the harness.

He was all business, but my stomach fluttered when he pulled at the strap on my waist and checked the tightness of the cinches around my thighs.

"Don't worry," Vincent said. "Boone wouldn't have paired you with Davis if she wasn't good at this."

"I'm sure it'll be okay." With Vincent at my side, my anxiety about jumping had been replaced with nervousness of another sort. Maybe if I kept him close I wouldn't stress out about dangling from a helicopter.

Once we were loaded and the door was closed, the helicopter took off. Boone spoke with Rider about what they were going to do, then he tested Rider's harness.

When Boone came over to check on me, Vincent stayed close as he put on his harness. I could feel that Vincent was uncomfortable with Boone being there, but he didn't say anything and didn't hover.

"Did Davis explain everything?" Boone asked.

"I think so."

Boone nodded and went around to each person, checking everything over, and giving last-minute instructions to his team.

I tried to put on a facade of calm, but I'm not sure it worked. Vincent could sense I was nervous, but he almost always knew what I was feeling; one of the benefits of sharing a soul—or one of the drawbacks, depending on how you looked at it.

Far too soon, they were opening the doors. Tolman and then Renick disappeared over the edge. One by one, I watched them go. The equipment went down next.

When Vincent stepped down, I held my breath until he was out of sight.

Pushing my fear back, I followed Davis. She showed me how to step down, and even though I had watched everyone else, I appreciated the instruction.

Boone hooked us together. "Don't hold on too tight."

Davis steadied herself. I held on, and the moment my feet left the skids, I'm pretty sure my heart stopped. Closing my eyes seemed like a good idea, yet I couldn't help but look around. The forest was beautiful.

The drop wasn't free fall, but my stomach flipped as though it was. Before I knew it, we thudded down on solid ground. My insides felt as though they were trying to catch up. Renick unhooked us and helped me out of my harness. It surprised me that he didn't have some annoying comment. However, I guess when it was time to get to work then he did just that. That made me feel a little better about him.

But only a little.

The harness and the lines went up.

"This way," Davis said.

She led me to our supplies. Back in the hangar, there hadn't appeared to be a lot, but now it looked like so much stuff. In the past, our few days here and there in the woods had been short trips and we hadn't needed to carry weeks' worth of food and supplies.

Davis passed me a rifle and I slung it over my shoulder. After that, I pretty much just stayed out of the way. About ten minutes later, Rider joined me. His eyes were like saucers and his hair looked wild.

"What did you think?" I asked.

"Jumping straight from the helicopter would be easier. If they had gone a little lower, we could have."

"Landing the helicopter and stepping out on firm ground is my preference."

Rider started to look around once he was handed weapons. I watched the helicopter fly away. When the noise died down, it felt as though our final cord to civilization was severed.

In a way, that's exactly what happened.

When I turned around, Rider was gone.

"Rider?" I called quietly.

He stepped out from behind a tree yards away.

"Stick close, okay? This isn't like the woods back home."

"It smells like..." Rider breathed deeply and exhaled loudly. "It smells like the forests in my world."

Rider never spoke much about his home in the other dimension, but I knew things weren't good when he left. From what it sounded like, when his father died, his family had gone to pieces. His brother killed his sister and would have killed Rider if he hadn't left.

"Where did you put your gun?" I asked.

Rider tapped the holster on his leg.

"The other one," I said.

He went to a tree and picked it up, but held it out to me, arm outstretched. "The chemicals in these tranquilizers smell different than ours."

"I've got live rounds. I'll trade you," I said. "Bring it here."

While we traded guns, Boone came over. "We have a few hours of daylight left. Tolman and Renick are checking the immediate vicinity. Rider, Logan said you'd know where he is."

Rider cocked an ear and listened for a moment. "He is in that direction." Rider pointed. "Not far."

"He told me he'd stick close," Boone said, nodding.

"Where are Vincent and Davis?" I asked.

"They're checking reference points to make sure we know where we are."

"I'm glad *someone* knows," I muttered, looking around.

"You didn't get a chance to try out your pack back at the base," Boone said. "Let's get it fitted now."

"Fitted?" I asked, setting the tranq rifle to the side. "I thought they were pretty much one size fits all."

"Sort of," Boone said. "But if you have them adjusted wrong it's a lot more work to carry around."

Boone lifted the pack and I put my arms through the straps. When Boone let go, it felt as though the thing was filled with lead. Having been stuck in the middle of nowhere recently with almost no supplies, I decided I liked the weight. It was a reminder that things weren't too dire.

Boone adjusted the clasps at my waist, then buckled the straps together across my chest. "How's that feel? Too heavy?"

"It's not bad."

He moved the bag around some and made some more adjustments as Davis joined us.

"We've noted three points," Davis said, speaking louder and more forceful than I expected.

"Excellent," Boone said, pulling a strap to take away some of the slack. "Good work. Let's gear up and move out. Rider, do you want to... Where's Rider?"

"I am here," Rider said, coming back into view from the other side of the clearing.

"At least you have your gun with you this time," I said.

Rider nodded, but he wasn't really looking at us. His eyes roved everywhere and he really seemed to like what he saw.

"Let me know when Logan's on his way back," Boone said. "I'm assuming he can find us, right?"

"He said he will catch up to us very soon."

"Rider," I said, watching him walk into the woods again.

"Yes?" He asked.

"Will you stick with us?"

"I will," Rider said.

"In sight, please," I said.

Rider stepped back into the clearing. "Your sight or mine?"

"Mine."

Rider frowned, but nodded.

Vincent and Davis had already donned their packs and Boone was putting his on.

"Grab your kit, Rider," Boone said. "Let's move out."

Boone led the way and Vincent followed. Rider picked up his bag and tossed it over his shoulder as if it weighed nothing.

Davis was watching him, as though she were sizing him up. When she saw me looking at her, she waved me over. We followed behind the others.

The clearing had grass—dense, tall, and heavy. Once we stepped under the trees, I saw there were vines coming down and bushes or small trees going up. Even following people that had already forged a trail, it was difficult to navigate.

"Do you mind if I ask you something?" Davis asked, speaking low and watching the others in front of us.

I kept my eyes firmly glued to the ground, making sure nothing unexpected tripped me up.

"Sure," I said, uncertain if I actually minded or not.

"I've seen Vincent's eyes go black, and I've seen them swirl with a kind of dark color, like ink spilled across water. Why do they do that?"

"Sometimes it's just a natural response to what's in front of him. When did you notice this?"

"Back at the base when we first saw him. His eyes were flat black. Then, when he and I came into the clearing to report to Boone, they started to turn black, but stopped."

I sighed before I could stop myself. Vincent and I really needed to have a talk about Boone. He was seeing something that wasn't there. Why had he needed to spend so much time away? We could have worked it all out by now if he had talked to me.

"Did I say something wrong again?" Davis asked.

"No, he probably saw something he didn't like."

Rider wasn't in sight again. He was usually partnered with Vincent, and Logan and I generally teamed up. The four of us only worked together on larger cases. I felt the need to keep track of my friend.

"And Rider?" Davis asked.

"What about him?" I asked, trying not to get preemptively defensive once again.

"How much can he lift?"

"Um... I'm not sure, really. More than most people would expect, I know that."

"Davis, is the team on their way back?" Boone called.

Davis halted and I stopped next to her. A faraway expression appeared.

"They are," Davis called up to Boone.

"Mind if I ask you a few questions?" I asked once we started moving again.

Davis grinned. "Only seems fair."

"How do you know if they're on their way?"

"It's hard to explain. The three of us can kind of... sense one another."

"What about other people?"

"No, just them."

I wanted to ask what else she could do, but felt that would be really invasive. It would also leave her open to be able to ask me, and I didn't want to have to try to explain.

"The undergrowth is thinning out," I noted, trying to change the subject.

"Good," she said. "It would suck to have to walk through that crap all day."

"It's going to get dark quick under the canopy," Boone said. "I want us to get as far as we can tonight."

"Are we going to the village?" I asked.

"Not the one you're thinking of. A survivor turned up in another place, so we're going there first," Boone said.

"Why didn't we land there?" I asked.

"These people are primitive," Boone said. "Extremely primitive. If we go in by foot, we might be welcomed. At the very least someone should talk to us."

"What language do they speak?" I asked.

"Most of these tribes have their own language," Boone said. "Some of them can be pretty hostile, so we have to keep up our guard."

"So, how do we talk to them?" I asked.

"I'll be able to help there," Logan said, striding up behind us.

Davis jumped and turned, but tried to play it off once her brain caught up with the fact that it was Logan.

"One of these days I'm going to remember the bells," I said under my breath. I knew both of my light-footed partners would be able to hear me.

"You think you'll know their language?" Boone asked.

"Could be," Logan said, passing Davis and me. "What was your plan for talking with them?

"Sometimes there are people in the tribe that deal with outsiders. Someone might know Spanish or Portuguese."

"Let me try first," Logan said. "We might get further if we're actually speaking their language."

"Do we want to see them tonight?" Rider asked.

"No," Boone said. "There's not enough daylight left."

"We should stop here," Rider said.

"There might be a decent spot on one of the rises," Logan said. "Rider, why don't you check it out?"

Rider smiled and bounded off, almost immediately disappearing.

"You don't think we can get any closer?" Boone asked, turning back to us.

I had forgotten that Boone always tried to look for an explanation as to why a suggestion was made, unless he really trusted that person. I thought he trusted Rider in that way, but I must have been wrong.

"Rider would know better than the rest of us," Logan said. "Sounds like we have a place to bed down for the night."

Without another word, Logan disappeared into the woods.

"That's a good point," Boone said. He started to follow, but then stopped. "Cassie, do you mind leading the way?"

If he was asking, it was because Logan really had disappeared. I wasn't sure of the specifics, but elves are really good about disappearing, and they make no noise when walking in the woods.

Logan probably hadn't appreciated Boone second guessing Rider, so he was going to let him figure out where to go on his own.

"Sure." I closed my eyes and mentally stretched, making the jump into the Path. I tried to hold back some of the strength, hoping it would hide me from other things that lived in the Path. I knew if I could see them, they could see me, but I didn't know if they could see me at any other times.

Looking around, I spotted Rider's Path, which was the easiest to find and follow.

The rest of the world was too much of a distraction to actually move. The green canopy above glittered and swayed. A current of swirls wound through the area, showing the Path the air took. Streaks filled the sky, possibly left by birds from earlier in the day.

"Cass?"

The truly unique thing about the Path was the fact that it was virtually untouched.

"Cass?" Vincent's voice snapped me back to the group.

"Right. Yeah. We're going this way." I followed Rider's Path up the hill, though I couldn't help but watch my surroundings. Animal trails crisscrossed the forest floor and ran up the trees.

I didn't drop the Path when we walked out into a rocky area where Logan and Rider were waiting. The most vivid orange I'd ever seen in the Path came through here. Usually, animal Paths were weaker because they ran on instinct and didn't think deeply enough to make an imprint on the world around them.

The glittering orange flow called to me. I could see that it was an animal Path; the instinctual fluctuations were still there.

This is their world. The Path remembers them so deeply because it belongs to them. We shouldn't be here.

Looking back, I noticed the Paths of the others contaminated the surrounding areas. It was almost sad to see. I turned to follow the orange thread and found Rider blocking my way.

EIGHT

He didn't say anything, but then again, he didn't have to. With a sigh of regret, I took one last look at the world around me, then closed my eyes and stepped back into the real world. Color bled out of the surroundings and the vibrant forest turned drab.

"Your home was like this?" I asked him.

"Parts of it were," Rider said. "The best parts."

"I can see why you keep wandering off into the woods."

I set the rifle to the side and started working my way out of the straps. Once I put the gear aside, I realized how worn I felt. I wondered briefly how far we had gone today. Looking around at everyone setting up, I realized I was probably the only one that didn't actually have a clue as to the distance of our hike.

Is judging distances something that can be learned? At this point, if I hadn't learned it yet, I probably wouldn't be able to.

I rolled my shoulders to loosen them and opened my bag. Water was my main goal, but I also dragged out my hammock. There were plenty of trees, but not all of them far enough apart to be useful for hammocks. As the camp began to take shape, I saw that we were scattered around the area.

While I was working, Renick and Tolman caught up.

"What kind of knot is that?" Vincent asked.

I raised my eyebrow to see if he was kidding. "The knot kind."

He had trouble hiding the grin on his face. "Mind if I rework those?"

I shrugged. "Sure. I'd rather not have my tarp falling down on me in the middle of the night."

"Oh, it would stay up," Vincent said as he started trying to untie one of my knots. "It just might not come back down tomorrow when it's time to leave."

"I see." I started to untie the other end.

Looking around, I saw that no one seemed to be paying much attention to us.

"We should talk," I said.

"We need to," Vincent said.

Neither of us said anything for a while as Vincent worked on retying his side.

When he was finished, I handed off my side to him.

"We don't know how long we're going to be out here," Vincent said.

"That's true," I agreed. "Hopefully it won't be longer than a week."

"The point is," Vincent said, testing the new knot he'd easily put together, "we're going to be working with this new team."

"We are." I was leery of where the conversation was going. I grabbed my tarp, ready to throw it over the new guideline.

"I think things might work better, you know, as a team, if we kept our distance."

My mouth fell open. "What?"

"It's not what I want," Vincent said, grabbing my hand that was holding the tarp. "But they'll get along better with you if you aren't around me." He took the tarp and stepped away, throwing it over the guideline.

I took a quick look around the camp. "If they don't like it, that's their problem."

"It's only until we get home."

I didn't say anything. At that moment, I didn't trust myself even to open my mouth.

"Look, I've seen the way they stare at me. It's for the best. They need to know they can trust you and vice-versa."

If I opened my mouth, it was either going to be to cry, which would embarrass me to no end, or to yell at him, which wouldn't be much better.

He finished staking down the tarp, then came back over to me.

"We're okay, aren't we?" he asked.

"No," I said through clenched teeth. "We really, really aren't."

Worry pulsed in the Path. I could feel it without the need to Read.

"It's for the best," he said.

I crossed my arms and glared at him. "I'm not okay with this."

"It's for the best," he repeated. With his stone-like mask set in place, he left.

My mind warred with itself, fighting to determine the best way to deal with the situation.

Boone and Logan had already agreed there would be no fire except for the small one for cooking, so the camp darkened quickly. They also assigned Davis and me to first watch.

Luckily, I had pretty good night vision. As my mind grappled over a course of action, I watched Vincent talk to Rider, who looked in my direction anxiously a few times.

"I need your kit, princess," Renick said, stepping into my line of sight.

"Where does it need to go?" I asked.

"It'll have to go with all the others."

I went to pick up the bag, but Renick beat me to it.

His grin died away when he looked in my direction again.

"What's up, big man?" he asked.

"Up is where the supplies belong," Rider said from behind me.

Renick apparently didn't know what to think of Rider yet, so he walked off.

"Vincent sent me over," Rider said once Renick was gone. "He does not like Renick."

"Oh, no. That is not happening."

"Vincent means well."

"Is that what you really think?"

"I do."

"Well, I think he's being an ass, and you can tell him I said so."

Rider wrung his hands. "I do not know what to do."

"About what?" I asked.

"Do I really say that to Vincent?"

The wind went out of my anger. "No, I'm just frustrated. Don't worry about it." I wanted to tell Rider that if Vincent wanted something done and it involved me, make Vincent do it himself, but that seemed hypocritical to have Rider deliver a message like that. "I'm going to grab dinner."

"We should meditate."

I almost said not tonight, but I thought better of it. My powers weren't working well, and when my mind was mixed up, it seemed to be worse. The last thing I needed was to be out here and not be able to handle the blinding pain using my powers could cause. Even worse, I wasn't always alone in the Path anymore, which was unnerving and could cause even more issues.

"Sure," I agreed. "Let's find something to eat and then find a comfortable place."

We quickly grabbed some food, but there was very little time to eat. Where had the day gone? Rider was patiently waiting for me when I finished.

"Over here," Rider said, leading the way.

He found a place slightly away from the camp, for which I was glad. Meditating with a bunch of people staring would be difficult.

When I closed my eyes, the shattered pieces of my soul were waiting for me at the edge of my mind. At the moment, they seemed to be moving with each other, which was good. When the shards started grinding against each other was when I had problems.

Twenty minutes later, I opened my eyes to full darkness.

"Time for guard duty," I said, rising to my feet.

"We should ask Vincent to join us tomorrow night," Rider said.

"I'm not sure he'll want to be included." I looked up and spotted Vincent watching us come back into camp. "Besides, if he were there, it might make it more difficult."

"You do seem rather upset with him."

"He's being unreasonable."

"He is trying to make things easier for you."

"Yeah, well, he's making them harder. Never mind him for now."

"If that is what you want."

"I'm going on duty. Get some sleep."

I met up with Davis at the edge of camp.

"How's your first day going?" Davis asked.

"Not the best," I admitted.

"Renick?" she asked.

"No, Vincent's just... being himself, which can sometimes be as annoying as Renick."

Davis chuckled. "You haven't seen anything yet."

"How's your first day going?"

Davis shrugged. "Tolman is being difficult, but then, that's the way things go sometimes. We'll work it out."

"Is it the change of having new partners?"

"That's possible. He doesn't deal well with other people."

"I know exactly what that's like."

"It really is nice having another woman as a partner." Davis beamed. "Okay, we need a plan."

"We're more in your element here. I'll take your lead."

We walked the perimeter together once, then went our separate ways. The first shift worked well for me. By the time I carefully woke up Rider to take over, I was out of steam and too worn out to worry anymore about Vincent. After one last reminder for Rider not to wander off, I went to bed and almost immediately fell asleep.

The next morning, I avoided contact with Vincent, though not because of his ridiculous request. It was more an issue of not wanting to yell and to be further ticked off first thing in the morning.

I could tell Rider felt torn. At first, I was worried that he thought I was upset with him. Instead, I learned he wanted to fix things between Vincent and me.

We left quickly the next day and staggered out once again. Rider took the lead with Davis. Vincent and Tolman were behind us all. Imagining what stellar conversationalists they both were I knew there wouldn't be anything in the way of team bonding happening between them.

We had only gone about a mile before Rider slowed to a stop. Logan and Boone joined Rider and Davis. Tolman and Vincent were only a short distance behind and arrived before Renick had the chance to be annoying. It wasn't long before Logan signaled. The elf had an amazing whistle that mingled with the air to create something that was seemingly natural, yet completely distinguishable as coming from him.

When we approached, Boone and Logan had their bags off and were in deep conversation off to the side.

"Everything okay?" I asked. Following Logan and Boone's lead, I took the opportunity to take off the backpack.

Rider shook his head. "It is not. The village is ahead. I can tell that people have been in this area, but from the town, I only smell blood."

CHAPTER
NINE

"Smell blood, huh?" Tolman said. "I don't suppose it's animal blood."

I was surprised to hear from the almost silent man. His voice sounded gruff, probably from disuse.

"It is human and there is a lot of it," Rider said.

"We're going in together," Boone said, joining us.

Davis looked a little surprised by the decision, but said nothing.

Boone might have noticed her look, because he began to fill in details of the decision. From our time together, I knew from experience that Boone was the type to just give orders, or at least try to, and expected them to be followed. Maybe while in the gremlin world I broke him of the idea that everyone around him was a soldier.

"We don't know what we're dealing with. If the nightmare did this, we don't know how or even if it's still in the area. There are more things—worse things—that can be found this far away from civilization. People could have done this, or another animal. We stick together. Everyone stay in sight of someone else. *Visual sight*," he added after the slightest of pauses.

"We'll fan out," Logan said, "but we'll want to stay close enough together to hear each other as well as see. And we'll move slow. Rifles and handguns at the ready. Until we know what we're dealing with, it's not a time for tranqs. The supplies stay here."

Boone pulled a net out of his bag and Logan grabbed a thick rope out of his.

"The supplies aren't going to be safe here no matter what we do with them," Boone said. "But if we keep them in the netting and high up, they'll at least have a chance."

Once our supplies were stowed, we moved quietly to the village. It wasn't the time to talk, which was good. For me, at least, wondering what we might find was filling my mind to the point that there wasn't room for conversation.

When Rider indicated, Boone gave out hand signals, ordering us to fan out. It was only because he had taught me a few of the signals that I knew what his instructions were. Even then I didn't understand exactly what he was saying, just enough to get by.

We spread apart and inched forward. I had my gun in hand, but hated the thought of using it. The tranq rifle slung over my shoulder would have been preferable. It always was when dealing with the Lost.

However, Boone had mentioned the possibility of people doing this. With people, I felt safer with the gun in hand.

The thought took me by surprise. A raging minotaur could be rampaging toward me and my first instinct would be to dart him and run like hell. Put a few attacking humans together and I wanted a gun in my hand. Granted, my first instinct would still be to run like hell, but I was getting better at tamping down that urge.

Which also might not be a good thing.

I gritted my teeth and pushed the thoughts out of my mind. Stalking toward a blood-splattered village wasn't the best time for introspection.

The trees began to thin and I could hear running water. A stream, maybe? It was too bad I didn't have the maps of the area memorized like Davis did.

By the time the first hut came into view, the smell of blood became noticeable. When we stepped into the open air, the stench permeated everything.

With a few more hand signals, we broke into smaller teams and began to walk by the first row of huts. When we stepped away from them, I was surprised to see the actual size of the village. It wasn't huge by modern standards, but it spread out. The homes seemed to have been erected in a haphazard manner, but most faced each other and a well-worn Path between them was practically a street.

We came together again.

"We're going to split up and search the area," Boone said. "Look for any threat. We also need to talk to any survivors we may find."

Together, we all moved up the road and then broke into groups, two by two, to check in and around the homes. Once the area was cleared, we went back to the road and went a few houses up to the next one that needed to be checked.

It was methodical and something that both teams were familiar with. Once all the huts were finished, we merged again and carefully moved forward into a clearing with a long building.

This place had been built with some thought. It was fully enclosed, whereas some of the huts had only three walls. Strong wood made up its construction. The roof was still thatched, like most of the other dwellings.

"This is not good," Rider said.

He didn't have to say why. The stench of death was strong here.

"Do you hear anything?" I asked.

"Not here and any other smells are being masked by blood." A gruffness was in his voice that worried me.

Rider's gaze was fixed on the building. Logan and I were the only ones who took notice of the strange tone. I watched my friend almost as much as Logan.

There was a difference in Rider's face. His skin looked darker and his hands were stretched out. Rider's black hair usually laid flat and smooth. Now it looked as though it was growing bushy. The most noticeable difference was his eyes. A glow was in his eyes that would have looked beautiful, except when combined with the rest of the changes.

With all these together, Rider was scary enough that I wondered for a moment if it really was him.

I glanced at Logan, but he looked at a loss as for what to do.

Boone breached the building.

Rider automatically stepped forward to follow the others in. I wasn't sure it was a good idea for Rider to be any closer to this mess, so I stepped in front of him, making sure to lower my gun first. Rider kept his weapon gripped tightly. Thankfully, his finger wasn't on the trigger, but he looked agitated.

"Rider, why don't you come with me," I said, trying to remain all smiles while my friend had a gun pointed in my direction. Not *at* me, per se. But when someone is ready to storm a building, you have to expect a gun to be pointed at you if you stupidly step in front of them.

He lowered his gun. For a moment, I was relieved, then I saw that his hands were balled into fists.

"I sure hope you have the Path open," Logan said.

"That might not be a good idea," I said. "It affects him

when I open the Path."

"Cassie, step away," Logan said, keeping his voice quiet and careful.

Glancing his way, I saw that his own face had elongated and looked more angular.

"What? No, I'm not going to step away." I looked back at Rider, frowning now. "Rider and I are friends. He's not going to do anything to a friend, are you, Rider."

"I think the smell of so much blood trumps all that," Logan said. "Step away. That's an order."

"That's what?" I yelled at Logan. "No. We just need to take a step back. Rider and I are going to go check on the bags and bring back some water. Right Rider?" It was the best I could think of. We could search the village again, but I didn't know what he'd do if he ran into any other pools of blood.

"Clear," voices called out in the building.

"It's better that we're gone before they come out." I turned my attention directly at Rider. "My friend isn't going to let me walk out into the jungle on my own, right?" Using an extreme amount of willpower, I walked toward Rider. It looked as though he tensed for a moment, but I brushed past him and moved toward the tree line.

I wanted to turn around to see if he was coming, but for some reason, I thought that would be a very bad idea. Rider wasn't in his usual frame of mind. He might decide to go back into the village if I didn't have faith in him. When I walked into the woods, I listened hard for any sounds of Rider behind me.

There was nothing.

But, of course, Rider moved silently in the woods. I wouldn't hear anything even if he *were* behind me.

In a few more steps, I heard a twig break behind me and I smiled.

"Feeling any better?" I asked.

A growl behind me made me stop dead in my tracks. Shadows grew thicker around us, but it only lasted a moment. He'd made that sound before. It was a threat.

Once my heart decided to unfreeze, I took a deep breath and moved forward, slowly. At this point, I had to make it clear to him I wasn't running, just moving forward.

We moved silently like that for some time. It took me a while to relax my fear enough to pay attention to anything else besides Rider.

"Shit," I said, mostly under my breath. I sighed and looked at the terrain. "I have no idea where we are."

I turned around. Rider was standing right behind me. Close.

Too close.

With my heart pounding in my chest and my brain telling me to run, I looked up at Rider's eyes, which was a long way up, especially this close.

He wasn't even looking at me. Even better, he looked like my Rider again. Relief welled up, but I tried to play it off.

"I don't suppose you have any idea where we are?"

He seemed to be ignoring me, so I looked around, trying to find something familiar.

My trek through the woods had left an obvious trail, which was good. We'd entered the village far away from where we exited, but we were traveling in the same direction.

"Let's go this way," I said, while mentally trying to map out the forest in relation to the village.

With Rider this close, I could sense his movement behind me, but he dropped farther back.

"You know," I said after a while, "I think you worried Logan back there."

"I did."

Hearing his voice back to normal lifted some of the weight

of worry that had started weighing me down.

"Any idea what he told the others?" I asked.

"I was not listening." He paused before adding, "I should have been listening."

I shrugged. "Why? I wasn't."

Rider chuckled softly.

Even with a light laugh, I could tell he was still straining or wrestling with something.

"Want to talk about it?" I asked.

"About listening?"

"That's not what I meant and you know it. If you want to talk about what happened back there, I'm listening. If you don't want to talk about it, that's okay, but I need to know when you're feeling well enough to go back." I stopped and stared up at the trees. "Although, I wouldn't mind also talking about where the hell we are."

"We are close."

Looking around, I saw the direction he motioned for us to go in. I'd like to say that I had been heading in the right direction, but it would be a stretch.

At least we didn't have to go back the way we came.

There was movement out of the corner of my eye. Even though I turned my head quickly, I didn't catch what it was.

"Did you see that?" I asked, stopping once again.

"I did not see anything."

"Are there any animals close by?" I asked. "Close enough that I could see?" I added.

Rider pointed up a tree. "I am not sure what that is. A kind of monkey, maybe?"

"Awww, it's a sloth." If anyone else had been here, I would have been embarrassed by that, but not with Rider alongside me. "He's cute. He's also slow though—not what I thought I saw."

It crossed my mind to ask if he smelled anything strange around, but I didn't want him to think of smells right now.

I looked up at the sloth again before moving on.

"There is a large snake over there," Rider said.

When I glanced the way he pointed, I also involuntarily took a step back from that direction.

"How large is large?" I watched for a moment until I saw a large mass move on the ground. "Nope." I sped up, trying to go wide around the creature. "Nope, not dealing with that."

Rider chuckled, a real laugh this time.

"Do me a favor and warn me if you see another one of those. I don't care how far away it is, I want to know about it."

"I will do that," he said. "Right up there."

He pointed straight ahead of us and up.

I stumbled backwards. "Another snake?" My voice went squeaky.

"Our supplies."

I put a hand to my chest to try to calm my racing heart. This time, I followed Rider until we stood under our gear.

"I should have thought this through better," I said.

"You said we would bring back water, correct?" he asked.

"Yeah, although since we're here, we may as well grab power bars or something for everyone's lunch."

Rider untied the rope holding the bags in the air and started hauling them up until they were almost touching the branch. He then climbed up the tree.

"Is there anything I can do to help?"

"It will only take me a few minutes," Rider said.

While Rider worked, I looked around. It was beautiful here. Gorgeous, even. If it weren't for the blood waiting for us back at the village, I might have even enjoyed the jungle.

A blur appeared and disappeared at the corner of my vision. I slowly scanned the landscape, trying to catch sight of anything out of the ordinary. Since I had no idea what was 'ordinary' here, it didn't narrow things down much.

When Rider joined me, I was squinting in the area I had seen the blur.

"Are you well?" Rider asked.

"Can you go over there by that tree and tell me if you see or hear anything around there?"

Rider slung a bag over his shoulder and walked to the spot.

"Over the past two days there has been nothing here except for us and a large cat."

"Oh. Thanks." I looked around a little more, but saw nothing. "Do you want to go back?"

"We should."

I gave up my search for invisible movements and smiled at Rider. "That's not what I asked."

"I was... taken by surprise. I will be ready once we reach the village."

"Don't worry. They've probably already cleared the building. We won't have to go in there."

"I must go inside."

"Why?"

"A werewolf was killed inside."

"A werewolf, out here?" I didn't bother asking if he was sure. Rider could identify anything familiar by smell.

"She is someone I once knew."

"Rider, I am so sorry to hear that. Of course you were upset."

"Angry," Rider corrected. "Very, very angry."

"Is there anything I can do?" I asked.

Rider looked confused. "She is dead. I do not think you can help."

"I mean... I'm not sure what werewolves think of death. I

don't know how *you* think about death, especially of someone you know."

"I understand."

"Vincent and I both might need you to tell us what you need along the way." I thought about mentioning Logan, but he wasn't friends with Rider the way Vincent and I were.

"I will attempt to do that."

"And we're going to make mistakes, but know it's because we want to help you."

"Thank you."

I stood awkwardly, not sure what to do at that point. Thankfully, Rider took pity on me.

"I would like to return to the village now."

"Of course," I said, setting off at once.

"It is the other way," Rider said after I had gone a short distance.

"Of course. Sure. It's... that way?" I pointed behind us.

Rider moved my arm. "That is the correct direction."

"Thanks."

It was interesting to me that Rider didn't wander as he normally would. Instead, he stayed close by. Close enough to enter my personal space, but then Rider had never really understood people did not normally stand that close together. At least, we usually didn't back home.

I caught the blur once again, but I didn't stop this time, only hesitated.

If I was seeing parts of the Path without trying to, I was going to be upset. Who knew what lurked in the Path?

However, if I could see it in this world, wouldn't Rider be able to see, hear, or smell it? What kind of thing could avoid—

There was something that Rider couldn't pick up. And if you saw them, it's because they wanted to be seen.

Leprechauns.

TEN

The realization stopped me in my tracks. I didn't look around; it wasn't worth it. If leprechauns wanted me to see them, they would show up no matter what I did.

"Is there something the matter?" Rider asked.

"Um, no. I'm good. Sorry, I got lost in thought." I hurried to catch up to him.

I could tell Rider, Vincent, and Logan about my suspicions, but not the others. Most people would be tempted to try to catch a leprechaun if they knew they were there. If the military and AIR were using the Lost in experiments, there was no way I wanted either one of them to know that leprechauns even existed.

That meant I had to be very careful talking to my team. Who knew what skills Boone's people had?

We were near the village when Logan came out to greet us.

"Howdy, partner." His smile was more of a twisted grimace that looked all wrong on the elf. "We all good here?"

Glancing at Rider, I saw that his attention was already on the village.

"Yeah," I said. "What did you tell the others?"

"I told them I sent you and Rider to check the outskirts of town and grab some water. Which is what you did, right?"

"Rider has the water and we brought some food as well," I said. "What happened after we left?"

"We haven't found any survivors yet. Boone has his team searching the area," Logan said. "I want you two to stay down by the huts. Search again and look for clues to what might have happened. I don't want you anywhere near that lodge."

"Rider needs to go to the building." I leaned in and lowered my voice, which I didn't have to do for Logan's benefit, but I didn't want any others to hear until Rider was ready. "There is a werewolf in the building. One that Rider knew."

"I didn't realize," Logan said, his attitude shifting. "There were two bodies in there that definitely weren't locals."

"Any clue as to why they were there?" I asked.

"From the looks of it, they'd been settled here for quite some time," Logan said. "Rider, why don't you go on? Wait for me before you go inside, though. I need to talk with Cassie here for a minute—in private if you don't mind."

Rider nodded and walked away.

I watched Rider. "How bad was it in there?"

"Bad. Really bad. Listen, Cassie, this isn't like home out here. I need to know that if I give you an order, you're going to follow it."

"What?" My eyes narrowed and honed in on Logan.

"This is a whole different rodeo. When I give an order, it's to keep you or someone else safe. You're going to have to consider the fact that I have more experience, and listen to me when I ask you to do something."

I could feel my face start to flush red. "Most of the time I have no problem with that. If you *ask* me, chances are I'll do it."

Logan raised an eyebrow. "Chances are?"

"If you tell me to step aside when a friend or one of my partners needs me, then maybe *you* need to consider not giving the order."

"You don't think I could have helped Rider?" Logan asked.

"Help him by doing what?" I hissed, stepping closer. "You were ready to fight, not help."

"What makes you think—"

"You were already starting to go all strange. The only times I've ever seen you elf out are when you're ready for a fight."

Logan rubbed his chin as though checking the contours of his face. "I hadn't realized."

"How could you not realize?"

"We'll talk about it later," Logan said. "I'm going to catch up to Rider and make sure he's okay in there."

"I should go—"

"I'll have Vincent join me if you want," Logan said. "Why don't you go down by the huts and see if you can find anything?"

"You don't want me to go into the lodge?" I asked.

"Hell, I don't want *anyone* inside that building," Logan said. "I just thought you might want to take a few minutes to catch your breath."

He was probably right.

"Call me if you need me," I mumbled and walked off, out of the tree line and into the village.

Standing between the rows of huts, I did take a minute to calm down.

Everything felt wrong here. I'd never seen Rider upset in this way, except one time when he was accidentally drugged. Was he close to changing? He had never done that around me before. To my knowledge, he hadn't changed with anyone around.

Then there was Logan. Damn that elf had some nerve. I gripped my hands hard into fists, then relaxed them. After doing that a few times, I felt a little better. Logan was just upset about the experiments. We all were.

And Vincent... well, I guess he was being normal, just ridiculous. As Gran had said, he was getting in the way of himself. In order not to do the same, I probably needed to stop being aggravated with him.

Maybe I was just homesick. *The faster we find what we're looking for, the quicker we get home.* Then things could get back to some semblance of normal.

This is normal, I reminded myself. Chaotic and hectic and unrelenting. Usually I liked it. This time, though?

Not so much.

I worked my way back to the hut closest to the lodge. Thankfully, that was far enough to make the smell less pungent. At least to me.

Carefully, I started going through the buildings. The first two had four walls and a roof. Although calling them walls wasn't quite right either. It was more like four patches of walls, with a door and windows punched out of reeds. If the wind ever picked up, it would keep out most of the blowing rain. It also blocked out most of the sun, which cooled things down more than I would have thought.

Some of the buildings had a few belongings inside— pottery mostly, some with ornate pictures carved around the edges. There were a few tools scattered here and there. Toward the middle of the town, most of the huts had three walls. The structures blocked the sun and caught the breeze.

What I didn't find anywhere were clues as to what might have happened. There were footmarks in the dirt, most of them ours, but some indicated that the person who'd left them wore no shoes.

Toward the other end of the village, a large, primitive-looking loom stood close to the entrance of a four-walled building. The loom itself fascinated me, but what looked like a splash of blood on the partially woven cloth was what kept me in the place.

Nothing looked out of place in the footprints. There was no indication something was here that wasn't human or human shaped. From the only known carvings of the nightmare, it didn't look human.

I was giving up hope of seeing anything more than the splash of blood, when then I came to the buildings furthest away from the lodge. There was more than just a little blood here.

At the edge of town, there was a platform near the trees. There I found our first hint of what might have happened. Drag marks in the mud showed something large pulled out of the town. More importantly, there were two animal tracks imprinted as well.

The creature had to be heavy to have made such deep prints and they were larger than anything I had seen. I glanced nervously into the surrounding woods. The thing's prints looked larger than my head.

"Logan," I called, raising my voice only a little, "I need something to mark a spot."

Boone's team was out in the woods, I knew that. They would know if anything was close by, right?

I wiped sweaty hands on my pants and edged away.

"A few areas, actually," I added when I approached the pool of blood. "Not that this one really needs to be marked."

Seeing the bloodshed here made me want to go back to the building with the loom, but I thought it might be better to get the others first, so I started toward the largest building, what the others had called a lodge.

The track was well worn, all the way through the town and even to the edge that I had just left.

A guttural howl pierced the quiet village. Expecting large monsters, I turned, getting ready to grab the Path.

It was almost a relief to see a dark-skinned man running toward me. Then I took in his wild, dirty appearance, and the crazed look on his face. A lone fighter I knew I could take on, especially if the person didn't have a weapon. Crazy is harder to handle. Nothing they did was expected, and they could get lucky when they were flailing around.

Still, I knew we wanted a survivor to talk to. The dried blood that coated the man was a testament that he had lived through something horrific.

I turned to the side, making myself a smaller target, and—despite wanting to run the other direction—I stood my ground, steeling myself to grab the man as he quickly approached.

Mentally I prepared to reach for the Path, just in case.

A loud BANG rang out, causing me to jump.

The man's trajectory changed slightly and his momentum brought him to me. Instinct made me try to catch his fall, but when I saw the blood, I staggered back, letting the man fall to the ground.

The hole in the side of the man's head was larger than I ever wanted to see again.

"Cass!"

I didn't turn to my partners. Instead, I looked in the direction the bullet had come from.

Tolman walked into the clearing. He had his gun slung over his shoulder, and for the first time ever, I saw his smile.

The man wasn't looking at me, but at the body on the ground. The look on his face was both proud and predatory.

I shivered and looked back down at the body.

"What happened?" Logan asked, arriving first.

The only thing I could do was wave down at the body.

"He attacked you?" Logan asked. Looking around, he saw Tolman as well, and didn't take his eyes off the man.

It was only then that Tolman's face reverted to its usual bland expression.

"The man wasn't armed," I said at last. "He—I was just going to subdue him and..."

"So he didn't attack you?" Logan asked.

My other two partners arrived. I could see Boone approaching quickly as well.

"He was charging her," Tolman said. "He was a threat."

I stepped back, wanting to fade into my team. As much as I hated to admit it, I needed a minute.

"You saw that he had no weapon?" Logan asked.

It was a leading question.

Tolman shrugged.

"Cassie, what happened, exactly?" Logan asked as Boone arrived.

"He," I waved at the body once again, "ran toward me. He didn't have a weapon, so I was going to subdue him. So we could talk to him."

"And then?" Logan prompted.

"The shot fired." I closed my eyes and took a deep breath.

"What about the blood?" Logan asked.

Looking down, I saw that my uniform had a large smear of blood down the front.

"I wasn't thinking," I admitted. "I started to catch him, but then thought better of it and stepped back."

Stepped back, staggered back, flinched back—it was all the same, right?

"Anything else?" Logan asked.

"He didn't look like he was in his right mind," I admitted.

"Which direction did he come from?" Logan asked.

I indicated the direction, back toward the pools of blood. The man had no other marks on him aside from the obvious one that we had just made.

We? I thought.

Well yes, we were a team now, like it or not. We had done this.

"Why don't you get a drink and go show Rider and Vincent what you found," Logan said. "Boone and I will take care of this here."

I nodded, and without another word, I walked away, back the way I had come.

"Tolman," I heard Boone say, his voice the one of command. "Back to it. We'll talk later."

The building with the loom was closest, so I ducked inside, Vincent and Rider following. The idea of Tolman lurking back in the perimeter of the woods made me uneasy.

I had to shake that thought off. We were a team. As a team-mate, he probably acted exactly as he should have. He'd thought I was in trouble and he did what he could.

The look on his face... maybe I had imagined it. I'd been in shock or something. That was possible, right?

"Cass?"

"Hmmm," I said, still trying to pull myself out of darker thoughts.

"Are you okay?" Vincent put a comforting arm around the small of my back.

A part of me wanted him to pull me closer until the darkness in my mind faded away. However, this wasn't the time or the place.

"Yeah," I said, taking the water bottle Rider handed to me and using that as an excuse to step away from Vincent. "I just need a minute." With Vincent so close, the temptation to keep him around me was too high.

I took a drink and passed the bottle back.

Vincent looked upset, but Rider searched around the room without any of his usual curiosity. It looked like it was more something to do than anything else.

"What about you, Rider?" I asked.

"I am upset," he said without looking at anyone.

His bluntness made me wish I had been honest as well.

"Is there anything we can do?" I asked.

"Not that I am aware of," Rider said. "Why are we in this room?"

The question took me by surprise. I thought Rider would have noticed the smell of the blood, even if he hadn't spotted it yet. Although, how he could have missed it was beyond me.

"The loom," I said.

"Maybe this should wait," Vincent said.

"No," I said, "it shouldn't. We have to do what needs to be done."

"I'm glad Tolman was there," Vincent said.

"What? Why?" I asked.

"He neutralized the threat and kept you safe."

My temper flared. "You don't think I could have handled one guy on my own?"

"Doesn't matter. You didn't have to," Vincent said.

"Stop." Rider's voice was hard and direct.

I blew out a rush of air that I had been ready to use to argue with Vincent.

"Is this the only blood in the room?" Rider asked.

"As far as I know. Do you smell anymore?" I asked

"The only thing I can smell is blood," Rider said.

Guilt washed over me. I needed to stop thinking about Tolman and start paying more attention to what Rider needed.

"That's all the blood I found inside here. Unfortunately, there's more outside." I led the way out of the building and down the street.

Nothing could be said about the drying pool of blood. Rider and Vincent looked around and found no more than I had.

"Over here is where I found what we might be looking for." I waved them over to the drag marks. Logan was approaching while the others checked the area more thoroughly than I had.

When I showed them the footprint, the elf arrived.

Logan whistled, and not the sweet melodious whistling he usually did. This whistle seemed to say, 'Uh oh, we're in trouble now.'

"That's a mighty big varmint," Logan said.

"It looks like it grabbed someone and dragged them into the forest," Vincent said. "I don't see any indication that it came into town."

"Could it have circled around and gone to the lodge?" I asked.

"Something this size couldn't have fit inside," Vincent said.

"Probably not," Logan said, "but we can try to find out. You up for it, partner?"

"People did what happened up there," Vincent said. "The weapons are there. There's evidence everywhere. There's no reason for Cassie to try to go back that far."

"I don't think it's that far," Logan said. "All this had to have happened less than a day ago. Twenty-four hours, tops."

"Where do you want me to start?" I asked.

"Maybe we can get a look at the thing that—"

"I would like to know who killed the people," Rider cut in.

Logan tilted his head and looked at Rider. "What are you going to do when you find out what happened?"

"I will know. That is enough," Rider said.

"Are you going to be happy with whatever answer you get?" Logan asked.

Rider looked at him in confusion, but there was anger built up as well. "Why would I be happy with an answer to this?"

Vincent looked torn. "He means, are you going to feel any better for knowing?"

"Nothing will make me feel better about this," Rider said.

"So finding out is worth having Cass see what happened?" Vincent asked.

"You don't have to answer that, Rider," I said. "Let's start around the lodge."

On the way back, we found Renick reporting to Boone.

"So far, we haven't found any other threats," Boone said as we approached.

My mind was already on the task ahead. I hadn't seen inside the lodge yet, and I wasn't sure if that worked for me or against me.

"What areas have been searched?" Logan asked, stopping to talk.

"A short perimeter. Not far out yet. What did you all find?" Boone asked.

Logan briefly told him.

"Hold up," Boone said, stopping the rest of us from continuing. "We could use some more eyes out there. In this situation, it's better if we're in pairs. We have no way to know what's out there."

"Well," Logan said, "we're about to try finding out. Vincent and Rider can meet up with Davis and Tolman, though."

"That's a good idea," I said, trying to curb Vincent's protests. "Too many Paths around might make it harder."

Vincent glared at me, but I tried not to notice.

"Rider, do you want to meet up with Davis?" Logan asked.

"Will it make it easier if I am not there?" Rider asked, looking at me.

"I think so. Substantial Paths and ones with strong emotion could make it harder." *And as a bonus, they won't see me if things go bad.*

"What are you doing?" Boone asked.

"Cassie's going to try to rewind the day," Logan said.

"I don't think I've seen that before," Boone said. "If you want, I can work with her."

Vincent gave Logan a hard look. "I'm staying."

CHAPTER

ELEVEN

Are Vincent's eyes getting darker?

Logan looked like he was going to argue the point, but then changed his mind. "That's probably best. Rider and I will be able to hear what's going on in case there's trouble. We'll catch up with Davis and Tolman."

I put a hand on my hip and glared at Vincent. He looked at me blankly, but I could sense his resolve.

"Holler if you need us," Logan said.

Boone turned towards us. "In that case, Renick and I are going to check the area around the river to see if we can find anything else."

Renick winked at me and grinned. "Good luck, princess."

They all took off in different directions.

I rolled my eyes, but when I saw Vincent clench his hands, I grabbed his arm and tugged him gently away. "Come on."

He didn't need any encouragement to walk with me.

"That guy's an ass," Vincent said.

"And he's going to be more of an ass if he knows it bothers

you." I paused to think about what I'd said. "Well, maybe not to you, but leave him be."

"You don't have to go in there," Vincent said.

"It'll be good to know. The faster we find what we're looking for, the faster we can go home." After we walked a little farther, I realized I hadn't asked him his plans yet. "You *are* coming home with us, right?"

He took my hand and squeezed it. "I am."

Energy flowed between us. A tingling sensation rose up my arm. My own irritation and nervousness melted away and I could feel Vincent's Path get lighter.

As much as I wanted to, I didn't complain when he pulled away.

"I'm not sure where you should start," Vincent said as we approached the long building.

"It all happened inside," I said. "Most of it, anyway. Otherwise, there would be blood out here too."

Vincent winced.

I looked at the building and wiped sweaty palms on my uniform, careful to avoid the blood.

"I'll start outside." I was such a chicken.

Looking around at the real world once again didn't lessen my anxiety, so I closed my eyes and plunged into the Path.

When I opened my eyes to the shimmering world, I frowned. "There are dozens of Paths here."

"Any of them look odd?" Vincent asked.

"Not yet." The brightest of Paths had to be those of the team. My partners' and Boone's I was familiar with. Our newest team members had odd Paths, but I knew that wasn't what we were looking for. I made a mental note to Read their Paths later to see if I could discover why they were so... uniform.

I bypassed those and went to the older ones. "Logan's right, the Paths aren't that old. There's dozens of them." Like peeling an onion, I went layer by layer. My heart twisted when I found the one that I was looking for, the werewolf.

Something moved out of the corner of my eye and I twitched away, bumping into Vincent. While we were touching, Vincent's whole being reached out to me. Our energy wrapped around each other. All other thoughts beyond him were forgotten.

He steadied me. "What's wrong?"

When he drew away, it was like losing the sun on a perfect day.

"Nothing." Sighing, I got back to work. "I'm going to look back."

When I was younger, I couldn't go into the past of an area most of the time, because I didn't have the power to do so. After Vincent shattered my soul, I had the power, but no control. Now that I had power and control, it made things a little easier to move backwards.

Sometimes.

Pushing my way back to the werewolf's Path was easy. It was almost as though it wanted to draw me in.

The Path's flow appeared to slow and I began to see ghosted images of the past.

"Doing okay?" Vincent asked.

"They were running." I turned and looked back toward the town. "Not at first. The ones that reached here first were confused and kept looking back."

As we stood outside the building, the past shadow of the door slammed open and shut dozens of time, but it was just villagers. They all seemed to belong there.

"The people at the back of the rush were running hard by

the time they got here." I reached out a hand and let it hover over one of the Paths. "They were scared." I looked back to the village. "No, those weren't the last, there were others farther behind."

Many of the people had been yelling, and the newcomers were no different, except they pushed one another. More than one person veered off and went into the woods. I gasped and pulled back, unnerved when I discovered the man that had rushed at me earlier. His past self approached at a dead run.

An arm wrapped around my waist. Now that I was expecting it, I knew it was Vincent.

"Maybe you should come back," he said.

"The guy that we... saw earlier today. He was terrified. He ran inside like all the others."

Taking a deep breath, I plunged in and opened the door to the lodge.

The stench was almost unbearable and I gagged—not something you want to do around a crime scene. I covered my mouth and nose, trying to block out the worst of the smell.

Seeing the room was a thousand times worse. The terrified people in the past stood in groups, shaking and trying to keep their fear at bay.

Then there were the bodies in the present.

The door in the past snapped closed; the man Tolman had shot barred it and then stepped back. The man gestured and yelled words in an unknown language while not taking his eyes off the wood holding back whatever unknown terror was outside.

A shifting pattern in the Path caused me to move my attention from the scene to the Path itself.

I jumped when something banged against the door in the past.

"You should give me an update," Vincent said in equal parts annoyance and worry.

"They're all inside and they blocked the door," I said dismissively. "His Path, though..." Quickly, I turned to look at the others. "Several Paths in fact. The people that came in last."

"What about the Paths?" Vincent asked.

As I watched, a dark purple cloud seemed to flow from the Path of their past to their Paths that ended in the room. The man in front of the door stiffened and he gripped his knife. I moved closer, held my hand over the man's Path, and felt as the cloud moved.

"It's... I'm not sure," I admitted. "Something seemed to be affecting their Path. No... *infecting* them."

The deep purple stopped moving. It found its target and it had surrounded the man.

I blew out a deep breath, and making sure to keep my hand over my mouth and nose, I readied myself to touch the man's Path in order to feel what he felt.

The man turned and looked me straight in the eye. I gasped and stepped back. It couldn't be me that he was looking at. That wasn't possible.

For some reason that made me look around for the werewolf. She was on the balls of her feet, ready to run or fight.

What could take down a werewolf?

The man yelled a string of words and my attention snapped back to him. He lunged forward and raised the knife. I fumbled back and screamed when his knife met my skin. My arm screamed when the blade sliced through it.

Chaos erupted around us.

Vincent was the only thing that kept me from falling to the floor. The man went to strike again when someone else rushed at him. Everyone was fighting.

No, *most* of the people were fighting.

"The last of the people that came in, they're... they're... Screams of men, women, and children rang in my ears.

Vincent hauled me to the door, but I couldn't look away. At first, I drew some hope that Rider's werewolf friend could help. She moved some children behind her and growled. Her form began to change, but then two of the men rushed at her. They wrestled her to the ground. She managed to slash open a throat, but one man was replaced with another.

Someone stabbed her in the side. It only seemed to piss her off, which was good. Then, the man that had barred the door jumped on her and stabbed her. Not once or twice, but over and over and over.

The vision blurred as I began to cry. So many tears came that they couldn't fall fast enough.

Vincent turned me around and grabbed my face, forcing me to look at him. When I concentrated on his eyes, the screams seemed to die away. One by one, they winked out.

"We're getting out of here," Vincent said.

When he took my arm, I could feel him shaking, or maybe it was me. He went to the door and appeared to walk through it. He was gone.

"What?" I cried. I banged on the door. Hands from outside pulled at me through the solid surface. "No, open the door!"

Looking around behind me, I saw why silence fell. The man stood there, covered in blood, knife in hand, and he watched me.

I tried to push off the bar of the door, but it wouldn't budge.

The man yelled something at me.

"Oh, shit," I said under my breath.

I turned and faced him, ready to do what I could to defend myself. Trying to pull at his Path was like running my hands across a patch of oil in the ocean. As I tugged on it, I only wiped a little off the surface.

Touching his Path, I felt his madness. It was as though I was stuck in this man's nightmare, or maybe I was causing it.

The man yelled and ran forward. I tried to keep my hands loose, ready to grab him.

Rider moved in front of me. He wrapped his arms around me and dragged me outside. As we went through the door, he staggered. The man's screams still echoed in my mind when I opened my eyes, back in the present.

"Drop it," Rider ordered.

Taking a deep breath, I nodded. Not even looking around one last time, I closed my eyes and pushed the Path away.

For one panicked minute, I thought it wasn't going to go. It felt as though the Path was tugging me back.

I'm the Reader, I told myself. *I use the Path, not the other way around!*

The Path fell away and the world returned. Rider had leaned down, nose to nose with me. My legs threatened to give way, but he kept me on my feet, supporting my weight.

He looked up and growled at something or someone, but I didn't see what it was.

My heart was racing and my breathing was fast and shallow. When I stared back at the building, I shivered.

Forcing my feet to stay under me, I stood mostly on my own strength. "Let's move away from here."

I was surprised at how steady my voice sounded. I was also surprised that I could walk almost on my own. Getting away from that place was enough to keep me moving.

Once we were closer to the huts, I stopped and leaned against a tree. I closed my eyes while trying to force the images out of my head—the children, men trying to retaliate, and Rider's friend fighting them until she went still.

"What happened?" Boone sounded out of breath.

Someone gently lifted my arm and I opened my eyes to see Rider twisting it this way and that.

"We do not know," Rider said. He placed my arm where it had been before he picked it up. Then he began to circle me and the tree I was leaning against.

"I'm pulling the others in," Boone said.

"Don't," Vincent said. I could hear the attempt to restrain his anger. "The fewer people the better right now."

"What can I do?" Boone asked.

"Logan went to get a first-aid kit," Vincent said. "Where's the water?"

"I'll get it," Boone said.

Rider pulled me away from the tree, and although I wanted nothing more than collapse to the ground and sleep, I stood and watched him.

He walked around behind me and then lifted my other arm. When he was done, he let me lean back against the tree. From there, I sank to the ground and shut my eyes again.

"You're bleeding all over the place," Vincent said. "Take off your shirt and let's take a look."

My eyes snapped open and I frowned at Vincent, but then realized he was talking to Rider.

Rider looked around, trying to twist himself to see his back. He turned in a circle a few times in an effort to see.

Vincent shook his head, but anyone could have seen the grin that seemed to lighten his spirit.

I smiled. It lightened mine, too.

Vincent stopped him after he circled the third time. "I'll find it for you."

I let my mind float on the surface, ignoring everything that I had seen.

"It is only a scratch," Rider said, but he took off his shirt anyway.

Vincent inspected Rider's back. "If it was a scratch, it wouldn't be bleeding like this. Any idea what did it?"

Rider glanced down at me, seeing that I was watching. "Was it those that are in the Path?"

I shook my head and watched the two, trying to keep my mind blank.

"What's in the Path?" Vincent asked.

"You have missed a lot," Rider told him.

"Catch me up."

"I am sure she will let you know when there is time."

That's Rider, ever the optimist.

"You are frustrating," Vincent said.

Rider laughed, then winced and clutched his back.

I couldn't help but agree with Rider. Vincent calling others frustrating was an ironic thought.

Then I noticed, really noticed the wound in Rider's back. "You've been stabbed." It came out as a plain statement as I tried to stamp down thoughts of what happened.

He nodded. "It happened when I took you out of the building. I did not see where it came from, and you were the only living person in the room."

I scrunched my eyes up at the reminder of the other kind of people in the room.

Boone appeared. "Here's the water. What happened to you?"

"He's been stabbed," Vincent said. "Put some water on this so I can clean it up."

"It will heal soon," Rider said.

"Who stabbed him?" Boone asked.

Vincent's eyes darted to me and the back to Boone.

I sighed. "He was stabbed by the man that Tolman shot earlier."

Rider was the only one that didn't look at me as if I was crazy.

"Here," Boone said, passing me the water. "I grabbed a protein bar."

The idea of eating right now made my stomach churn.

"You should lie down," Boone continued, "and maybe elevate your feet."

"What?" I asked.

"She's not in shock," Vincent said. "It was... Something went wrong."

Vincent gave a quick rundown of things from his point of view. "It wasn't until she couldn't leave the building that I realized how bad it was."

Logan arrived and took over for Vincent, dressing Rider's wound. Vincent sat down next to me and started to roll back my sleeve, but the cut was too high. Instead, I took off the outer shirt. I hadn't realized how hot I was until I was left in short sleeves.

He took some antiseptic and carefully began to clean the cut. I winced at the sharp sting. The cut was shallow, which had to have been dumb luck.

Or maybe... I looked around, but I saw no signs of leprechauns.

"This also appeared from nowhere," Vincent said.

"It came from the past," I said. Using as little description as I could manage, I told them what I had seen.

By the time I was done, I had three men looming over me, and one who was next to me. It was strange to think that with the seemingly endless and empty forest around us, I was starting to feel crowded.

"At least one other person went into the forest?" Boone asked.

"I think there were more. The one I noticed ran in that direction," I said, waving off into the forest.

"You say these people were infected by something?" Boone asked.

"Yes."

When Vincent was done with my arm, he remained sitting close enough that he could keep contact with me, which made me feel somewhat better.

"We should have you Read the other end of the village," Logan said. "Let's get a good look at what's behind all of this."

"Not today," Vincent said, rising to his feet.

"A quick look—"

"Let's give her some breathing room," Vincent said, cutting Logan off.

"I'll pull the team in closer. Now that we have a possible direction to check, I'll send two out to scout that way," Boone said.

"We need to make a decision on what to do with," Logan waved his hand in the direction of the building, "everything."

"We also need to find a base of operations," Boone said. "We could be in the area for a few days."

"I can look for suitable sites," Vincent said. "I need to chat with Logan for a minute first, though."

"I'll send Tolman with you when you head out," Boone said.

"Rider, take it easy until your side heals some," Logan said. "Keep an eye on each other."

They walked away, leaving Rider and me alone. He sat down next to me, and said nothing. I leaned my head back against the tree and closed my eyes. With the sun shining down on the village not far away, and the sound of birds talking and animals moving around, it almost felt serene—as long as I kept my mind blank.

The silence Rider and I shared was a comfortable one, despite the challenges of the day.

Sometime later, Logan called Rider over and they chatted for a while before Logan returned, taking Rider's place.

"He'll be back shortly," Logan said. "I'm not sure how werewolves treat the dead in their own world, but here, he's going to take a minute to say goodbye to the werewolf that died inside."

"What are you going to do with the place?" I asked.

"Burn it," Logan said. "We don't know what caused people to turn on each other like that. Sterilizing the area seems like the best move."

When I didn't respond, Logan began to whistle. The two sounds he made blended into a beautiful harmony. I loved to hear it, despite the fact that it was Home on the Range, which I'd heard about a million times over the past year.

"I don't need a babysitter," I said once he stopped.

"There are several people that might have turned crazy and they're running around out here. From this point on, we stay in pairs. No exceptions."

"What about Rider?"

"Boone is with him."

Feeling the need to be productive in some way, I started to get to my feet. My legs shook and I had to lean against the tree to keep upright.

"How're you doing?" Logan asked.

"I could use some caffeine," I admitted.

"Funny thing is, Boone thought of that. The first-aid kit comes complete with caffeine tablets."

Logan combed through the supplies and handed two over.

I popped the pills in my mouth and followed them up with some water. "What should I be doing?"

"Until you can stand on your own, not much," Logan said.

I rolled my eyes and forced myself to stop leaning on the tree. "Now what?"

Logan looked around, scanning the landscape carefully. "Are you up to getting back to work?"

"That's what I'm here for."

"Let's go for a walk."

CHAPTER

TWELVE

It wasn't until we started walking through the village that I realized he was taking me to the place where someone had been dragged into the woods.

The last thing I wanted to do was admit I was spent, but as we approached the small pool of dried blood, I realized I'd have to say something. "I'm not sure there's much more I can do in the Path today."

"That's what the caffeine was for," Logan said.

I stopped and stared at him in surprise. "Is everything okay?"

"*Nothing* here is okay," Logan said.

"I mean with you. Not just here, but back at home, too. You haven't been yourself lately."

He looked agitated. "Are you suggesting there's something wrong with me because I want you to Read the Path?"

"No, I'm saying this because you've jumped the gun at several things lately. Back at the office, then here with Rider, you became worked up over something that you'd normally be calm about."

"Rider could have done some serious damage if he had lost control."

"Yeah, but you weren't even considering another option beyond fighting. That's not like you."

"So, you're not going to do this?" Logan asked.

I looked at the trail the creature took through the woods, wondering what I should do. On the one hand, I wanted to help all I could. On the other hand, I didn't want to fall flat on my face. It didn't help that I was scared of what I might see.

And of what might see me.

"Later," I said. "If I do any more right now, I'll drop from exhaustion. That's going to make me a liability."

Logan looked around at anything except me.

"It left a pretty obvious physical Path in this world," I reminded him. "We could follow it."

"We should know what we're up against first."

I bit my lip and mentally took stock of the energy I had remaining. There was a reason I could hardly stand earlier. With my energy this low, I had nothing to work with.

Logan's forlorn look turned into a smile, which he actually aimed at me. "Even if we did find something today, there's nothing we could do with it. You know, a year ago, you would have jumped in with no questions. Your grandmother would be right proud of you."

I felt a little better, but it was tempting to dip a toe into the Path to see if he was still upset.

"So am I. When you push your luck, there's going to end up being a time when you push it too far," he said.

"While we're over here," I said, trying to deflect the attention. "We could decide where we're going to start work tomorrow."

"Let's concentrate on what this thing might be. We can

ignore the rest of the village, and start closer to where it went into the woods."

I glanced back to where the ground was stained by drying pools of blood.

"No need to bother with that. We've all seen a bit too much today. No one more than you."

"Do you think we should follow it into the woods tomorrow?"

"Probably. We're going to burn the lodge, so we'll need to make sure the fire is taken care of first. Right now, that lodge is the most dangerous thing out here."

"More than the crazed people wandering around and something called a nightmare?"

"You can bank on it. If left alone, the smell is going to pull in every animal for miles. After all, to them it's a free meal."

"I never thought about that."

"And I know Rider said your soul might not attract the kind of attention it did before, but some predator could still be interested. I'd rather not test it out here."

"Agreed."

Logan went still, and after a minute, his ears rolled out to their points.

My first instinct was to ask what he'd heard, but knew that would be stupid. Instead, I tried to breathe quietly and wait as still as possible.

"You know that Path you saw back in Boone's office?" Logan asked. "The strange one that came through the wall?"

"Yeah," I said.

"Is that a Path you could block out?"

"Yes. If it's here, I might even be able to do that now since it should be completely in the present."

Logan's ears twitched and rolled back down until they

resembled human—although lumpy looking—ears. "Not now, but tomorrow, we need to talk."

"You and me?"

"And Boone."

"What about Vincent and Rider?"

"Not for this one. Besides, Rider will already hear us, and it would look too suspicious if we all huddled together."

"What do you know?" I asked.

"It's more about what I suspect than what I know."

"And that is?"

"Tomorrow. Today, I need to go help Boone. Rider's on his way. Maybe you two could go down to the river and clean up some."

Looking down at myself, I saw the smears of blood on my arms and on my pants. Luckily, my undershirt had survived almost unscathed.

"Soul shattered or not, that'll draw attention." Logan tipped his hat and started to walk away.

"Logan," I called, getting him to stop, "you never answered my question."

"Which one is that?"

"Are you okay?"

"Sugar withdrawal?"

I'm not sure if Logan meant it as a question, but it sounded as though he were trying to gauge if I would believe him or not.

"You're a bad liar," I said.

"It's nothing that can't wait. Talking about it at home will be better than out here."

I knew that was the only thing I would get out of him about it for now, so I only nodded.

"If I forget myself or don't sound like myself, call me out on it."

"I can do that," I said. "Although, if you're all elfed out, I may hide behind Rider before I say anything."

Logan laughed melodiously.

Being around a happy elf is always nice. Their good mood was contagious, like it or not.

As Logan walked away, I briefly wondered if that meant his other moods were contagious as well, but I dismissed the idea.

When I was alone, it felt once again as though I could close my eyes and imagine I was in some sort of tropical paradise. If I closed my eyes for too long, though, I was sure grim pictures would take over.

I could see Rider and Logan talking where they met on their way through the village, so waved before I stepped into the woods to get out of the sun. Even though I was feet away from the clearing where the village sat, it almost felt like a different world under the canopy.

A flash of color and the sound of something moving in the undergrowth had me checking the ground. Nothing stirred for a moment. When I turned to face the woods in the direction the creature had gone, I saw a hint of brown close to the ground, which darted from one tree to another.

I stood stock still and watched the spot. Shortly after, a small head poked out from behind the tree. I glanced back to the village to make sure I was still alone, but Rider wasn't far away.

When I turned back, there were two of them standing there.

"I thought I saw you out here," I said quietly. After checking the ground for snakes, I squatted down. "Can you understand my language?"

The two didn't move any closer, but watched me with wide eyes.

After a moment, I looked around. "Where's your friend? Aren't there always three of you around?"

They looked at each other, and then disappeared behind the tree.

I stayed put for a moment, but then stood. It was probably for the better that they didn't stick around. Who knows who might have been listening.

When I looked at the spot they disappeared from, one poked its head out again and beckoned me forward. Glancing back, I still had a few minutes before Rider was here.

Anxiety about going farther into the woods on my own threatened to roll over me. Before it had a chance to take root, I followed the little leprechaun.

If I yelled, Rider and Logan would hear me. Keeping that in mind, I became a little more comfortable with following someone I didn't know into the rainforest.

Thankfully, they didn't have to lead me far.

A stand of what looked like vines created a small hollow at the base of a tree. Sitting in the center was a leprechaun, presumably the third in the group, tied up in small but tight ropes that looked as though they were spun from thin tendrils of a plant.

The moment the leprechaun saw others, it struggled against its bonds ferociously. When standing it might be three feet tall, but even though he was small, the violence at which it struggled made me back up a step.

One of them said something, then the other picked it up, when that one stopped, they turned sadly to the third. I felt a pang myself. They always worked in threes, but their friend was obviously not in his right mind.

"I'm sorry," I said, my chest growing tight. "I don't under-stand what you're saying."

They looked at each other for a moment as though

communicating silently, and then one disappeared and almost instantly returned with twig. The leprechaun stepped inside, but stayed well away from his struggling friend. Using the twig, leprechaun two began to draw in the dirt.

When he stepped away, I saw what I had been dreading. The crude drawing looked very much like a cat with more than one tail. The leprechaun pointed at the cat, then the village, then the cat, and finally their friend.

"How long has he been like this?" I whispered.

The two only looked at me, as though waiting for me to do something.

If it was the nightmare that attacked the village and the leprechaun, I had an idea of what was happening. Moving closer, I looked into his eyes.

The eyes were wild. More like that of an animal than of a person.

I licked my lips and looked around. Would they let me bring someone else back here? Would they let me take the little man with me?

The answer to both of those, I knew, would be no.

Remembering what I had seen in the lodge caused me to shudder, but I tried to keep my mind on what the Path had done to the survivor in the village. He had been okay, or at least seemed okay, until the other Path encircled him, trapping him in a shell of madness.

When I knelt on the ground, my knees were instantly damp.

The two healthy leprechauns sat in front of me, all of us turned toward the snarling creature in the middle.

One of the two took out a small stone that looked sharp. My mind told me it was a dagger, but I didn't want to believe that. It pushed the point into the ground so that it stood straight up and down.

"I don't know what it is you're thinking," I said, "but you can stop thinking it right now."

Neither of them looked at me.

I wasn't sure if I could fix this, but I knew I had to try. Grabbing hold of one of the thick vines lining the hollow to steady myself, I closed my eyes and stretched myself until I snapped free and into the Path.

Whatever had affected the villagers, whether it be a nightmare or something else, was also affecting the leprechaun.

The dark purple had solidified, building a shell around the man, driving him stark raving mad. I felt the surrounding stream of Path, trying to find some sort of crack or hold over the smooth surface that encompassed him. Not locating what I needed, I put a little more power into it. Then a little more.

Finding the faintest of openings, I wedged a part of Path into it, and as if I were using a crowbar, I pried away the affected area. When a piece broke off, I held it, not allowing the Path to flow away, worried it might affect something else.

How did the nightmare catch a leprechaun? They made no noise, didn't have a trace of a smell, and only showed themselves to those they wanted to see them. It seemed impossible for one to be caught.

Unless it was silent and stealthy enough that the leprechaun ran into the nightmare.

At first, I wasn't sure if the ragged breathing was coming from the bound leprechaun or from me. It took me a while to realize it was both. One of the leprechauns scooted forward on his knees, looking relieved.

"No," I snapped, holding up a finger to show I needed more time.

He froze, but didn't move away. The two began talking again. This time, the third joined in.

While they chatted away incomprehensibly, I scoured his Path for any remaining trace of infection.

"Cassie," I heard Rider call.

"Rider, stop. Wait where you are," I said. "I need a minute."

The leprechauns were in a frenzy, wanting to move their friend away. Finally, when I was sure there wasn't a hint of contamination left, I dropped my hand and nodded.

The newly healthy leprechaun and one other sped away.

I was still holding onto the infected Path. Gripping the root, I fell back on my butt and turned to lean against it.

The other leprechaun waited somewhat nervously. When I was mostly steady, it began to gabble at me.

I sighed, then pointed at the sun. "When that goes down." I drew an imaginary line down to the horizon. "You bring him back to me." Hoping that the hand gestures were somewhat universal was the best I could do at the moment. "The elf, the man with the long ears," more miming, "can talk like you."

The little creature cocked his head as though waiting for me to make sense.

I shook my head and made a shooing motion. He looked confused and I sighed.

"You do not sound well," Rider said.

"One more minute." I turned my attention to the Path I had gathered. Although I couldn't see my own Path, I felt it, and I was trying to keep the contaminated Path well away from me. My mind was starting to get fuzzy. Since I had no idea what to do with it, I sunk the Path into the ground.

I pushed it deep and hoped it wouldn't harm anything. With that done, I made a shooing motion again and the leprechaun finally took the hint.

"I think I'm going to need your help, Rider," I said in a normal voice.

When I heard him moving toward me, I pushed away the Path.

I wasn't sure if I was actually swaying or if I had a bad case of vertigo. Either way, the world moved in ways it had no business moving.

"I am not sure who you were talking to," Rider said.

Before I could protest, he pulled me to my feet and started to look me over.

"You didn't hear anyone else?" I asked.

"I did not."

"Do you smell anything else?"

"My nose is not as it should be. Who were you talking to?"

"There has been one other time that you couldn't see or smell a Lost. Do you remember?"

"The old man?" Rider asked.

"Not him, the others. We were in the middle of the woods there, too."

Rider's eyes grew wide. "The le—"

"Shhh," I said. "I think it's best no one else knows."

"That is wise. I am... uneasy out here."

"Can you help me to the water? Logan suggested we clean up."

"I would like that."

Letting me hold his arm for support, he led the way out of the woods and back to the edge of the village, where he turned toward the running water.

We walked upstream until we were on the other side of the village. When we passed the flames, we said nothing, and I tried to avoid looking at the building altogether.

"They have found a spot to stay the night," Rider said as we reached a stretch of river that wasn't flowing quite as fast as the rest.

"Let's get cleaned up, then we can give them a hand with making camp," I said, walking out onto a rock.

"How is your arm?" Rider asked, taking off his shirt to wash it out.

"Better now that I can clean it. How's your side?"

"It should be healed by tomorrow morning."

"Thank you for getting me out of there."

"Thank you for going in." Rider hesitated. "Do you know what happened to the werewolf inside?"

A hundred thoughts went through my head. *Do I tell him? Do I want to think about it? What will happen if he knows? Does he really want to know?*

Many more questions flew by before the big one came up. *Why did I go in there if I wasn't going to tell him?*

After too long of a pause, I took a deep breath. "She tried to protect the children in the room."

Rider watched the far riverbank. "That explains why she did not run. It does not explain why she did not survive."

I splashed water on my arms and even tried to wash the blood off my pants, but it was all stalling.

Rider waited patiently, letting me approach it at my own speed. When he was done at the river, he sat on the bank.

Once I had cleaned up as much as I could without jumping in, I told Rider what happened inside.

With the words came the horror of everything I had seen. I had to stop a few times to sniff and wipe my eyes. By the time I finished, I had gone numb. It was the best defense I had. Maybe the only one.

After sitting for a while, I forced myself unsteadily to my feet and moved away from the water. I wasn't the only one that was having a hard time with the details, so I gave Rider some space for a little while. Black smoke filled the sky, and I watched as I waited.

"I think I will go for a run," Rider said.

"That's not a good idea. Not with that thing out there."

"I gotta say, I agree with her," Boone said as he arrived with Logan.

Although Logan was as quiet as Rider was, Boone was not. Somewhere in the back of my mind, I'd heard their approach.

"I will hear anything if it comes near," Rider said.

"That's true," Logan said.

Moving to my feet again was an effort of willpower. "I don't think you will, though."

CHAPTER

THIRTEEN

"You think this thing is quiet?" Logan asked.

I wondered once again what could catch hold of something that could hide itself as thoroughly as a leprechaun could. "Either that or it lays in wait for someone to stumble over it."

"What makes you think that?" Logan asked.

I felt worn to the bone and standing in place talking wasn't helping any. "I've seen... evidence."

"In the Path?" Logan asked. "Did you see what it was?"

My brow furrowed and I shifted my weight from foot to foot. There was no way I could mention the leprechauns in front of anyone. "I didn't see it, and I can't tell you what I did see."

Logan raised an eyebrow and waited for more.

It had been a long day and I really didn't like having everyone staring at me. I kept my mouth shut in case I said too much, or, a rising possibility, in case I got ticked off at someone.

There was movement behind them, which caught my

attention. Something was coming straight at us, fast. The only thing I could do was gasp before ripping into the Path and solidifying it.

Or almost solidifying it. The spear that was being hurled at us slowed as though it were stuck in jello before it finally fell to the ground a few feet before reaching its target. Logan and Boone turned as the weapon thudded to the ground. Rider ran toward the forest, having already seen what caused my distraction.

When the spear hit the ground, I let the Path flow normally once again.

"We need him alive," Logan hollered, running after Rider.

Boone already had his gun in hand and followed.

It was one step too far. My legs wouldn't hold me, but when I fell, I managed to stay sitting up, alert for more spears or other projectiles. Rider reached the forest first and disappeared. Logan wasn't far behind.

Boone was more cautious. I watched him switch directions, then go into the woods off to the side.

The sound died away and I was alone. It took a few tries to push the Path away, which was a mark of how tired I was. Once it was gone, even sitting up was difficult. I felt as though I was on a boat, going out to sea.

It would be really stupid to lie down right here, I repeated to myself a few times.

Maybe for just a minute.

That was all the convincing I needed to give myself. I lay back on the ground, then rolled over to stare at the sky. Moments later, I heard feet pounding on the ground, coming in my direction. I tensed, ready to enter the Path once again and use up the last of my dying embers of power.

"Cassie," Boone's voice came out as a command and I relaxed.

"I'm going to need a minute," I said, not using the effort to raise my voice. "A minute and a crap-ton of caffeine."

Boone's pace slowed. "Damnit, you scared me." His voice was more relieved than agitated. "I thought you were right behind me."

The world spun, but I still managed to sit up. There was no way I was going to lie there and have someone standing over me.

"I was. I was just really far behind you."

Boone chuckled, but I think it was more of a tension reliever than anything else. "I'm pretty sure that doesn't count."

"Did they catch who threw the spear?" I asked.

"No idea," Boone said. "I rounded back when I realized I'd lost you."

He watched the forest closely, gun still in hand.

"We need to get out of the open," Boone said. "You saved us once, I'd rather not put you to the trouble again."

I wanted nothing more than to lie back down, but when he held out his hand, I took it.

He hauled me to my feet, where it took me a minute to catch my balance. When I did, it was only because I was leaning heavily on Boone that I could go anywhere.

"This sucks," I said, not quite under my breath as we moved into the woods.

"I'm sure they've already caught the culprit," Boone said, trying to keep his voice light.

I shook my head, but said nothing. The sucky part was feeling useless. Rider had been stabbed, for goodness sake, and he was back in action. It wasn't as though I wanted to go running around in the forest, but I really hated being a burden.

When Boone picked a spot under cover, I sat back down

and leaned against the tree. He stood, alert and ready to fire on anyone that approached.

"It's getting dark," Boone said. "We'll need to start making our way to the camp."

"How far away is it?"

"About a mile."

"Yeah, right. I'll race you there."

"I can throw you over my shoulder."

"Ha! That's so not going to happen."

"Right, then, back on your feet."

I had to bite back a moan when he pulled me up once more. At this point, though, there was no use complaining—Boone was doing most of the work. It might even have been easier for him had he thrown me over his shoulder.

We hadn't gotten far when worry began to creep in.

I started to look around for my other partners. "Where are they?"

"I'm sure they're fine," Boone said. "If we don't hear from them by the time we reach camp, we'll send some of the squad out to help them."

"If Rider or Logan turn crazy, we're screwed. You know that, right?"

Boone chuckled, but it was forced. "You haven't seen what the others can do yet."

"Maybe she'll get the chance."

Boone started to bring his gun around, but then the voice seemed to register with him.

Davis stepped out of deepening shadows, Renick close behind.

"What's the situation?" Davis asked.

"Here, help her," Boone said, shifting me over to Davis.

"This sucks," I said under my breath again.

"She just saved our lives, but it had a pretty high cost,"

Boone said in way of explanation. "I'm going to run and check on Rider and Logan." He hesitated for a minute. "They'll hear me, right?"

"You can't go alone," I said. Boone started to say something, but I cut him off. "No exceptions." I grinned at him. "If you walk away on your own, we'll just have to trail behind. Way behind, in my case."

Boone grinned. "Right. Davis, you're with me. Renick, get her back to the camp."

Davis got me on my feet and I sagged against a tree. Then, they were gone.

Renick watched them go before turning to me. "Come on, princess, let's move out."

"I need a minute," I said.

"Saving the boss man may give you a free ride with him, but not me. Let's go."

"Remind me to punch you in the face once I get my strength back." I pushed myself away from the tree, then wavered.

Renick put his arm around me, helping me stay on my feet while keeping his gun in hand. "You might break a nail doing that."

"More like break my hand on your hard head." Once I steadied myself, I was able to lean on his arm and walk on my own.

"I can't believe it's only been one day out here and you're already falling down."

"Pissing me off isn't going to make me move any faster."

"You all are civilians, for Pete's sake. We spent the day running around in the woods and you all did what? Look for clues? This isn't the city. You're not going to take fingerprints and match them up to find the killer."

"I'm beginning to hate the sound of your voice."

"Well, princess, you need me right now."

"What I need is to stop for a minute."

He sighed, but I ignored him and leaned against a tree, trying to pull some vestiges of strength together.

"Did you twist your ankle and fall on Boone to save his life or something?"

"What is your problem?"

"We're just trying to figure out what use you are out here."

We? "Well, I walked through the past and got attacked there, then I watched people slaughter each other. I found out that whatever the hell this thing is, it infects people, driving them crazy, and it either moves silently or lays in wait. And you did what today? Walk through the woods?"

He shrugged. "Something like that. Don't think you and the Walker are the only ones around that can do things."

"I'll keep that in mind."

"Ready to move out?"

"Yes, the sooner we get back the better."

Talking with Renick made my blood pressure rise. For a little while, I managed to move through the woods on my own. However, when I started having to keep myself up by pushing myself from tree to tree, Renick moved in to let me lean on him once again.

"You know," Renick said after a while, "that Walker friend of yours has gotten all buddy buddy with Tolman."

I tried to find a point to what he was saying. "So? We're working together. Like it or not, we're a team."

"So, if I was about to be bludgeoned to death right now, you want me to believe you'd help instead of run away."

I rolled my eyes. "Of course I would. Unless I was the one doing it of course."

His laugh was a dry chuckle. "So, we're supposed to be all friendly and braid each other's hair now, is that it?"

"Well, it might be nice if you stood still when I punch you in the face, but," I mock sighed, "I know I can't get everything I want."

Renick laughed full out.

"What's going on?" Vincent asked.

Seeing him lifted my spirits considerably, despite the flat black of his eyes. Not caring if others were around, I moved away from Renick to be with Vincent. Even without the Path, I could feel him about to go off on someone.

"He thinks it's funny that I want him to stand still when I punch him in the face."

Vincent shook his head. "I mean you. I warned Logan that you were running on fumes."

Renick left, still grinning, and went over to Tolman, who was cleaning his gun.

"Not much of a choice," I said. "Someone chucked a spear at us."

When I filled him in on what happened, I turned to include Renick and Tolman.

It was hard to concentrate while leaning on Vincent. After a month away, it felt good to have him back, even if things were awkward. Trying to figure out where you are in a relationship —or if you even really have one—wasn't easy when you were surrounded by people you didn't know.

Vincent may have taken my distraction as a sign of exhaustion, so we moved to a rock. I sat down and my heart fluttered when he joined me on the same rock. Reminding myself I wasn't a schoolgirl with a crush didn't help drive the feeling away.

"I could use some more caffeine," I said.

"What you need is sleep," Vincent said.

"Food first," I said, "I'm starving."

"Food's almost ready," Tolman said. "We have coffee heating. If you aren't taking a shift tonight, though, you might not want it."

Hearing Tolman talking to me came as a surprise.

"She won't be," Vincent said.

I wanted to disagree and say I would help them guard the camp, but I wouldn't be any use to anyone if I fell asleep on the job. The feeling that I wouldn't be able to pull my own weight really started to grate on my nerves.

"I'll still take the coffee, though," I said, giving Tolman a tired smile.

The food wasn't great, but it wasn't the worst, either. Not that it mattered much, as I ate it so fast that the taste barely had time to register. Around us, night closed in.

"We found tracks earlier while we were canvasing the area," Renick said. "Well, I say tracks. Two prints were all we found. Whatever it was disappeared into some pretty dense jungle."

"If it was dense, wouldn't it have left some sort of trail through the undergrowth?" I asked.

"It should have," Tolman said, as though the creature had purposefully fooled him.

"Yeah," Renick said, "but it didn't leave a trace behind."

Something that big had to have put its mark somewhere.

I thought hard about the catlike look of the cave drawings we'd been shown. "The prints, were they deep?"

Renick shrugged. "Anything that big is going to leave some pretty deep prints if it walked through mud."

"When you were around the prints, did you look up?" I asked.

Tolman's eyes unfocused for a moment. It felt as though he turned inward to remember.

"We didn't see anything in the trees," Tolman said.

"But did you look *at* the trees? I'm wondering if there might have been claw marks or something," I said.

"You think it might be a climber?" Renick asked.

"It might explain why it disappeared," I said. "I can't imagine something that big, and presumably heavy, flying off. If it can become insubstantial and pass through things, I think we're screwed."

Renick grinned.

There was noise in the distance and I worried about what might be coming.

"It's the others," Tolman said.

Looking around I couldn't see anyone. Minutes later, the rest of the team trooped out of the darkness.

To know what caused the noise, Tolman must have super good hearing, or like Davis, he sensed where she was.

Rider looked gloomy and slumped down onto the ground nearby.

"No luck?" I asked.

"Yes and no," Logan said. He found a log to perch on. "We found the guy, but he put up a fight. When he realized he wasn't going to win, he slit his own throat."

I shivered from the graphic images my mind opened up. Vincent shifted closer in a comforting sort of way.

"From what it sounds like," Boone said, moving around the camp, "realize may be a strong word."

"True," Logan said. "There didn't seem to be much going on besides the aggression and insanity."

Davis, like Boone, seemed to be walking around the camp checking on things.

"How are you holding up?" Logan asked.

"Better, now that I've eaten and been caffeinated," I said.

Logan nodded. "Boone, I think I'm going to take a wide walk around the camp. Make sure everything looks in order."

"Good idea," Boone said.

"Why don't I come with you," I said. It was the last thing I really wanted to do, but a leprechaun was still out there that I needed to check on.

While in contact with Vincent, I could easily feel his disapproval.

"If you're up for it," Logan said.

I downed the now-lukewarm coffee, then grabbed a headlamp and my gun.

Once we had walked away from the camp far enough to not hear the others, Logan rolled his ears out. A little farther and we started to circle around in the dark.

"That was quite a save earlier," he said after a while. "How are you really feeling?"

"The coffee helped, but right now I feel like I could sleep for days. Other than that, I'm fine."

"Long day."

"Yeah," I agreed, "too long."

We walked in silence again for a while. The red setting on my headlamp cast an eerie glow, but the canopy was thick here, so there weren't as many plants to trip over.

"So, why the sudden interest in our perimeter?" Logan asked.

"I don't have one beyond wanting to know it's safe, but I may need your help with something."

"This is the thing you couldn't tell me about earlier," Logan said. It wasn't a question.

"It is."

"Want to fill me in now?"

While we walked, I also kept an eye out for the leprechauns, so I decided to stall. "I'll let you know when I can. I want to make sure there's no one able to listen in. Hopefully closer to the end of our walk."

We walked in silence for a short time.

"We think there's another villager out here," Logan said. "We saw signs of someone on our way back to camp."

"From what I saw of the past, there could be two others."

"Even if we manage to find someone living, I'm not sure they're going to be much use to us."

At least I had hope to share in that area. "I might be able to help there." I bit my lip and wondered how I could explain without mentioning the leprechauns. Their secret wasn't really mine to share.

"Are you thinking about spreading around a lighter atmosphere?"

"I didn't even think of that," I admitted. "That's a really good idea, though."

"It works well on the Lost when you need to calm them down."

A flicker of movement caught my eye, and I smiled.

"What were you thinking of doing?" Logan asked.

"Hold up," I said coming to a stop. I flipped off the red light. With good night vision, I could see enough for this meeting. "Is anyone nearby?"

"Everyone's still in the camp."

"I'm going to Read the area."

"You sure that's a good idea? We're only about halfway around the camp."

I closed my eyes and reached into the Path. "Trust me, now's the time."

When I opened my eyes, the night looked like day once again. The vivid colors of the Path lit the world, just for me.

"Kneel down," I said, sitting. I searched through Paths, though I didn't see any out of the ordinary.

Before starting, I called out using a light, peaceful tone, "I'm here." I pointed to Logan's ears, which were more than obvious when they were at their peaks. "I brought someone to help us out."

That was the best I could do. He would either show himself to meet Logan, or he wouldn't and I'd look like an idiot.

"Now what?" Logan asked.

"When you left me at the edge of the woods to go help Boone, I walked into the forest a short way." Bringing a calm, trusting thought of Gran to mind, I spread the contentment around the area. I wouldn't be able to hold it up for long.

Instinct told me to look out for other strange Paths, possibly coming from the camp, but I found none.

Logan sighed. "You found someone, didn't you? One of the other missing people. What did you do with them?"

"*I* didn't exactly find someone. They found me."

Behind Logan I could see a leprechaun peering up at him, as though analyzing to decide if he was willing to appear or not.

"They? And you didn't tell anyone?"

"I sort of told Rider, in a roundabout way, that they were here."

"They who?"

I nodded behind him and Logan turned, finding himself nose-to-nose with a leprechaun.

Logan froze and watched the leprechaun. The elf had met enough Lost to know not to move too quickly or make any snap judgments unless absolutely necessary.

After the leprechaun had his fill of Logan, he came over to me.

"And this is?" Logan asked.

"I don't know his name, but I was hoping you might be able to translate."

The leprechaun started talking and pointing out into the woods. Logan closed his eyes and listened.

"I'm not sure what you mean," I said to the leprechaun.

He started babbling again, and after a few moments, Logan interrupted. He spoke slowly at first. The two spoke in short spurts back and forth.

"He says he owes you," Logan said.

"Tell him I need to see his friend to make sure he's still okay."

Logan spoke and the leprechaun looked sad. He looked from me, to Logan, and back to me again. Finally, he stepped behind some undergrowth and was gone.

"He didn't look too happy," I said.

Logan, however, wore a wide grin. "I can't believe they even came out. What did you do?"

Now that they had decided to let Logan see them, I told Logan about the struggling leprechaun that had been bound.

"You pushed the Path into the ground?" Logan asked.

"Yeah, but I'm not sure if that was the best thing to do or not, though."

"Hard to say. I guess it all depends on what's down there."

"I didn't think of that."

"Likely the worst we'll get is some sort of ticked-off milli-pede," Logan said reassuringly.

Two leprechauns arrived, completely silent. It was hard to tell which was which, but I think the one I helped was the one shaking. Their other friend appeared not long after.

I inspected every inch of the leprechaun's quaking Path while they stood there, silent and looking forlorn.

"I think he's still okay," I said. "That happened hours ago and he's still clean of the infected Path. I think I can help coun-teract the effects of this thing."

Logan passed on the good news to the leprechauns, who now looked confused.

"Are you sure you're using the right language?" I asked.

"As sure as I can be."

"Ask them where the leprechaun was attacked."

Once it was translated, the first leprechaun started talking while using expansive hand gestures. The other three picked up the litany, each in turn. I could tell they thought it was a whopper of a story because of their voices and their gestures.

"It's a few miles from here," Logan said. "The nightmare creature attacked them before they knew what was happening. He says he owes you and he's ready to settle the debt."

I shook my head. "He doesn't owe me anything. Can you explain to him that this is what we do?"

Logan started explaining, and there was some back and forth once again. The leprechaun walked over to me and tapped my forehead. Then he took out a small knife and plunged it into the ground in front of me.

"He said he doesn't want to meet the others in the camp. I told him it was best if he never lets anyone else see him again. Ever."

"Good, that's better for everyone."

"We have a problem, though. Seems like you've been marked as a friend to their race."

"I was, back when I met them the first time."

"That means the debt can't go unpaid. If I'm understanding him, I think he's saying the debt is luck for saving a life."

"Their luck is tied to their life. At least I think it is—I'm not really sure how that works."

"He says it's up to you to take the luck."

I could feel my face flush. "That's just... dumb. And ridiculous. What kind of friends do they have?"

"If you aren't ready for him to repay the debt, he will follow you."

"Great, that's all I need."

Logan grinned. "They really are something. Turns out that's the way it's always worked with humans. Any time humans have helped them, the humans received luck in exchange."

I took a deep breath and tried to remain focused, but I was losing my strength once again. "He can't follow me and I won't take his luck. It would kill him."

Logan started translating when an idea crept in.

"Wait," I said. "They *are* the luck. We can use that."

Logan raised an eyebrow at me. "Are you saying you want something from them?"

"Yeah, and it'll make us both happy. Ask them if they know where the nightmare is."

Logan came back with an affirmative, but he still looked disapproving.

"Tell them the luck was us meeting them, and if they tell us where the nightmare is, the debt is paid, because that's the best luck we could get right now."

Logan grinned and passed on the message.

I swayed and closed my eyes while the conversation went on around me. It felt almost as if I was outside myself, but I didn't want to drop the calming feeling I was generating for the leprechauns. Could a person sleep sitting up? I'm pretty sure I couldn't Read the Path while sleeping.

"It's done." Logan sounded muffled, as though he were talking through a pillow. "Cassie?"

His voice was distant, but when he shook me, it brought me back to myself.

"You need to stop Reading," Logan said.

He didn't have to tell me twice. I let the Path fall away and I fell with it.

CHAPTER

FOURTEEN

There was arguing, but it was being done quietly. Although I was half-asleep, I could still feel Vincent trying to dam back a crushing amount of emotion. His voice betrayed none of that, though, which is the only reason the argument remained quiet.

Drowsily, I stared up through the bug net and saw a star peeking out through a gap in the canopy. It winked out, it appeared, and then it was gone again. I wished that whatever breeze was swaying the tree tops would come down here and join us.

When it reappeared, I realized I had the perspective wrong. The swaying was much closer, and the thing moving was coming toward me, down from the tree.

"What the hell is that?" I hadn't meant to ask so bluntly, but I had a dawning suspicion that the thing was slithering down.

"What is it, Cass?"

"What's the... the—the big thing, coming down from the tree."

"Oh wow."

I hated how he sounded so calm. How could anyone be calm with a giant snake on the loose?

With my hands shaking, I searched for the zipper to the bug shield. My fumbling fingers seemed to take forever to get the flap unzipped. In my rush to get away, I stumbled out of the hammock, but Vincent kept me on my feet.

Vincent helped me stay upright, but he wasn't moving away. Why was he not running?

"It's only a snake," Vincent said. "It's not poisonous or anything."

"Just a snake?" I squeaked. When faced with a giant snake, I felt that I had the right to squeak.

It reached the strap to my hammock and I moved to hover behind Vincent.

"I'm sure he only wanted to get warm," Vincent said, watching the creature.

The thing was holding on to a limb and had already stretched down what had to be twenty feet.

"Wow, princess, you found tomorrow's breakfast." Renick laughed at his own joke.

At least I thought it was a joke.

"What do we do with it?" I asked.

"We can encourage it to leave or move it," Logan said.

Tolman walked up, looking cranky, and I realized I must have woken him up along with everyone else.

An acute case of embarrassment arose.

Tolman glared at the snake as though it had personally harmed him.

The snake twitched and fell out of the tree. Tolman didn't say a word—he only turned and went back to his hammock.

The snake twitched a few more times, then it laid still.

My mouth dropped open. Eyes wide, I looked at Logan.

He gave the tiniest of nods.

"I didn't want it dead, just... just..." My voice came out as barely a whisper. I'm sure my partners heard me, even if Tolman couldn't. I sniffed and tried to pull back from the situation. "I just wanted it gone."

"I know," Vincent said, stepping closer. "It was a misunderstanding, that's all."

Now I was shaking for a whole other reason. This felt even worse. *Who does that to an animal? I mean, yeah, if there had been it or me, then you should go for it.*

I chanced a glance at Renick. He looked pissed.

Then, he noticed me watching him and his attitude shifted, hiding any agitation he might have felt. "Looks like it's all better, princess."

Vincent went still and I put my hand on his arm to dissuade any action on his part.

"Renick," Boone barked, "get rid of the snake. Take it well away from the camp. I don't want scavengers to show up."

Renick grumbled under his breath, but grabbed the snake and stomped away into the night.

It had been my fault. I should have been quieter.

Could Tolman do that to a person?

Not that it mattered. The man always seemed to be packing as much firepower as he could lift. If he were going to attack a person, it was probably easier to open fire.

I felt better than I had earlier—power wise at least—but I knew I needed a lot more sleep in order to make it through the day tomorrow.

I eased toward my hammock once again and I looked up into the tree wondering if the snake had any friends up there.

"You can switch with me," Vincent said.

When I saw that he was the closest hammock to me, I smiled. "Are you sure you don't mind?"

"Not a bit. I'm on duty, so I'll be close by, and I'll also keep a lookout for any other adventurous animals."

"Who are you on duty with?"

Vincent cringed slightly. "Renick."

"Play nice." After checking for anything that slithered or crawled, I leaned against a tree by Vincent's hammock. Lowering my voice, I added, "I didn't mean to wake everyone up."

"Boone and Davis are going back and forth, keeping an eye on the fire. Rider's still asleep, though."

"He's had a hard day."

"So have you. How are you holding up?"

"I'm fine," I lied.

He moved closer. "You know I can tell how you're actually feeling."

I forced a smile. "Then why do you ask?"

Vincent took my hand and leaned against the tree next to me. "I've been gone a while, I could be wrong."

His close contact made our energy twirl together. A tingling anticipation arose inside.

"Staying away from you didn't work so well today," I said.

"I know."

We stood silently for a while, listening to the sounds of the others settling in or, in Renick's case, walking around. I had hoped Vincent would say something else, like he wanted to be near me. The truth was, though, I knew he did, much the same as he knew how I felt.

Still, it would have been nice to hear.

"I should get back to work," Vincent said. He squeezed my hand before stepping away from the tree.

I gripped his hand, holding him near me so he didn't have a chance to walk away. My mind was a swirl of things I wanted to say to him, but none of them seemed right or appropriate.

"We have a lot to catch up on." It was the best I could come up with. It seemed like an understatement and left so much unsaid.

"I feel like I've missed a lot," Vincent admitted. "Before I left, you broke... I wasn't sure what I'd be coming back to."

I frowned wondering what my broken soul had to do with it. "I'm not sure I know what you mean."

"Neither am I." Vincent sighed, and I could see a chink form in the walls he built around himself.

Reluctantly, I let go of him.

I could sense more than see that he was trying to bottle up whatever was trying to break free.

"I need to get back to work," he said.

"Of course." *This isn't how I wanted things to go.*

He didn't move, so I did, turning my attention back to the hammock. After checking the bug net to ensure I didn't let anything inside with me, I got in and after a bit of rearranging, I managed to get comfortable.

Moments later, I heard Vincent walk away.

THE SUN WAS WELL over the horizon when I peeked my head out of bed the next day. My need for caffeine was high, but I made sure to check the tree and ground for any surprises of the reptile variety.

When I stumbled away from the hammock, Davis poked her head out from around a tree.

"I wasn't expecting you up yet," Davis said. "They made it sound like you'd be asleep much longer. I would have had some coffee ready."

"Thanks, I can make some," I said, looking around the site. "Where is everyone?"

"Your team is at the village along with Boone."

"What are they doing back there?"

"We can't move out until the fire is all the way out."

"I didn't think about that. Where are the others?"

"They're tracking. Trying to see if there is another person from the village out here."

"That's a good idea. If we find someone, we can find out more about what did this."

Davis's smile seemed to freeze. "I doubt anyone we find will be sane enough to be helpful."

"Maybe," I said, sidestepping the issue. "What are we supposed to be doing?"

"As soon as you're up to it," Boone said, walking into camp, "you two can go relieve Vincent and Rider for lunch."

Logan came soundlessly out of the woods. "Howdy, partner," he said, tipping his hat. "It's good to see you up and about."

I couldn't believe it was already lunchtime, so I grabbed a protein bar and a caffeine pill. "I'm up for it."

Logan looked me over. "You look like you can manage for the afternoon, but take it easy over there. I think we should send Rider and Vincent out to search for any other survivors."

"That sounds good," I said, grabbing water and hurrying off before either one of them changed their mind.

Davis and I walked in silence for a while.

"Do you mind if I ask you a question?" Davis asked, once we were almost to the village.

"Sure," I said, curious, but worried about what the question might be.

"Is this a typical mission for your team?"

"Typical? No, not that there really is a typical case. How about you?"

"Mostly they're like this. We have our orders, we go in, we do the job, and we go home."

"I see what you mean," I said. "Our orders aren't usually as straightforward as this."

"You seem to have a lot of down time," Davis continued.

I could feel my face start to turn red. "I wasn't exactly expect—"

"No," Davis rushed in. "I don't mean that as a bad thing. I just meant that you use your power a lot on the job."

"Oh." I'm not sure if that was any better or not. "Don't you all use yours?"

"Not in the way people may think," Davis said.

"What—"

"You are looking well," Rider said, interrupting as we approached the town. His smile looked artificial, which wasn't like him.

"Thanks," I said. "So are you. How's your back?"

"It is healed," Rider said.

"We weren't expecting you so soon," Vincent said, his usual blank face firmly in place.

"I'm rested enough to sit around and watch a fire," I said.

There was a flicker of a smile out of Vincent.

"You all should get back, though," I said. "I think Logan and Boone want to send you into the woods."

"The fire is almost out," Vincent said. "It should be done by this evening. You all have everything you need?"

"Yeah," I said, "we're all set."

With a nod, Rider melded into the woods and Vincent followed.

"Well," Davis said, "we're here; we may as well get clean."

She headed out to the section of the river closest to the lodge.

I really wanted to ask her what she meant about not using

her powers the way people think, but anything I thought of seemed rude—or worse, left me open to answering the same questions.

"I'm going to check the lodge first," I said.

"Sure thing," Davis said. "I was out here half the night. I'm sure it hasn't changed much since then."

I found a stick and poked at the ashes, spreading a few smoldering coals away from each other. Davis took off her hat and headed toward the river.

Shots rang out.

Jumping and turning toward the forest, I saw a mass of birds rise as two more shots were fired.

I waited, watching, expecting something else to happen.

"That was Tolman," Davis said.

I jumped. She was right beside me, yet I hadn't heard her moving. She looked anxious.

"Is he okay?" I asked. "I mean, can you tell if—"

"I need to get to them," Davis said, jerking forward toward the tree line.

"Wait! No one alone, remember."

"Come on, then," she said.

I looked at the smoke rising over spots. *It probably wouldn't hurt, right? I mean, it's a rainforest.*

Picturing hundreds and thousands of acres of rainforest on fire made me pause.

"Come on!" Davis said. "What if it was your team?"

I blinked at her. "You're right. It is my team." The burning embers were still visible and I was at a loss for what to do.

The fire had to have a Path, right?

"I need one minute," I said.

I jumped into the Path and found the Paths of massive amounts of heat in both the present and past.

It wasn't the only thing I found there. Two blurry shapes vibrated toward the village, and they were headed my way.

I bit my lip, grabbed every Path that was heat related, wrapped it into a ball, and threw it into the river.

They were getting close. Too close. With one last glance, I jumped out of the Path.

It wasn't until I caught my breath that I noticed I was trembling. I looked at Davis to see if she noticed. Her face was white and her mouth was open. She looked out over the river.

I followed her gaze and saw masses of smoke had risen from the stream. It was like a sauna near the water.

Crap!

Davis turned toward me and it looked like she was sizing me up. There was no fear or worry; it just appeared as though cool calculation was taking place.

"Let's go," I said to distract her. I hurried by and didn't look behind me. It took her a few moments to catch up. "Is Tolman hurt? Or Renick?"

"No, they're fighting, and they aren't in a good frame of mind to tell Boone what happened. I need to get to them before he does."

Alarm bells clanged around in my mind, but I stamped them down.

"How far away are they?" I asked.

"A little over three miles, but they're closer to the camp."

I didn't get a chance to ask much else. My breath was needed for keeping up with Davis.

What kind of frame of mind would they be in to not explain what happened. Was she afraid they wouldn't tell Boone something or tell him too much?

My energy lasted for two miles. I knew this because Davis kept up a litany of how far away Tolman and Renick were.

Sweat poured down my face. I shouldn't have worked so

quickly in the Path. There had to have been a better way, one that didn't require so much energy—maybe one that didn't turn me into a huge spectacle.

Pushing forward was difficult. I wasn't sure why we were running to get to Renick and Tolman when she knew they were okay.

It wasn't until I heard raised voices that I understood what Davis meant about them not being in the right frame of mind to talk to Boone.

Tolman, who was always so quiet, was yelling at Renick. Not much, though, Renick wasn't leaving much space to talk.

Davis put herself between the two and glared from one to the other. Both stopped talking, but I got the feeling the conversation actually continued.

I leaned against a tree to catch my breath. Back home, running was nothing like running here. This air was like breathing water. Looking around, I didn't see a convenient rock to sit on. That's when I saw the body.

"What happened?" I asked.

"I'd like to know that myself," Boone snapped from the forest.

Davis glared at Tolman. "Tell him."

Tolman didn't look happy about having to explain himself. "This person was a threat. I neutralized the threat."

Boone went over to check the body. "Davis, I'm not sure why you and Cassie are here. Go back to your post."

"The fire's out," Davis said.

"Unless every coal is extinguished, there's still a fire," Boone said. There was a vein pulsing in his neck—a sure sign he was pissed off. "You know that."

Davis looked at me. "You said it was out, right?"

I could feel my face turning red. Thankfully, after running

while breathing more water than air, my face was probably already flushed.

"You know the fire's out?" Boone asked.

"It is," I said.

"I don't see a weapon on this man," Boone said, aiming his gaze at Tolman. "Do you want to explain?"

"He came out of nowhere," Tolman said. "Looked like he was getting ready to attack Renick."

Boone looked at the other man.

Renick stood a little stiffer. "That's what happened," he said.

"Get back to the camp," Boone said. "I'll take care of things here."

"Um, I need a minute," I said as the others passed by. I gave Boone a meaningful look, hoping that he could read it.

"Course you do, princess," Renick said, but he kept his voice low enough that even I barely heard.

"Cassie will come back with me," Boone said, his voice finally starting to lose its hard edge. "Let the others know we're about an hour behind."

When they walked off, Logan stepped out of the woods.

"You got here before I did," Boone said. "What did you see?"

I found a spot on the ground to sit and got as comfortable as I could. "Tolman and Renick were arguing. Davis broke it up."

"What were they fighting about?" Boone asked.

I shrugged. "It sounded like Renick was being his usual charming self."

Boone rubbed his forehead, then squatted down next to the body.

"Three holes," Logan said. "One in the head and two in center mass. Your boy is a good shot."

"He's an impossible shot," Boone said. "He always hits his mark within a thousand yards."

"Always?" Logan asked.

"Under any conditions," Boone said. "I've never seen him miss."

"Why didn't they use tranqs?" Logan asked.

"Tolman wouldn't have been the one to carry the tranqs," Boone said. He looked at me. "Why were you here?"

"I have no idea," I said. "At first, I thought someone might be hurt, but then... I'm not sure. I think Davis was just worried."

"Could be," Boone said. "She probably thought they were killing each other."

"Do they not get along?" I asked.

"They get along fine most of the time," Boone said, "but their arguments can get more than a little heated."

"I think she knew they were fighting," I said. "She said they wouldn't be in the right frame of mind to tell you what happened." I looked at the body. "What do we do with him?"

"If he's contaminated, there's only one thing we can do," Boone said. "Do we know what happens to the contamination after they die?"

Logan shook his head and they both turned to me.

I looked around and wiped my sweaty palms over my fatigues. Seeing outside the Path wouldn't do me any good. I knew that, but I looked all the same.

Closing my eyes, I stretched my mind and jumped into the Path.

The body had no contamination. Frowning, I got to my feet and moved closer to the man's Path.

"Do we need to take him to the fire?" Boone asked.

"No, he's not infected," I said. His older Path wasn't infected either, which was surprising. Maybe the purple blight disappeared once its victim died. I bit my lip and glanced around, happy to see that I was alone in the Path, but I wasn't happy with what else was there. "You remember that Path I saw in your office?" I said, narrowing in on a Path leading into the woods. When I said the words, the Path disappeared. "Never mind. It's gone now."

Logan gave Boone a searching look.

"I'm going to look back a short way," I said before they could get into any other discussion. "I want to see something."

"It's not a good idea," Logan said. "Speaking of which, you put out the fire?"

My face heated up once more. "Yeah, I was worried someone was hurt at the time."

Before he could argue, I pushed back into the past Path. I winced when I saw the man get shot, but moved even farther back.

"The nightmare never got to this man," I said. "Even before he died, his Path was clean."

"I wonder why he was attacking then," Boone said.

I pushed back farther, but met with resistance. When I finally got through, I was left wavering.

"Time to come back," Logan said.

I watched the scene play out. "Renick was ahead of Tolman by quite a bit."

"We don't need to know this that badly," Logan said.

"The man was hiding. When Renick came by, he popped up out of hiding. He ran."

Logan laid a hand on my shoulder. "Your grandmother will have my ears if you burn yourself out."

"Right," I said vaguely, still watching the area.

"Cassie!" Logan snapped.

I jumped. "Okay." I let the Path push me up to the present and I stepped out.

Logan griped my shoulder harder to keep me from falling. Then, he lowered me to the ground and sighed.

"I don't suppose anyone brought caffeine?" I asked, lowering my head to keep the vertigo at bay.

Boone passed over two caffeine pills.

"My hero," I said, taking them dry.

"You need to go easy on those," Logan said.

"You said the man was running," Boone said. "Are you saying that Tolman shot an unarmed man moving away from Renick?"

I shook my head. "Yes and maybe no. From Tolman's point of view I could see why he might think the man was a threat."

"Giving him the benefit of the doubt?" Logan asked.

I nodded.

Boone and Logan started making decisions on what to do with the body. In the end, they decided to cover it and let nature take over.

It was a long, slow trip back to camp and we didn't arrive until it was fully dark.

CHAPTER

FIFTEEN

My dreams were full of nightmares. Past and future, fact and fiction, life and death were all jumbled together and had me waking in the night sweating. No one should have to see what we'd found out here.

And it had only been a couple of days.

The hammocks were technically built for two. When you laid down, the material cocooned over you nicely. To see out, you just put a leg over the edge.

When I woke up, the sun was rising and the humidity tried to rob me of oxygen, replacing it instead with water. Listening to the sounds of the camp, I heard that others were up, so I peeked out of the hammock Vincent had loaned me and looked around.

Rider was up, but moving silently. He stalked the grounds with his nose flaring. Vincent appeared to be asleep in my bed.

Logan was also up, but it seemed as though the elf never really slept. Davis and Tolman were keeping an eye on him. It took a few moments for my sleepy mind to realize why they watched him so intently. Logan's ears were at their points.

Then my eyes landed on what looked like a lumpy ball of orange nearby.

"Did someone bring a basketball?" I asked, not bothering to raise my voice.

Rider and Logan turned their heads in my direction, appearing confused.

"It's too lumpy to be a basketball," I heard Vincent say.

"Too large to be one, too," I added.

Davis and Tolman began to take notice as well.

"Is that...?" Davis trailed off.

The mass twitched and jerked back.

"*Hell no!*" Davis half yelled. She began to try to pull Tolman away.

Tolman's eyes grew wide, and Davis couldn't move him.

The creature scuttled around, allowing me to notice the legs for the first time.

"That's not—" My brain couldn't form the word spider. *They don't get that big.* It had to be a dog or something that had extra legs.

When it turned my direction, my heart stopped. I began to scramble in the hammock, trying to climb up one side of it to where it was lashed to a tree.

"Cass," came Vincent's calm voice. "Stop moving."

I froze. "Is it attracted to the movement or something?" It came out as a hoarse whisper in case sound was something that grabbed its attention.

"No," Vincent said. "You're climbing toward another one."

My eyes scrunched shut in self-preservation. *How can he be so calm?*

"Logan?" I called.

"They don't seem to be ready to attack or anything," Logan said. "They look curious, that's all."

"Curious as to how I taste, you mean. Someone, tranq them already!"

"Now, hold on," Logan said. "These tranqs will take down a raging minotaur. It could hurt them. Besides, *we're* the ones disturbing *them*."

"They aren't venomous," Boone said.

I wasn't shaking in fear at this point. Instead, I was well past that point—far beyond a world where rationality could be found. Opening my eyes a minuscule amount, I looked sideways, trying to see where the other creature was.

It was an effort not to scream. The spider was right there. A foot away from my head. If it stepped onto the bug net, it would be on top of me.

"Who cares if it's venomous? It's a spider the size of a dog!" *How could they not get this?* "Are there any more of them?"

"Only the two," Logan said.

"Is someone going to tranq this thing?" My high-pitched whisper barely came out.

"We need to consider that this might be a type of Lost," Logan said.

"It's indigenous to the area," Boone said.

"So?" Logan said as though speaking to someone slow on the uptake. "Where do you think you get half of your insects? Where do you think mosquitoes come from? Just because it's indigenous to the area now doesn't mean it didn't, at one time, come from another dimension."

"I guess it would explain why the spiders are so damn big," Boone said.

"Okay, okay," I said, more to myself than to anyone else. "It's fine. A giant orange spider—" My voice cracked and I had to restart. "A giant orange spider in the middle of the jungle. Just where you would expect a giant orange spider to be."

"Two," Logan reminded me.

"Thank you for the reminder," I said.

"I could catch one," Rider suggested.

The one on the ground inched forward.

I jumped into the Path and tied the air around me like a safety blanket.

Slowly, I slid back down to the center of the hammock. The spider on the tree tensed.

I fumbled for the zipper to the bug net. Before I could get outside, though, the spider pounced.

As far as the others could see, it landed on air.

I heard a whimper. At first, I thought it was me, but my breath was going in and out in short sharp bursts that didn't allow any room for noise to escape.

When I stood, I turned and looked eye to eye with the massive spider. The Path wavered for a moment, and I shuddered at the thought of this thing reaching me. I made sure to hold onto my shield as though it was a lifeline.

It certainly felt like it was.

The one on the ground came up to me. Neither was being aggressive. Like Logan said, they seemed curious. When I stepped away, the one hanging in the air jumped to the ground. It looked as though it had a little trouble landing with that fat body.

As I stepped farther away, they followed.

"Why?" I snapped at the spiders. Then I felt silly and sought out Logan. "Um, I'm not sure what to do at this point."

"Getting them away from the camp would be preferable," Davis said in a voice higher pitched than normal.

She appeared to have frozen in the act of pulling Tolman away. Tolman himself hadn't moved and he watched the spiders intently. His face appeared rigid. I imagined his mind full of multi-legged terrors.

I looked at Logan for suggestions, but he didn't appear happy to see these things either.

A spider leg reached out and tried to go through or maybe climb up my protection.

"Cass, you're burning through a lot of power," Vincent said.

I noticed that it wasn't until I had moved away, taking the spiders with me, that he got out of his bed.

"Yep," I said, "and I'll keep burning it until these things are far away from me."

"Can you convince them to go?" Logan asked.

"What?" I asked, beginning to lose all patience with anyone who wasn't suggesting tranquilizing the spiders. Since I was the only one suggesting tranqs, I was losing my patience with everyone.

"Maybe make them afraid of the camp," Logan suggested.

"Oh, you want *scared* giant orange spiders," I said, forcing as much fake sincerity into the statement as possible.

"Well, you might want to move over here first," Logan said. "I'd rather them not run this way, if it's all the same to you."

I looked at the nearest one, which appeared to be tapping at my enclosure. "It's worth a try. Just make sure you don't run away as well. Any of you."

When I circled around to stand by Logan, the creatures watched my trajectory. It was only when I was standing in front of everyone that I shifted gears.

Thinking of something intensely fearful wasn't difficult. Using my own terror, I began to fill the Path.

The spiders stopped their inquisitive approach.

"They're hunkering down," Logan said. "Anyone know what spiders will do before they run away?"

"What do you mean?" I asked.

"What's their natural response to something they're scared of?" Logan asked. "Do they run away or attack?"

"*What?*" I screeched. "No one said attacking was a possibility."

One of them scuttled back, then turned and sped across the forest floor faster than I would have expected it to move.

It wasn't long before the other followed.

Once they were out of sight, it felt like a great weight had been lifted, but I couldn't look away from where they'd disappeared, worried that they might return—possibly with reinforcements.

"Cassie," Logan said, "you might want to let up now."

The effort to look anywhere other than the direction of the spiders was great, but I had no idea what Logan was talking about.

Vincent wore his look of stony indifference. Boone appeared to be trying for the same, but he was straining. Even Logan and Rider looked like they were ready to run.

Davis and Tolman appeared to be fine, though—much better than when faced with the monster spiders.

Switching gears, I grabbed a memory of watching Gran cook in the kitchen. Contentment washed over the camp and everyone appeared to relax.

Except for Davis and Tolman.

It wasn't that I could control someone's emotions, but I could cool down or heat up the atmosphere, influencing how someone feels. It didn't affect Davis or Tolman, though.

Pushing the Path away left me feeling drained.

It was early morning and I was already exhausted. This day was going to suck.

"Okay," Boone said, "back to it."

Back to what, I had no idea, and I didn't care to know.

"Coffee?" I asked Logan.

Logan shook his head. "This isn't a great way to start the day."

"I agree. Someone should have tranqed them," I said.

"Get more rest while you can," Logan said. "We'll need you later."

The need to disagree was almost overpowering, but logic said he was right, so I held my tongue.

Back in the hammock, I listened to the sounds of the camp until I fell into an uneasy sleep.

When I woke again, the sun was high and the camp was quiet. Birds spoke to each other and the branches in the canopy swayed. If it weren't for all the murderous creatures and crazed madmen, the forest would have been bearable.

"It makes me uneasy when you do that."

I peered through the bug net and found Rider giving me a strange look.

"Do what?" I asked, stretching out.

"The humming," Rider said.

"I didn't realize I was."

"I think that is the root of the issue."

I sighed and let my head fall back, watching the sky again. "I don't know what you mean."

"It was the elf humming."

"Logan?" I asked, feeling even more confused.

"No, the elf in you."

Crap. I didn't know what to say. My soul had been imprinted by the lives of many. It wasn't often that I slid into a trivial part of another life as though it was my own.

"Ignore it." It was the best response I could give right now.

Rider said nothing.

The idea of borrowing part of a life that wasn't mine didn't sit well with me.

"Where are the others?"

"They are in different places."

"And you're stuck here with me?"

"I am partnered with you," Rider said, looking unsure. "I do not appear to be stuck."

I smiled at him. "Any signs of giant spiders?"

"They have not returned."

"What are we supposed to be doing?" I asked, ready to brave the world outside of the bug net once again.

"After lunch, we need to finish packing up the camp. I think we should take the chance to meditate as well."

My mouth watered at the mere mention of food.

Rider and I worked well together. After eating something that had once been freeze-dried, we put away any remaining equipment. By the time we were done, it was barely noticeable that we had been there.

"Logan and Boone will be returning soon," Rider said.

"No one else is with them?"

"Vincent and Tolman are searching the area to see if we can find any other former residents of the village. Davis and Renick are scouting ahead. They will be finding our next—"

A shrill howl filled the air, cutting Rider off. Birds took flight. It seemed as though the noise was coming from every-where at once, and whatever was making the disturbance sounded close.

While the din continued, I moved closer to Rider. The sound cut off after what seemed like forever.

"Where did it come from, Rider?" I asked the moment I knew I would hear his response.

"I am not sure."

"Do you hear Vincent?" I asked. "Is everyone okay?"

Rider cocked his head and listened intently. "Boone and Logan are returning now. Vincent and Tolman are unharmed."

"Davis and Renick?"

"I do not hear them. They have disappeared," Rider said, as though he didn't believe what he was saying.

"What—"

"No," Rider said, interrupting. He came close to me and lowered his voice. "They have moved. They are over a mile closer."

"Are they running?" I asked.

Rider shook his head. "They are... Now they are closer still. Moving from one spot to another."

"You mean they're teleporting?"

"I do not know that word, but they are walking now." Rider shifted from foot to foot, looking so worried that I patted his arm. "I must have misheard. The sounds, they bent oddly. That is all." He shrugged off my hand, not unkindly, and moved away.

"Is everything okay?" I asked.

"Vincent is hurrying back," Rider said.

"That's not an answer."

"He has been very worried about you."

"Why won't you answer me?"

Rider's shoulders slumped, and when he dropped the facade, he looked tired. "It is not an easy question to answer."

I looked around the camp at a loss. "I guess it was a stupid question to ask. I'm really sorry about your friend."

"I knew her, but we were not friends."

I smiled. To werewolves the word friend took on a next-level meaning that was hard to explain. "Is there anything I can do?"

"I need... something."

"What? Whatever it is, I'll help."

Rider let out a frustrated growl. "I need to run. I need to smell something that is not blood. I need for the people of this world not to be like they are back home."

I bit my lip. Having no idea how to give him those things made me worry. "Which people?"

"The new three and the people in the village. Everyone that is not our family."

Maybe that's what friends were in Rider's world—family.

I couldn't really do anything for him, so I did the best I could. I wrapped my arms around him and hugged him tight. He was breathing heavily as though he had been very active.

Little by little, he calmed down. He returned the hug and didn't let go until I heard others approach. Even then, Rider seemed reluctant to let go and remained close.

"Maybe you can go for a run," I suggested. "Surely, Logan would understand."

Rider shook his head. "After. When there are not as many people around that want us dead."

"Where we go, the crazies tend to follow."

"We usually do not let them get so close."

Close? "Was the thing that yelled out nearby? Or other people from the village?"

Just then, Vincent and Tolman arrived, looking as though they had rushed the whole way.

"Do you know where it came from?" Vincent asked, wiping the sweat off his face.

I couldn't help but notice that Vincent was inspecting Rider and me, looking for signs that something might be wrong.

"It is difficult to tell for sure," Rider said.

Logan and Boone arrived not long after.

"I didn't get a line on the source either," Logan said. "I think we're moving in the right direction, though."

Boone began to pack up the remaining items. "We need to be ready to move out in five."

I moved back to Vincent's hammock, which I had vacated not long before, and started unstrapping it from the tree. Vincent went to the other side to help.

"We can split up the rest of Davis and Renick's gear," Tolman said.

"Never mind that," Logan said. "We'll grab them as they are."

Tolman looked as though he was ready to argue, but Logan snagged one of the bags and threw it over his shoulder as though it was weightless.

"Rider, you take the other," Logan said.

"Do you think that it was the nightmare that made that noise?" I asked.

"It's the best explanation we have," Logan said. "I can't think of anything from this world that can make sound move that way. And only a few Lost—none of them sound like that."

"Rider and Tolman, you two pull ahead. Don't stop until you reach the others—unless you catch sight of this thing."

"Let us know your progress," Logan called after them.

"Cassie, you're with me." Boone said.

I finished shoving the bug net into its pouch, then passed it off to Vincent. Vincent barely noticed, since he was glowering at Boone, who studiously avoided noticing the look.

"We'll catch up," Boone added to Logan.

The moment I grabbed my bag, Boone started leading the way out of the camp. It made me nervous to leave so quickly, but on my last look around, I didn't see anything that I had forgotten.

We moved silently for a while. For some reason, even with the urgency that had sprung up back at camp, I felt more relaxed when I was alone with Boone.

"So," Boone started, "is there some sort of trick to get your boyfriend to like me?"

"He's not my—" I stopped, then changed directions. "It's not that he doesn't like you. He just doesn't know you yet."

"I know Vincent's a nice guy and all, but I have to say, it's unnerving when someone with his power glares at you like that."

"Vincent and I have been through a lot together. Then you and I disappeared for a few days and..."

"Yeah, I guess if I bring his girlfriend home barely alive, I shouldn't expect him to like me too much."

"That probably has a lot to do with it."

"How have you been holding up since then?"

"It's been strange. How about with you?"

"Possibly stranger," Boone said.

"Strange enough to call in backup. That's saying something."

"Speaking of that, I wanted to have a word with you in private while we can."

"Is that why we're going in a different direction?"

"No, we're going to the village. You're the only one that has a chance of getting to know this creature better."

The idea of Reading a Path that was days old sounded exhausting. We knew what had happened in the village lodge, seeing the mayhem on the other end of the village didn't sound like a great way to start my day. "I guess it's a good thing I got a few extra hours of sleep."

"Whatever it was you did in the lodge the other day, you're not doing that again today."

I raised an eyebrow, which Boone couldn't see since he was walking ahead.

"I mean," he corrected himself, "it's better if you don't. Not without Rider around. Plus, we're going to need everyone in peak condition when we face whatever this thing is."

"What is it you want me to do, then?"

"I'm just hoping you can get a feel for this thing. We know it's an aggressive predator, but that's about it."

I thought about that for a minute. "Do we know it's aggressive?"

"We know it attacked at least two villages."

"My guess is it's not an herbivore and it seems to cause aggression, but we can't even be sure of that. We don't know what these people may have done to it before it attacked."

"You're pleading defense on its behalf?"

I noticed Boone's grin. "I'm not pleading anything. I just think we need to consider the options."

"You think it might have attacked because it was hungry, or maybe in retaliation for something?"

"Or both. Or it could just be a vicious monster. The point is, I don't think we should automatically assume this thing is killing people just for the fun of it."

We tromped through the woods in silence for a while. Boone slowed the pace when we neared the huts.

"You know, I've missed working with you," Boone said.

"Me too, but next time we get together, can it be a bit closer to civilization?"

Boone chuckled, but lowered his voice. "Normally, I'd clear the town again just in case someone came back since Logan and I left. We're in a hurry, though, so I'll watch your back while you do your thing."

We moved quietly across the village to where it looked like the creature had dragged someone away. An eerie feeling had fallen among the empty huts. When we were close to the spot where the person was dragged away, we stopped and dropped our gear. I stretched and looked around, uneasy about getting started.

"Remember, if you wear yourself out, I'm not going to have to worry about Vincent," Boone said, "I'll be answering to Logan at that point."

"He won't blame you for something I do," I said, not really paying much attention.

Before Boone could say anything else, I stepped into the Path. I looked around, seeing wisps of Paths that were days old.

"I think it came in over by the platform," Boone said. "I'm pretty sure they had a guard above ground level."

While only Reading a small stream of the Path, I meandered around, narrowing in on the edge of the village. I sensed Boone nearby, but to be polite, I purposefully avoided Reading his Path.

Close to the forest, I stopped, catching a faint tinge of something impacting the Path in a big way.

"Do you see it?" Boone asked.

I waved my hand at him and studied the surroundings. Only allowing myself to Read a small bit saved on power, but it wasn't going to be enough.

Taking a deep breath, I let the Path pour over me.

Which was a mistake.

SIXTEEN

The Path bore angry reds, vivid blues—leaning toward black—and a streak of white-hot fire threading around. It surrounded me, poured over me, and made me fear for my life.

"What is it?" Boone asked, keeping his voice low and calming.

It was then that I noticed I was breathing fast. The stark terror rooted me to the spot. I began to tremble, and when someone touched my shoulder, I jumped and inhaled sharply.

"It's me," Boone said. "You're safe. What is it that you see?"

"I see someone frightened to the core. It's like... It's like the person's mind broke and nothing remained but the fear."

"Anything of the creature?"

Something moved faster than I could follow. The strange vibrating presence that lived in the Path had found me again. I wondered briefly if the thing out here was attached to the village.

Knowing I was running out of time, I jerked myself unsteadily into the woods. It was easier once I was out of that terrible Path. The experience permeated the area, but without the direct assault, it was easier to handle.

"I don't see anything else," I said, walking alongside the Path. "I think the person that was taken wiped out any traces of anything else."

"I'm not sure what that means," Boone admitted.

"It's as though their experience created a blight in the Path. Nothing else in the Path would be able to be seen."

"How long does something like that last?"

"It's hard to say. Logan left his mark in the woods a few years ago when we discovered a fairy had been killed. That anger is there, frozen in time, affecting the past and the future."

"So we have no hope of finding anything?" Boone asked.

"Unless the person is still alive, my guess is this has to end somewhere. It's a matter of finding the end."

Boone was quiet for a moment, so I kept moving.

"Let's leave it here," Boone said at last.

Frowning, I turned to face him. "We could track—" I froze. There was something standing behind Boone.

No, not something—someone. It took me a moment to figure out if it was real or in the Path.

Boone noted the look on my face. He turned. His puzzled look when he faced me again gave me the last hint I needed. The thing was in the Path. Shaking, I closed my eyes and pushed away the Path.

"What's wrong?" Boone asked.

"Um... nothing. Nothing is wrong."

"You're a bad liar."

I shook my head. "Something else was there, but it's nothing unless I'm in the Path."

"You've stopped."

"Yeah."

"Let's go." Boone turned and nearly walked into the area exactly where the thing in the Path had stood.

I grabbed his arm. Wordlessly, I dragged him back, and then circled wide.

"Can you still see it?" Boone asked, keeping his voice low.

"No, but it's... I would just feel better all-around if we avoid going where it stood."

"Was it a person from the past, like yesterday?"

"No, this is different. Don't worry about it."

"Hard not to after seeing the look on your face."

I smiled at him, but it felt weak. "It doesn't affect anything out here."

"Not even you?"

"Honestly? I don't know. Whatever they are, they see me, but I haven't let them get close."

"They? Are there a lot of them?"

"Hard to say. I don't know if I'm seeing the same thing over and over again, like they're following me, or if they're generally almost everywhere."

"What does your team say?"

"Not much. Vincent doesn't know and I try not to talk about it with the others much."

"Why not?"

I thought about that for a while. "I think I'm worried they'll look at me strangely."

"What makes you say that?"

We stepped back into the clearing and went for our supplies.

"Seeing what no one else can see can be difficult," I said once I had the bag situated on my back. I didn't look at Boone. Not directly, anyway.

"It must have been hell growing up," Boone said.

"Things weren't bad until college. I had Gran and Mom

around before that. Even though Mom pushed her power away, and wanted me to do the same, she never once thought I was making things up."

"And when you went away to college, you didn't have that anymore."

"Actually, I did. I went to school at the local college." I gave Boone the shortest version I could of my college years with Zander while he and I trooped through the rain forest.

"What an asshole," Boone said when I was done.

"Most people wouldn't be able to handle what we see and what we do. At least not right away."

"Dating is difficult."

"Do you have someone you're close to?"

"Not really. A few people I served with know the score, so I can at least talk to them, but the job has always come first. Once I left the service, I thought I'd be more settled. But this assignment..." Boone sighed and pulled to a stop. "Let's take a break."

"Don't we need to catch up with this thing?" I asked.

He looked at the sky. "I'm pretty sure Logan will be bringing everyone to a halt soon. We don't want to face the creature at night."

"How do you know where they are?"

Boone dropped his gear and grinned. "I forgot you don't have a good sense of direction. Think of it like this. They went straight, and we'll meet up with them by angling in."

"I'll take your word for it."

He chuckled before digging out a protein bar and water.

We ate in silence, listening to the birds chirp.

When I was halfway done with what I would laughingly call lunch, I heard another noise. "What's that chittering sound?"

"Monkeys, I think. While it's just the two of us, can I ask you something?"

I nodded and wolfed down the last of my meal.

"We can have a private chat." I smiled. "That's our code on the team. Logan and Rider won't listen in."

"It's not them I'm worried about. I'll try to make it quick, though," Boone said.

"Wait, let me check something." I glanced around and jumped into the Path. Looking around, I didn't see any signs of the strange Path that I had spotted yesterday and back in Boone's office. "Okay, I think we're good."

"You're Reading?" Boone asked.

I nodded.

"What do you think of the team so far?" Boone asked.

"Davis and I get on okay. Tolman and Vincent seem to have hit it off too."

"I'll have to get Tolman to tell me his secret."

"He doesn't look like he tells anyone much of anything."

"You're not wrong. And Renick?"

"He's an ass."

"That seems to be the consensus. Now, tell me what you've noticed. You see things others can't."

I wiped sweaty palms on my pants and looked around the forest. "The thing the other night with the snake. That was... odd."

"Telekinesis is only one of the things they can do."

"No, not because he could do it," I explained. "It's because it looked as if there was no thought behind the action. He saw something bothering him and just killed it."

"I've seen something like that before from Davis."

"Then there was the way Tolman killed the guy in the village. That's been the only time I've seen him look happy, except a few times I've seen him and Davis together."

"I wondered if something may be going on between the two. Are you sure he wasn't just excited that he saved you?"

"*Thought* he was saving me," I corrected. "And yes, it's a possibility."

"Then there was this morning."

"I didn't notice anything this morning."

"When I used the Path to scare the spiders away, it didn't affect those two the way it did everyone else. Afterward, when I stirred up some other emotions, it didn't seem to faze them either. It could just be they're immune to my charms."

Boone chuckled again. "It's a possibility. Anything else?"

Should I tell him what Rider said about us being close to those that want to kill us? "The rest is just a feeling. Like, I see Davis and Tolman watching us as though they were taking notes." I wasn't even sure what Rider had meant, so it was best not to speculate.

"You all are a good team. So, overall, what would you say? Does it look like they can handle everything?"

"If I was alone with the three of them on assignment, it might be a little creepy. Can they talk to each other mentally?"

"It's a possibility," Boone conceded.

"You don't know?"

"There was mention of it early in the experiments, but nothing later. I think they've started hiding what they can do."

"They're guinea pigs, so I don't blame them. I also suspect that they can eavesdrop while being fairly far away."

Boone sighed. "I think you're right there as well."

"It sounds like working with them would be lonely."

Boone raised an eyebrow and looked at me. "Lonely?"

"They're keeping things from you. If it's just you and them, well, it seems isolating."

"Taking it all into consideration, it doesn't sound like things are as bad as I thought."

"Maybe."

"You're not saying something."

"It's just... I wouldn't want to be alone on a mission with them. It may be because I don't know them, though. Let's see how the rest of the time goes. I didn't get a good look at their Paths. I could do that, if you'd like."

"I like the sound of it. What can you find out that way?"

"Mostly how they're feeling."

"Give it a shot."

I drank a little more water and felt alarmed that my supply had gotten so low. "What are we going to do for water when we run out?"

"Don't worry; we won't have to resort to drinking ditch water. We have charcoal filters and purifying tablets."

"Charcoal?" I was leery of the taste already. "Anyway, we should get going."

"One more thing," Boone said, getting up and putting on his bag.

"Yeah?"

"Logan said you had a direction on where to go to find this thing, but he wouldn't tell me the source. I don't suppose you'd give me a hint?"

"I'm sorry," I said, "but the secret isn't mine to tell."

"No one showed up in a dream or something?"

"No."

"Good, because I don't like the kind of help your grand-mother's boyfriend gave us."

"Trust me when I say there's nothing to worry about with my information." I thought about that for a second. "Well, except for the fact that it leads to something called a nightmare."

"Alright, I trust you."

"Thank you."

"You're not too worn out?"

"It's not bad yet. I'm letting go of the Path now."

"Let's move out."

WHEN WE GOT BACK to camp, everything was already set up and the sun was starting to set.

I had expected a look from Vincent, but was surprised that he just seemed to glance around when we arrived.

What I wasn't expecting was the uneasy look Davis and Renick gave us.

If Boone noticed, he didn't show it. He dropped his gear and looked around the camp with a proprietorial air.

"Good spot," Boone said.

Looking around, it appeared to me like almost any other spot we'd camped out in.

"We think we're at least five miles away from the nightmare," Logan said.

"Did someone see it?" Boone asked.

Logan shook his head. "It's only a guess. Rider and I hiked an extra three miles to listen a little better. We think we've narrowed down the location. Everything go okay on your end?"

"Not really," I said, dropping my bag. "The man that was taken, his own Path was so intense it blocked everything else."

Vincent, Renick, and Davis moved closer in to pick up our conversation.

"Did you follow it?" Logan asked.

I squatted down and busied myself with my gear.

"Only for a short way," Boone said. "We need everyone in top shape for tomorrow."

"Any problems?" Logan asked.

When Boone hesitated, I jumped in, "No issues, but there was some activity in the Path."

Logan may have heard the hesitation in my voice, because he dropped that subject.

"Well, you're right about needing everyone fit for tomorrow," Logan said, looking around at the others. "Any issues, see me or Boone. We'll set up the night-watch schedule."

"I can take a shift," I said.

Logan looked me over. "Get set up and take the first shift with—" He glanced at Boone.

"Tolman."

I gave Tolman a weak smile. He didn't return it.

SEVENTEEN

For the first time since we'd entered the rain forest, I was fully rested the next day. After days of breathing the humid air and hiking, I was starting to get used to it at last. The three-mile hike the next day seemed easy compared to the rest of the trip.

"After we leave this spot, don't talk unless you have to," Boone said while Logan hoisted our bags into the air. "We're using comms today, so make sure you get an earpiece from Davis and test it out."

"Why have we not used these before now?" Rider said.

"Power sources are thin in the forest," Boone said.

I took the tiny earpiece and turned it on, testing it before putting it in my ear. They were standard agency-issued comms, and it seemed strange to be using the technology after days of roughing it.

"Logan and Rider have found our target," Boone said. "In two miles there's a depression in the ground. It's maybe a quarter of a mile wide. That's where we're stopping. Any questions?"

No one said anything. There was anticipation in the air that was palpable.

"Okay, partner up. Davis and Rider, Tolman and Renick, Cassie and Vincent. Logan will be with me. Take our lead."

Vincent seemed mildly surprised at being teamed up with me. His face even showed shock when Boone asked for a private word with him. Logan hummed a little as we readied ourselves.

When Vincent and Boone were finished, we headed out.

Even though we couldn't talk, it was nice to be partnered with Vincent. Being close to him made walking through the jungle more bearable.

Two miles later, Boone made some complicated hand gestures that went far beyond my range of knowledge. Not that it mattered—I followed Vincent's lead and hoped for the best.

We crept over the hill to get a good look at the depression below. It looked like a large sinkhole. Or, once I thought about the geography of the area, maybe a mouth of a small volcano or lava flow.

There was movement. Around the rocky edge across from us, a hole was almost hidden behind the roots of a tree.

"It isn't much of a cave," Davis said, keeping her voice low. "There are breaks in the surface. If we can get the creature to back further into the cave, we can pick it off from above."

I glanced at Vincent, seeing my own worry mirrored in his face.

"I can get a decent line of sight," came Tolman's whispered voice through the comms. "The thing is moving around. If it settles down, I might be able to take it out from here."

"We have to make contact first," Logan said. He was quiet, but he had a finality in his voice that said his course of action was the one they'd be taking.

"We've seen what it can do," Renick said.

I wasn't as certain of that as Renick sounded. Closing my eyes, I stepped tentatively into the Path. The nightmare bent the Path in funny ways, so I wasn't looking forward to seeing what it could do this close.

"We haven't seen everything it can do," Boone said.

"Good point," Davis said.

It was a relief to hear her back off. The team would follow her lead, even over Boone's—I was sure of that now.

The Path in the general area looked normal until I turned my attention solely on the scene below. Stark fear spread through the area beneath me.

Vincent turned off his comms and moved closer. "What is it?"

"What?" I asked, my attention being wrapped up in the scene.

"You saw something. What is it?"

"It's afraid. Terrified. Not just now, but it's been living like this for days, maybe weeks."

Vincent breathed deeply and watched below, looking around while he took the entire scene into account. I could feel him concentrating on the landscape below.

"Is it intelligent?" Logan asked through the comms.

I turned my microphone on. "The Path isn't complex, but there's so much terror from the poor thing that I can't be sure. I don't think it's sentient, but it's hard to be certain."

"Can you help it?" Rider asked. "Calming the animal could allow us to remove it without anyone getting hurt."

I began to look for a way into the basin. "I can't from here."

"How close do you need to be?" Vincent asked.

"The closer I am the better the effect," I said.

My partners waited while I looked for a way. They knew me well enough to know I was going to try if I could.

"Fall back," Boone said. "One hundred yards and hold."

We crept away. Since we had been fanned out in a circle, when we fell back to what Vincent said was the right distance, I couldn't see anyone.

"Since we can't get close," Davis said through the comms, I think we need to take our shot when it comes."

"Cassie?" Boone turned my name into a question. He seemed to know I wasn't going to give up on the animal.

"I think I can climb down, but it might be noisy," I said.

"Can you deflect the sound?" Logan asked.

"I can try. The Paths of sounds bounce all over and I can't enclose myself and move," I said.

"Rider or I might be able to get you to the cave mouth without much noise," Logan said.

"Give me a minute." I looked at Vincent and thought over my options, then turned off my comms.

"I'm going with you," Vincent said as soon as we had as much privacy as we could get.

I smiled at him, liking the sound of that.

"But we could also get Rider or Logan to go with us if you want," Vincent said.

"More people may not work as well. This thing does something to people's Paths."

Vincent seemed to hesitate. "Would you rather have Logan or Rider with you?"

If Rider went with me and something happened to me, what would Vincent do? Vincent and Rider's friendship could be ruined beyond repair. Their friendship was Rider's type of friendship. Once it was there, it was there. The bond was as tight as family. If Vincent blamed Rider, Rider might not be able to handle the rejection from Vincent.

Logan might be a good choice, though. I looked into Vincent's eyes and saw the truth in what he was asking. His question felt deeper than just who I wanted to go into the basin with me.

I clicked on my comms. "Vincent and I are going to make our way there. I should be able to block the sound." There was no outward change in Vincent, but I could feel his relief without the Path open.

Even if I could never open the Path again, my bond with Vincent was enough that I'd always be able to tell how he felt.

"Davis and Rider, circle around and try to find openings overhead," Boone said. "There may be more than one way in. Tolman, find your spot. Shooting is a last resort, got that?"

"Got it," Tolman said.

Communications went quiet as we all signed off. I slung my tranq rifle over my shoulder. Then Vincent and I moved toward the nightmare.

"You'll stay here, won't you?" I said.

"I'm going with you," Vincent reminded me.

"That's not what I meant. When we get there, if I can't stop this thing..." I couldn't finish that. For some reason, I couldn't say, *Don't leave again. Don't go between the worlds.*

"I can't promise anything," Vincent said quietly.

I'm not going to tear up at work. I'm not. It's not going to happen. I bit my lip and looked around, trying to take my mind off the idea that Vincent could be gone again. Another month. Maybe more, maybe less. Was this what it was always going to be like between us?

"If anything—"

"Don't." I cut him off more sharply than I'd intended. I softened my tone. "Do what you need to do and I'll do the same."

Vincent stopped. I went a few more steps before I realized that he wasn't going to start moving again.

"What's wrong?" I asked.

It looked as though his mind was turned inward.

"What is it?" I asked, suddenly worried I had said something wrong.

"It's nothing," Vincent said, his voice as blank as he tried to make his face. "Let's go."

He started to move past me and I grabbed his arm. My hand began to tingle and warmth spread into me. For once, I tried to ignore it.

"It's not nothing," I said.

He pulled free and started moving toward our goal. "We'll talk later. It's not the time or place."

I sighed. "It never is."

Vincent rounded on me and I nearly jumped, startled by his change. "You said do what you need to, right?"

"Yeah," I said, feeling uneasy.

"What you need to do and what I need to do are two separate things."

"But the goal is the same."

"No, I need to keep you safe, and you need to keep your distance from me."

My anger boiled up, but I shoved it down before it could escape. If I said the wrong thing now, I'd regret it.

But what the hell should I say?

"Those two things are opposite," I said lamely.

"Outside of work they aren't."

"Is that really what you want?" I asked, trying to keep my heart together while shoving down my temper.

"Of course not," he said, "but it's what you need."

I rolled my eyes. "What I *need* isn't up to you."

I tried to think of this from the outside. Gran said that Vincent and I get in our own way. That was what was happening at that moment. Both of us weren't saying what we should have been.

Vincent shook his head.

What needed to be said? I had no idea.

However, I knew what I wanted. Right then more than anything. Glaring at Vincent, I moved right up to him. I let my anger boil out and roll away.

And I kissed him.

The world disappeared. There was no hesitancy on his part or mine. My rifle dropped to the ground, though I barely noticed. He squeezed me to him tightly enough that I knew what he had in mind if only we had been alone. At least not in the middle of the jungle.

We came up for breath and he laid his forehead against mine, his eyes shut and his breathing heavy.

"That wasn't what I had in mind," Vincent said.

I smirked at him. "You're a bad liar. Besides, it's what I was thinking and something I've wanted ever since I saw you at the base."

He sighed and pulled back some. "You can see this isn't going to work."

"We'll make it work. As long as you stop with this stupid idea that I should be with someone else."

"And if I leave again?" His body tensed in my arms.

I smiled at him and blinked innocently. "If it's a stupid reason, then I get to yell at you. Then you can make it up to me. Win-win."

He smiled. A real, whole smile. "And if it's for a good reason?"

"Then we'll have to make up for lost time."

"I like the sound of that," Vincent said.

Logan popped onto the comms and cleared his throat. "Slow up. We don't want to be there too much before Vincent and Cassie."

"But you have to stop with this whole 'we shouldn't be

together' crap," I said more seriously, while ignoring Logan. "It... it hurts to hear that."

Vincent looked momentarily embarrassed before he pulled me so tightly to him that I couldn't have looked at his face if I tried. I could feel a kind of embarrassed mortification flow from him. "I won't say it again."

"Or think it," I countered. "We belong together. You're mine now." Thinking about that, I added, "and I'm yours."

"You're mine?" He pulled back and looked at me playfully.

I was surprised to see the expression. "As much as you're mine," I said, warningly. Then I smiled. "And for as long as we want."

"Cassie, Vincent, give us a signal when you're in place," Logan said. He didn't sound unkind, but he was adamant.

I sighed and stepped back. "Fine," I said, not bothering to turn on the comms. "We're on our way." I snatched up my rifle and adjusted it. Then I looked around. "Did we come from that way?"

"No," Vincent said, grinning.

"So we're going that way?"

He chuckled. Vincent took my hand and led me in a new direction.

"One bit of forest looks like another," I grumbled.

So, this is it. Vincent and I are together. The thought gave me tingles in all the right places. It would take a rampaging mino-taur bearing down on us to make me lose my smile.

Or maybe a nightmare.

"I should be able to calm the animal down," I said.

"I know you can," Vincent said, squeezing my hand.

"And if something happens, hopefully I can keep it from hurting us long enough to tranquilize it."

Vincent said nothing.

"But if for whatever reason you have to leave, how long would you be gone between the worlds?"

"We're in South America," Vincent said.

"We are, yes. That doesn't answer my question."

Vincent seemed uneasy. "If you get my sister down here, it might not take more than a week."

"And if we didn't have your sister?"

"That's actually a situation I wanted to talk to you about." He lowered his voice. "But not out here. We need to wait until we get home."

"Sure," I said, wondering what could be that secretive.

It wasn't until we were close to our destination that I realized he hadn't answered my question. He seemed to get along well with his sister—he'd spent almost a month with her, after all. She would travel for him. I hoped she already had her passport.

"We're going silent," Vincent said.

"I'll muffle our sound as best I can," I said.

He dropped my hand when we neared the large basin. When he did so, I closed my eyes and reached for the Path. The intensity threatened to wash over me and sweep me away, perhaps to the past or a mysterious future. Before opening my eyes, I pushed back as much of it as I could and allowed only a trickle of the Path to be seen.

It amazed me how much easier it was to do work with the Path than it had been a few months ago. With that done, I sorted through the Paths and tried to make one solid enough to stop sound.

"I'll climb down first," Vincent whispered. "Wait till I reach the bottom, then start after me."

Looking over the edge, I saw that the drop seemed much larger than it had before. Could I even climb down this thing?

Vincent reached the bottom quickly. There were plenty of

handholds and places to put my feet. Vincent stealthily found one after another.

Taking a deep breath, I sat down, grabbed a rock and moved out onto the cliff face.

Once I was there, I realized calling it a cliff was a misnomer. It wasn't a straight drop. In fact, once or twice I was able to walk down a few steps instead of climb. Each step had me wondering about spiders and snakes.

Vincent would have scared them off, right?

Something brushed my hand. Too late, I realized it was a piece of foliage. Instinctively I let go, then skidded down the last few feet.

Vincent stood me up and scanned me silently. He gave me a questioning look.

Embarrassed, I made an okay sign and studied our surroundings.

I was able to dampen the sounds of our movement as we scrambled over the rough landscape. It wasn't until we were at the cave mouth that I realized the entrance was elevated. The idea of having my head appear to the animal before anything else didn't instill me with a lot of confidence.

Vincent started to move forward and I grabbed his hand. When he looked at me, I shook my head and closed my eyes. I thought pulling up a happy memory would be easy. I figured the fact that Vincent and I were together would be a great event, but those emotions were many and jumbled.

Instead, I thought about home. Not a particular time, but home in general. Gran in the kitchen, Molly pacing the house as she got to know her surroundings. Even Cici in the back garden. The memory was warm and inviting, so I let it fill me, and then spill out. I encouraged the emotions up and around, trying to overtake the fear in the Path.

Vincent looked slightly dazed, so I stepped past him and climbed up. Thankfully, he immediately followed.

I didn't go straight to the mouth of the cave. Standing with the light behind me would only outline my shape. It would make me a perfect target.

Instead, I slipped in through the side, keeping myself as close to the wall as possible.

I was putting more concentration into emotion and less into the sound protection, which I discovered was a mistake when I tripped over something and scattered several rocks around me.

A loud yowl filled the cave and two large dinner-plate-sized eyes glinted in the darkness. Fear pulsed through the cave. Vincent managed to get to me to my feet and then started pulling me to the cave entrance. I resisted, not ready to give up.

The noise turned into a low growl. At that moment, I realized the emotion I was pumping into the room might not be enough. I opened the Path wider and forced more to come through. The thing howled and backed up. The darkness turned into black fur when light hit it from above.

"Cass, we should get out of here," Vincent said.

"No," I insisted. "Stay behind me. I'm going to try something."

With the Path clear and fresh, I studied the creature.

"This place is littered with bones," Vincent muttered.

My mistake was clear in the Path. The animal's fear turned gray then blue, then such a dark blue that it could almost match the animal's fur.

"Oh, no. I didn't mean that," I said, trying to pull up something happier.

"What?" Vincent asked. "You can't say that without telling me what it is."

"I made it sad. Homesick, really. I didn't mean to."

Sadness had swamped everything else. To counter it, I opened the Path wide and put light emotions directly into the beast's Path.

With my senses fully opened, the streaming Path showed me more. I could see the creature clearly. It looked like a large cat, blacker than even the darkness of the deepest depths of the ocean.

It made me think of Molly. Sure, Molly was small now, but I knew she could grow to be huge.

The thing's tail flicked and it began to settle down. It laid its head down and blinked at me.

Cautiously, I stepped forward.

"What are you doing?" Vincent asked.

"I'm getting closer," I said, keeping my voice light and friendly. The truth was that the loneliness the animal felt pulled at my heart. Even now, with its Path turning green and brown, I could see that it felt hollow. Completely alone in the world. "It's okay," I murmured to it as I neared.

It didn't seem concerned with me getting closer. Then again, I probably looked more like lunch to it than anything else. Its tail flicked again and I noticed something new.

"The drawings were right about the two tails, weren't they?" My steps were smaller now that I was close. "You are beautiful." I hesitantly held out my hand. The thing raised its head and sniffed me before bumping its nose against my hand. They were close to the same size. When it settled its head down again, I ran my hand through her fur, much as I did Molly. "Such soft fur."

A deep rumbling came from the creature and I nearly drew away, ready to make the Path solid.

Then I stopped. "You're purring, aren't you?"

It rubbed its face into me. Since its face was as large as my body, it nearly knocking me over. I laughed softly, then continued petting it.

"Vincent, come here."

"I know Margaret likes to keep strays," I heard Logan say through the comms, "but I think she'll object if you take that giant thing home."

Vincent moved up and stood so close behind me I could feel the heat of his body. "You might want to dial it back some," he said quietly to me.

He was right, of course. I was starting to feel worn.

A loud crack overcame all other noise. The nightmare howled, but the sound died away as blood splashed over me.

An overwhelming sense of pain and betrayal crashed into us, knocking me to my knees.

It felt as though an imp sat on my chest. Breathing became hard. The agony poured into me from the burst the creature had put forth, although I could see now that the creature's Path was dead. The blight it made on the Path had to be permanent.

Noise filtered in through my comms, but I couldn't make heads or tails of it. The animal had thought I deceived it. Its last moments in this world were ones of pain and duplicity.

My breath came in short bursts and I knew tears were rolling down my face. More than anything, I knew I had to get out of that cave.

Vincent put his hand on my shoulder. I turned to him, ready to have him take me away from there.

It wasn't Vincent. I blinked vaguely at the thing standing in front of me.

Then I screamed.

The cat wasn't the nightmare. The true nightmare was standing over me. Its skin was rough and calloused, almost looking like bark. The eyes were black as coal, and when it opened its mouth to make noise, I could see sharpened teeth.

A hand clamped down on my shoulder hard enough for me to cry out. I felt a tug from somewhere deep inside me.

I screamed again. It was something I had felt before. My energy began to drain away and I instantly felt weak. If I hadn't been kneeling already, I would have fallen to the ground.

I pulled at the talon-like hand on my shoulder, ready to pry it off.

A tingling sensation leapt from the beast to me. The sensation worked its way up my arm.

This thing had swallowed up Vincent and now was coming after me.

The pull on my strength slowed and stopped. I slumped forward, but still gripped that taloned hand.

It wasn't right. None of this was. I looked at the horrible sight looming over me, knowing I was going to die. I Read the thing's Path, ready to try to use what little strength I had to grip it and throw it away from me.

It was Vincent's Path.

The creature knelt down in front of me, making harsh guttural sounds that made me want to run out of the shadowy darkness of the cave. It took my hand.

It was Vincent.

I closed my eyes and concentrated on the feel of Vincent. Leaning forward, I risked laying my head on its shoulder. Focusing on the Path, I saw the telltale signs of someone in the grip of the madness the nightmare caused.

Carefully, I began to chip away at it.

There were yells and other noise around me. I didn't want to look. I was afraid to see what kind of horrors were coming to greet us. When someone tried to pull me away, I swatted them weakly, all the while taking apart the contaminant piece by tiny piece until Vincent began to emerge.

My vision blurred. Too much energy used and too much taken.

I was pushed away and fell back.

"Get her out of here!" Vincent yelled vehemently.

The shock of hearing him so angry made me snap away from the Path.

When I risked opening my eyes, I could see... things around me. They were blurred from vibrating so quickly.

But I could see under the illusion of the nightmare now. The energy taken must have started breaking apart the madness, much as I had done to Vincent. Rider, Davis, and Vincent were all appearing underneath the nightmarish figures.

"Don't touch me," Vincent snapped, I could see him backing away. "Rider, don't let anyone else in here."

So much hatred and anger was in his voice that I wondered if I was still in the nightmare.

"I will do that," Rider said. "It will be okay."

"None of this is okay," Vincent snarled. "Get her out of here!"

"It might be better if she stayed," Rider said.

"No!" Vincent backed into a wall and slid down. "Take her away before something worse happens."

Davis helped me to my feet. I staggered a bit, but was able to move while using her as support.

I heard Vincent mutter something. Rider must have heard it, because he stopped Davis and me as we stepped outside. Even under the canopy, it was bright outside.

Rider lifted my chin and studied me. When he let go, he walked around Davis and me.

He stopped in front of me again. "Are you injured?"

I shook my head.

"Please say it," Rider said. "You have not spoken."

"I'm not hurt," I said, my voice listless and dull. "Just tired. Is Vincent... did I do something? Is he hurt?"

"He will be well. His mind is muddled. Did he—"

"I'm tired," I cut in. "Just tired."

Rider looked me over one last time before nodding and retreating into the cave.

"Come on," Davis said almost under her breath. "Let's get you out of here."

She helped me stumble away from the cave. I thought she'd stop close by, but she kept moving. Seeing Logan and Boone running over, I understood why. They looked pissed, and I knew there was about to be a bunch of yelling.

"I'm taking her back to camp," Davis called.

"Is she okay?" Logan reached us first.

"Just tired," I said. *And more than a little confused.* I knew why, though. It took a lot of effort to make my brain ignore what just happened. I stowed it away in the corner of my mind and put one foot in front of another until I could find the time to piece everything together.

"Stay on comms and give us updates," Boone said as he joined us.

Davis nodded.

"And get Tolman over here now," Boone continued. "He's got some explaining to do."

Her mouth was a thin line, but she nodded and moved on. Making it out of the bowl wasn't easy, but with Davis's help, I managed it. Before we were out of earshot, we could hear Rider arguing with Logan. True to his word, Rider wasn't letting anyone else into the cave yet.

I was leaning more heavily on Davis now, which I hated. "I need a break."

"Just a little farther," Davis said. "We're almost there."

There was no way we could almost be at the camp. "Almost where?"

Davis sighed and let me lean against a tree. She rummaged through her pockets for a minute while I closed my eyes and tried not to think of the nightmare in the cave. The animal or what followed.

"I'm really sorry about this," Davis said.

Ugh. I really needed a longer break, but I didn't say so. Davis was standing right next to me with a nervous smile on her face. I blew out a steadying breath. When she put her arm around me, I felt a prick on the side of my neck.

I slapped my hand up to swat the bug away.

"Really sorry," Davis repeated.

The tiredness grew until I slid down the tree. Walking was out of the question. Looking up, I saw Tolman and Renick approaching. After that, the world went blurry, then dark, and I fell asleep.

It felt only moments later when the sound of arguing woke me up. Looking around, I saw Davis and Renick yelling. It took me a while to care about what their disagreement was about. Mostly, I wanted for everyone to shut up or go away.

"She's up," Tolman said.

Davis and Renick went quiet, but it felt as though the argument continued. It seemed as though, if I entered the Path, I would be able to see words fly from one mind to another.

When I finally pushed myself up to a sitting position, a headache attempted to slice my brain open. I grabbed my head, trying to keep it together.

"Don't bother trying anything," Tolman said. "We've been built to stop psychic attacks."

"Psychic what?" I kept my voice low to prevent the words from stabbing into my head. At least it was dark out now. I didn't think I could have handled sunlight.

"Don't play dumb," Tolman said.

"Stop," Davis said. "She's here for a reason, remember?"

"It wasn't a reason we agreed with." Tolman indicated himself and Renick.

"You have your orders," Davis said. "You don't have to agree. Besides, we could use her on our side."

"Your side of what?" I asked. "What orders? Where is everyone?"

Davis gave me a sickly sweet smile and I subconsciously leaned away from her. She sat down near me, but stayed a measured distance away.

"We'll track them down," Davis said. "Soon."

"Except Boone," Renick cut in.

Tolman glared at Renick.

"Boone gets a chance, but so does Cassie," Davis said.

"A chance at what?" I lowered my hands and tried to ignore the pounding of my head. Something was happening around me and I needed to pay closer attention to my new partners. Without so much as blinking, I stepped carefully into the Path. Pain exploded in my mind, but I didn't dare let go.

"Our orders," Davis continued, "are to kill the Lost."

"I knew it," I snapped. "You were planning on killing the nightmare all along. It was an innocent animal. You didn't have to kill it."

"You're human. You get a chance to join us," Davis said.

An icy feeling started at my heart and began to radiate out. In the Path, I could see signals were indeed traveling from person to person.

"A chance to join you at what?" I asked.

"Actually, join may be a bit of a stretch," Davis said. "You just have to stay out of our way."

The iciness left me uneasy. To distance myself as best I could, I put up a sold wall of Path between the others and myself. My head roared with pain and I winced, but kept the wall steady.

"We're partners," I said. "How am I in your way?"

"We need you to let us do our job," Davis said.

"You already killed the nightmare." A hole opened in the pit of my stomach and I glared at Davis, daring her to say what I thought she was trying to tell me.

"One down, three to go," Tolman muttered.

I stood up like a shot. "You can't mean that!"

By the time I was fully standing, Tolman had his gun out, pointed straight at my head.

"You idiot," Davis snapped at Tolman.

It wasn't until I was standing that I realized how much power I had burned through. Not just here, but earlier as well. I wasn't completely done in, but I would be close if I didn't get out of here.

"Look," Davis said, slowly standing and raising her hands out in a slowdown gesture. It felt as though she were trying to placate me.

If she thought I was angry, I'd go with it. The fact was, though, I was too tired, confused, and scared to be angry as well.

"We brought you here to give you a chance," Davis said. "Please, stay here and let us do our job."

"And your job is?" I looked from one to the other in turn.

"To kill the Lost," Davis said.

"They don't belong here," Tolman said.

Renick's hands were clenched tightly, but he said nothing.

"You said three," I said, grasping for something to stall the situation until I could wrap my head around what was happening.

"Walkers don't belong anywhere," Tolman said.

"Wait a minute," Davis said. "Vincent is human and I know he means a lot to Cassie. Maybe we could let him live if Cassie will stay out of the way. What do you say, Cassie?"

"I say you're crazy." My voice came out a little screechy, but I didn't care. They were insane. That was all there was to it. "We're supposed to be your partners. Why would they ask us to work with you?"

"*Boone* asked you to work with us," Renick snapped. "Blame him."

"You've been brainwashed or something," I said. "Let's just go back to the others and we can talk about this."

"We're going back to the others," Tolman said. He looked at Davis.

Davis sighed. "We're doing that without you, though. I'm sorry, Cassie. I really liked—"

Tolman fired once.

I jumped back and fell over. My breath came in short, sharp bursts as I staggered back to my feet.

"What the hell?" Tolman asked.

I fed more power into the Path as Tolman fired a second time.

When I stayed standing, he fired again.

"What are you?" Davis asked. "Tolman doesn't miss."

Tolman emptied his clip. Each time, my power got weaker as it absorbed the impact.

"Knock it off," Davis said. "They'll hear us."

"We have miles of rain forest between us and them." Tolman dropped his clip and slammed another in. "In this dense forest, they aren't going to hear much."

"You idiot. They have good hearing," Renick snapped.

"They do," I said, trying to hide the fact that I was shaking, "and I guarantee they're coming for me."

"Let's go," Renick said. "I'm not dying just because you can't keep your gun holstered."

Tolman had been aiming his gun at me again, but he then swung it around to point at Renick.

Renick only grinned.

"She's right," Davis said. "Let's go."

"We can't leave her," Tolman said.

"We can and we are." Davis grabbed her bag. "She's not even our target. Let's move it."

Renick and Tolman followed suit, although the latter looked ready to rebel.

Something passed unspoken between them. Then, Tolman took one step and disappeared.

"This could have ended better, you know," Davis said. The accusation in her voice was clear. "We could have worked together."

"That's what we were supposed to be doing!" I yelled.

Davis shook her head. Within five steps, she too disappeared.

I turned to Renick.

"Sorry, princess, I'm a go-with-the-flow kind of guy. Do me a favor and stay away from your partners. I don't want to have to kill you." He turned and was gone.

I gaped for a few moments before turning and running like hell. I had no idea where I was going, but since I didn't know where I was, it didn't really matter much. With the Path open, night was like day in the flow of colors. Once I thought it was safe, though, or at least relatively so, I pushed it away. I jogged a few more steps before finding a tree root with my foot and a tree with my head as I tumbled forward.

I panted while sprawled out on the ground and waiting for my vision to become less blurred.

A deep-throated growl made me slap a hand over my mouth to stop the sounds of rapid breathing from escaping.

It sounded like a large cat.

It sounded like a nightmare.

Could there be two?

I pushed myself to my feet, staggered a little as the world tried to pitch me over again, and I was then forced to lean against a tree until my head stopped spinning.

Crap. I was covered in the blood of the first nightmare. Sure, some of it had been wiped away, but it was in my clothes and hair. I could feel it on me.

The noise came again, closer now.

It definitely sounded like the nightmare.

Could it be the same one? I thought wildly. *Am I still under the influence of the first nightmare? Has any of this really happened?*

The Path would tell the truth. It always did. I reached out. The light and color of the world blinded me. It felt as if it bore into my mind. All the beautiful flows slammed into each other. My stomach churned and lurched. Using the tree as support, I was able to lean over before I lost everything I had eaten since entering the jungle.

At least it felt like it.

I let the Path drop again. The sound stopped. I pushed myself away from the tree and stumbled off in another direction.

Or maybe it was the same one. Who could tell out here?

I hadn't gone far when a large creature filled the trail in front of me. It wasn't a nightmare and it wasn't a cat. It was a wolf. A very large, black animal, almost as deeply dark as the nightmare had been.

The other growl was more urgent behind me. I turned.

Not a nightmare, but definitely a cat. Jaguar, maybe?

Who knows? Who cares? I was stuck between a wolf and a cat, both of the giant variety. I tensed as I heard the wolf behind me launch itself forward. It brushed past me, then pounced on the cat.

The screech the animal made ripped through the night. The cat made its way out from under the wolf and backed up, swiping at it and growling. The wolf backed up as well, putting itself between the cat and me.

Somewhere in my mind, I knew that the wolf must be Rider, but I was having a hard time convincing myself of that.

The wolf backed up farther. The cat screamed and ran away. Rider sat still for a while, not turning to face me. After a few silent minutes staring into nothing, he shuddered and lifted its head, sniffing the air.

I was having a hard time connecting my mental image of Rider, my Rider, with the sleek black animal. The idea of reaching for the Path was instinctive, but I stamped that thought out. If this were Rider, he'd know if I opened the Path. He might think I was scared of him. This felt like a tenuous situation, and I didn't want to risk offending him in some way.

His nose looked like it was working overtime. Then he sneezed twice and pawed at his snout.

"I don't know if you're trying to smell the cat, me, or someone else. Davis, maybe. If you're looking for her, don't follow her. I think... Well, we need to talk first."

He looked over his shoulder at me. His ear flopped over, forcing me to bite my lip to keep from grinning. It was cute, but I don't think Rider would have appreciated me saying so at that moment.

I sighed. "And if you're trying to smell me, I'm over here."

Without moving his head, Rider turned the rest of his body

to face me. He approached slowly, then started to sniff me. He walked around me twice in a familiar pattern.

"I'm okay," I told him.

He moved behind me again and pushed the spot behind my knee, causing my legs to buckle.

"Okay, okay," I said. I sat down on the ground, trying to find a comfortable spot.

Rider rounded me again, then stuck his nose in my neck.

"That tickles," I said, leaning away.

He licked my neck.

I tried to nudge him away. "Stop that. I'm fine. It's just..." I waved my hand in the air in the direction I might have run from. She had drugged me. I'd trusted her. I had trusted all of them. I sniffed and closed my eyes, trying not to let myself feel upset.

It wasn't working.

"I'm so stupid," I said. "You warned me. You didn't trust them. Logan didn't. Hell, it was Boone's team and *he* didn't even trust them."

The large black animal form of Rider pawed at my leg.

I let my head drop.

Rider put his head on my shoulders, and without a thought, I hugged him. He was warm and furry, and I had to force myself to remember who he was and that I shouldn't cry on his shoulder. At least not while on the job.

"Cass!" Vincent called from some distance away.

CHAPTER
NINETEEN

Rider whined, but I didn't let go. I just needed a minute.

"Cass!" Vincent's voice sounded more urgent.

Rider whined again and pulled away. I finally let go.

I sighed again. "I'm over here!" This was such a crap day.

Little urgent noises of distress were coming from Rider.

"What's wrong?" I asked.

He bounded a few steps off. A look flashed from the direction Vincent was yelling from and back to me, then back again.

"You're worried about him?" I got to my feet in a hurry and looked around. "Vincent!"

Rider shook himself down from head to toe. He backed up a few paces and hung his head.

"You're worried about what he might say, aren't you?" I said. "We know you're a werewolf, I don't understand."

He looked distressed.

"I won't say anything if you don't want me to."

The animal seemed to breathe a little easier.

"We should talk about this," I added. "When we're back home, you and I or maybe the three of us—"

"Cass!" Vincent called, much closer this time.

"This way," I called. When I looked back to Rider, he was gone.

A black animal in the night in the rain forest. He may have only gone a few steps for me to lose track of him.

Flashes of light appeared around the trees. I searched the area a little more before giving up on catching sight of Rider. Instead, I concentrated on Vincent.

I moved toward the dancing light.

Vincent didn't even slow down when he came into view. He stalked over to me, looking disgruntled. The light of his headlamp momentarily blinded me when he put his arms around me and held me.

We said nothing. It had been a long day, and despite the sticky heat, neither of us seemed inclined to let the other go. I wanted to put time in a little bubble and stay there longer— ignore the craziness around us until it all went away.

Vincent was the first to step back, clapping a hand over the light when he saw me look away. He removed the light and handed it over. "Hold it for me for a minute."

When I went to turn it off to gain some semblance of night vision once again, he stopped me.

"Shine it here for me." As soon as he was satisfied with how I pointed the light, he cupped my chin and turned my head until he could look me straight in the eyes. Lines of worry stood out in the light.

I took his free hand. "You didn't do anything."

"I did," Vincent said. "It may be that I didn't cause much damage, but we can't pretend I didn't do anything."

"Did I—" I started, but then hesitated. The nightmare

caused in the cave was disjointed. "I don't really know what happened. Are you okay? Did I do anything?"

"I don't know much more than you. As it wore off, I knew what I tried to do to you, what I still thought I needed to do when I opened my eyes again, but I can't remember much else."

"They killed it," I said, flatly.

"Yeah, I'd like a word with them about that." He stroked the side of my face once before taking the light and covering it again. "You're bleeding. Did you hit your head?"

I didn't bother with an answer.

"I get why they took you away," Vincent said, "but not why they killed the nightmare."

Stunned, my mouth gaped open. Vincent messed around with the light, turning it from bright white to red. He didn't seem to notice my response.

"Let's get back to—"

"What do you mean you know why they took me away?"

In the eerie red light, Vincent looked uneasy. "Getting you away from me was the right thing. I would have sent Rider with you, but I needed him to keep everyone out of the cave until I had hold of myself again."

"You—I can't even—They—" I forced my mouth shut before I said something I would regret. Then I took a deep breath and shifted direction. "Where is everyone?"

"This way. We're setting up a camp nearby so we can work in the morning. We have a bit of a hike, though."

I started in the direction he indicated, then glanced back to look into the darkness in an effort to see if I could find the large black wolf. "Everyone is back at the camp site?"

"Logan and Boone are. Rider and I split up to find everyone else."

"What happened to everyone stay with someone else? No

exceptions, remember?" I stalked off in the direction I thought Vincent had indicated.

"The nightmare has been neutralized. We don't have to worry about it anymore." He steadily edged me in another direction as he walked beside me.

I pretended not to notice. "At least now I know I'm not the only idiot."

"What's that supposed to mean?"

"The nightmare hasn't even started yet."

"Hold up, Cass," Vincent said, pulling me to a stop. He looked me over. "You're still covered in that thing's blood. Are you sure you're alright?"

I took a deep breath, trying to steady myself. It didn't work. "I'm fine. I'm just pissed off." Thinking about it, I realized it was so much more than that. "I'm pissed off, scared, tired, dirty, sad about the Lost dying, frustrated, and hurt because you seem to think it was okay that people took me away when I didn't want to go."

Vincent looked at a loss. "What can I do to help?"

"You can start off by promising me that if I get taken somewhere against my will, you won't pass it off as being okay!"

"It's not like that. Of course, if Davis had—"

"If she had what? Drugged me, taken me somewhere, threatened to kill me, and oh yeah, given the okay to shoot me. How about if she had done those things?"

Vincent tensed. "Cass, what happened?"

"All of those things!" I stalked off again in a hurry to get to the others. Rider would beat me to them, but I didn't want to be too far behind.

"Wait up." Vincent walked fast to keep pace. "The nightmare—"

"Was murdered. On purpose. They want to kill all the Lost."

"It bled all over you. It affected both of us. Are you sure—"

"I'm positive."

"But—"

"Vincent, I'm positive."

"They drugged you?"

"Yes."

Vincent grabbed my hand and pulled me to a stop, looking frantic. "Did they inject you with something?"

That was a harder question to answer. "I don't know what they did."

"How can you not know?" Vincent said, running his hands over my arms as though he might still find a needle sticking out.

"I think it was one of our tranquilizer darts." I brushed the hair away from my neck and let him get a closer look. He blinded me with real light once again and I squeezed my eyes shut. "The tranqs we have out here are different than our usual ones, but it felt similar anyway."

His fingers carefully brushed over the surface of my neck. "The fact that you know that bothers me," he muttered.

I shrugged, but only slightly, not wanting to move his hands. "It was better I had been tranqed than to hurt someone."

Vincent's fear seemed to be subsiding and he was trying to put on his work face. "Start from the beginning. What happened after you left the cave?"

"Only if we're moving. We need to get to the others fast."

The amount of self-control Vincent showed amazed me. He kept hold of my hand and listened to my story—there was no change in pressure. The reassuring grip was the same that he might have at any other time. The only time his calm exterior demeanor changed subtly was when I stumbled over my words, carefully trying to pick them when Davis had said I wouldn't be going with them, essentially giving the go ahead to get me out of the way. His hand twitched, which was the only outward change I could feel. In the Path, however, it was as though a volcano erupted. Even without Reading, I could feel its effect.

"Who did it?" Vincent asked. "Renick?"

The fact that he didn't immediately guess Tolman made me want to tell him even less. "No, not Renick."

"Tolman shot at you?"

"Sorry, I know you all were getting along."

"Tolman wouldn't have missed."

"He didn't miss. If I hadn't been using the Path to protect myself, I'd be dead. If Davis had kept letting him shoot, I'd probably be dead. I don't think I could have held the Path for much longer."

"We should take a break."

"We need to get to Logan."

"You're about to fall down. We need to get to him with you on your feet."

I sighed and stopped. "You're right."

"I've got some caffeine."

I perked up like Pavlov's dog might. "That's fortuitous."

"We thought you might need it after what happened in the cave."

It wasn't until I let go of Vincent's hand that I realized how tired I was. I tried checking a tree for giant spiders or snakes, but too many places were there that I couldn't see. I settled down in open space instead.

Vincent sat down in front of me and handed me a caffeine pill and some water. "I'm surprised Rider hasn't caught up with us yet."

I kept my face impassive. "Didn't you all split up?"

"Yeah, but he had to have heard the shots. Even I heard them."

"Why did you think everything was okay if you heard shots fired?"

"I'm pretty sure if Tolman ran into another one of those spiders, he'd open fire." Vincent went quiet after he said it.

"Sorry," I said again. "I know you got along with him."

"We had a lot in common."

"On the surface maybe." I didn't believe, actually believe, they had anything at all in common, but Vincent seemed to.

"Doesn't matter."

It did matter, but I didn't say it. "The caffeine is starting to kick in. We should go."

Vincent didn't move. "You know this ends badly."

"I thought it already had. The nightmare is dead, the mission is over."

"I mean with Boone's team."

"We'll have to take them in."

"If we can."

I didn't want to think about any other scenario. "Come on. Let's get moving."

We got to our feet, and once Vincent chose the direction, we started back. I heard a twig snap not far away. Expecting Rider, I looked around, but saw nothing.

"We need to hurry," I said.

CHAPTER

TWENTY

The fire danced like a beacon as we approached the camp. I cringed at the sight of it, but how were they to know?

"I see you found our girl," Logan said. "Any trouble?"

"Lots," I said. "I think we need to douse the fire and move."

Logan didn't waste time asking why. He grabbed the water, and soon plumes of smoke rose in the air. As I filled them in, I caught myself glancing at Boone and wringing my hands. His expression grew stonier as each new fact lined up.

"We need a plan," Vincent said when I wrapped up.

"I knew there was something wrong," Boone said, almost as though it was to himself. "But I didn't expect this."

"But now we deal with it," Vincent said.

I looked out into the heavy darkness of the jungle. "We need to get Rider back here." I wasn't sure if Vincent was going to try to blame this on Boone, but I thought shifting his focus away from Boone might help. "Any idea where he is?" I asked, aiming the question at Logan.

Logan's ears were already at their points. "I lost track of him after he and Vincent split up, so I can't be certain."

Worry threatened to swamp me. Vincent moved closer, which was some small comfort.

"We need a plan," I said, repeating Vincent's sentiment.

"We find Rider, and then you all are getting out of here," Boone said.

"You think we should let them go?" Logan asked.

"No," Boone said, "but I can't ask you all to stay after this. Once we find your partner, I'll call for your extraction."

"No way," I said, not deigning to entertain the idea. "If you aren't on their side, they'll kill you."

"It's my mess," Boone said. "I'll clean it up."

"It's not your mess, though." My temper was starting to rise. "The military did this."

"AIR, too," Logan added.

"I shouldn't have brought you all here," Boone said.

"You should have," Logan said. "It's better to know what we're up against than to be surprised by it later on. Besides, if you die out here, there's no one around to tell the government what a horrible idea their experiment is. They aren't going to listen to us."

Boone shook his head. "You and Rider are direct targets."

"All the more reason for us to stick around and make sure this mess gets sorted," Logan said. "The military isn't going to like that their pet project went so wrong."

Boone looked at me. I wasn't sure if he was asking for my opinion or wanting me to convince Logan to leave.

"Leaving was never an option for me," I said.

"Or me," Vincent said. "They all need to be brought in."

"And if they can't be?" Boone asked, watching Vincent.

"If they leave South America, it's going to be in cuffs,"

Vincent said. "It's either that, or they don't walk out of here at all."

The idea of killing anyone also wasn't an option, at least not for me. For the others, I'm sure it would be a last resort.

"First, we need to take care of the nightmare," Logan said. "Then we find Rider and regroup."

"What do you mean take care of the nightmare?" I asked

"This project crossed humans and Lost to turn them into a weapon," Logan said. "I can't imagine what they might do if the government got their hands on the creature's corpse."

My nose curled up at the thought, then I realized something. "What kind of Lost can teleport?"

"Teleport?" Logan asked.

"That's how Davis and the others left," I reminded them.

"I thought that was a colorful turn of phrase," Logan said. "I don't know of anything that can disappear from one place and appear in another."

"That's not what they're doing," Vincent said.

Everyone looked at him in expectation. It was sometimes hard to remember that Vincent has tracked a myriad of Lost in his career.

"What are they doing, then?" Logan asked. "You can't tell me they added Walkers into the mix."

"If they did, we wouldn't stand a chance against three. It is a possibility to consider, though." Vincent's gaze flickered momentarily to Boone, and then he looked hard at Logan.

"I'll go take care of the nightmare," Boone said, taking the hint. "We'll burn it in the cave, and then collapse it if we can." He grabbed a bag and disappeared into the darkness.

I sat down next to the smoldering remains of the fire and rubbed my temples. The exhaustion was sneaking up on me again, and I didn't like that Boone had essentially been sent away.

Vincent waited until Boone was well out of sight before he continued. "Walkers have different skills. You all know some of what I can do, but you also know the rumors, that Walkers can step out of this world and step back in wherever they want. It's an exaggeration, but there is some truth behind it."

"How so?" Logan asked.

"My sister probably couldn't take a soul if her life depended on it, which I'm thankful for. But she can walk in and out of this world easily. It's kind of like instinct. She can sense where she is in both worlds at the same time." He looked at me. "I'm probably not explaining this very well."

"What you're saying is that it's possible," Logan said. "They could be Walkers, extra good at the Walking part."

"It's possible," Vincent said.

"But you don't think that's what it is," I said, reading his face.

"No," Vincent said. He shifted his stance as though uncomfortable. "I know you all have heard about the old ones. If they're found, it's in less-populated areas, like Midwest and out west on the east of the Rockies."

"You're saying the old ones know how to teleport?" I asked.

"The old ones are just a generic term for a whole slew of races that have been found," Vincent said. "Possibly for thousands of years. We're talking dragons, gods, gorgons, djinn."

Logan seemed to visibly pale. "Gods and gorgons are easy, but jhin? We might be really bad off if they're part jhin. I'm not sure they can teleport, though."

"Not teleport in the way you're thinking, no," Vincent said. "But there are races that can bend space. They can be standing somewhere, then pick a point miles away and pull it closer to them."

"That could be what they're doing," I said. "Rider

mentioned that they seemed to disappear and reappear closer. I thought it was just his senses in disarray."

"We'll have to tranq them," Logan said. "Did Boone have a real gun or tranqs?"

"I'll check," I volunteered.

"We don't want to risk you getting lost," Logan said.

I rolled my eyes, "I'll follow Boone's Path."

"Are you sure?" Vincent asked. "You've been working your powers pretty hard today."

"I won't need much energy to follow him," I said.

"At least start by heading that way," Logan said, nodding in the direction I should take. "You'll catch up pretty quickly. We won't be far behind. I want to make sure there are no traces of the nightmare left before we leave the area."

I grabbed my tranq gun and headed into the darkness in the direction Logan indicated. Thankfully, my night vision had fully returned.

Since I carefully moved through the terrain, I was also able to hear a few traces of conversation.

"This isn't a kill mission," Logan said.

I slowed when I heard the words.

"You know that, right?" Logan continued.

"Do you?" Vincent asked, not unkindly. "I know what you think of Boone's team. We're all thinking it."

"Almost all of us," Logan said.

I hurried on, not wanting to figure out if they were talking about me. Thinking it over, I knew Logan had been horrified of the idea of Boone's team. Building humans from Lost, whether it was DNA changed, gene therapy, or some sort of voodoo magic, it wasn't something I wanted to see the government doing. What was the point?

They thought they were building weapons, and they were, but why not just hire the Lost to begin with? In the case of the old ones, maybe it wasn't possible. Maybe they just couldn't find a Lost that wanted to do what they were asking. That was always a possibility.

Or maybe they didn't want to work with the Lost?

That idea seemed ludicrous. There were quite a few Lost working in AIR. Boone had also mentioned Lost working with him in the military. They wouldn't let the Lost be a part of those organizations if the government didn't want to work with them.

Would they?

It was true I never saw a Lost in the upper ranks of management. However, for ones like Logan, who lived a lot longer, surely they had the chance to rise higher, at least within AIR itself. Maybe not the people fresh from another dimension, but there were Lost born in this world. They were citizens like everyone else who was born in the country.

It was an uncomfortable thought. Remembering the changeling we'd encountered a month ago, it seemed that there were some Lost that were very anti-government. Maybe there were factions in the government that were very anti-Lost.

Boone might be able to fill in a few more blanks.

To ask him, I'd have to find him. I came to a stop and looked around, suddenly worried about being on my own. Without closing my eyes, I jumped into the Path. Stabbing pain came with it. Surprisingly, I was only a little off course. I mentally traced Boone's Path before pushing my power away. The color drained from the world, but so did the agony the Path had brought. I faltered, nearly falling.

I was forced to steady myself, which wasn't easy. It was the end of my day. The power had burned down to embers, leaving me exhausted. Once I found Boone and Rider, I needed to meditate. Something they added to the tranquilizers was throwing me off.

There was still so much left to do. Take care of the nightmare, find Rider, and make a plan for how to deal with Boone's team. Just thinking about it made me even more tired.

Feeling my limbs almost as weighed down as my mind, I trudged forward. Getting down into the basin where the nightmare's cave could be found was more difficult than it had been the first time. Luckily, there was bright light in the distance marking the cave where Boone was readying whatever it was he was putting together.

The idea of walking into the cave with the dead nightmare made me slow as I approached, which I hated. We had a job to do, and the sooner it was done, the better. The thought spurred me into the cave.

Boone had the cave lit in several areas, making the entire area bright. He was there, standing with his hand on his gun eyeing Tolman.

Tolman's gun was aimed straight at Boone's head.

My heart skipped a beat as I sucked in a sharp breath. Movement beside me made me jerk away as Davis attempted to grab me from the side.

She couldn't get hold of me, so she lashed out instead. Before my mind had fully caught up, she punched me in the face.

I reeled back. My foot caught on something and I fell.

The blow was doing nothing to help my brain catch up to the situation. On instinct, I jumped into the Path, despite what I knew it would bring. Davis pulled out her gun.

Knowing I had to stop her so I could help Boone, I grabbed Davis's Path and slammed it back into the wall of the cave, taking her with it. When I did, I noticed something off about the Path in the cave, but it wasn't the time for distractions.

I scrambled up to a sitting position, then I went for Tolman, but Boone had already launched himself at the man. Tolman's gun clattered against a rocky outcrop of the cave.

Tolman screamed and threw Boone back, sending my friend flying. The Path showed a great deal of power behind the attack.

Tolman yelled again. It was a gut-wrenching shriek of rage and pain. "You bitch!"

It seemed like a vast overreaction to what I had done. My mind flew to Davis, who wasn't moving.

I got to my knees as Tolman grabbed his gun.

My mind went blank. Time seemed to slow. Davis wasn't moving. Not a twitch, not a rise and fall of her chest.

She was still.

My body grew cold and I couldn't look away. I blindly started to scramble over to her as Tolman fired. I felt the sting of the bullet, but my mind was too wrapped in its own torment to take notice.

She couldn't be dead.

Tolman screamed at me again. Mind numb, I looked at him. His face was red and his eyes were bright. The situation slammed home in my mind.

I killed her.

He knew it.

In that moment, I knew I was dead.

He squeezed the trigger. The bang seemed to fill the cave and my whole world. Flashes of Gran, Rider, my mother and Logan all whirled by before my mind honed in on Vincent.

Tolman crumpled to the ground.

Somehow, I was in one piece. My eyes strayed to Boone who looked as surprised as I was. I followed his gaze and saw Renick. His face was twisted in pain and his gun was still pointing to where Tolman had been. It looked as though nothing else existed for him but the body of his friend. The man he had just killed.

Boone pulled his gun out and yelled at Renick to drop his. Renick did it without hesitation, looking as though he just didn't care anymore.

I watched it all happen in a detached way. It felt separate, apart from the world I was living.

Keeping his gun steady, Boone struggled to his feet. Only then did he stumble.

Renick went to help him.

"Stop," Boone said, struggling to point his gun again.

"You're half done in," Renick said. "Let's get out of this cave, and then you can shoot me."

"Stop!" Boone yelled, then shook his head.

"Boone," I said, my voice listless. "Don't."

Boone looked around, taking in the situation. He lowered his weapon, allowing Renick to come closer.

Rider ran into the cave, gun drawn, and aimed at Renick. I looked down at Davis. I didn't want to see Rider right now. I didn't want to see anyone. Boone would sort the situation out.

Vincent and Logan arrived. Logan looked tense, ready for action and his features looked stretched. Guns were pointed at Renick, and although Renick looked at ease, he stuck pretty close to Boone, letting the man lean on him.

"It's over," Boone said. "Renick's right, let's get out of here."

"There is a lot of blood," Rider said. His gun was still out, but it hung loosely in his hand, pointed at the ground.

Vincent's gun was still at the ready, but he worked his way wide around to me. "What happened?" he asked, keeping his voice low, meant just for me.

I didn't say anything. My heart—hell, my entire body—felt hollow.

Boone gave a quick recap, glossing over Davis. While he spoke, Logan's appearance began to smooth out as he returned to his normal everyday self.

Boone got to the part of tackling Tolman when Rider interrupted.

"He shot her?"

"Shot *at* her," Boone said.

Rider came over to me and squatted down. His nose was flaring.

My thoughts seemed almost random as they rose. "There's something wrong with the Path in here."

Rider took hold of the sleeve of my shirt, and as though he were tearing paper, he ripped the cloth at the hole that the bullet made. "I need a first-aid kit."

I put my hand over one of his. "I don't think people should stay in here."

There was some rummaging around in bags. I still couldn't make eye contact with anyone. Less than twenty-four hours ago, this woman had been my partner, and now she was gone.

I'd killed her.

"Thank you," he said, taking a first-aid kit without turning his gaze away from me. "Everyone should move outside," Rider said.

Rider helped me to my feet and we followed the others out. Vincent hovered at my side.

Rider took my chin and forced my face up. He studied my eyes. I'm not sure what he saw in there, but I squeezed them shut and turned. He let go of my chin.

"We are stepping away," Rider said. "Alone."

"I'm going with you," Vincent said.

"No," Rider said. "You are not." He said it as a simple statement of fact. "I will tell you when you can see her."

Anger began to radiate off Vincent.

Rider stood up and put a hand on Vincent's shoulder.

"Trust me," Rider said.

They stood there for a few moments before Rider turned to help me up. Not saying anything, we started away from the others.

"She will later appreciate it if you assist Boone," Rider told Vincent as we passed. "He is more injured than I think he realizes."

Vincent didn't acknowledge that he'd heard what Rider said.

I braced myself for Rider to start talking, asking me something or saying things. Instead, he said nothing as we moved well away from the cave and into the fresh air. I looked back at the cave, cementing the picture in my mind. Once the mouth of the cave was out of sight, I sat on the ground with Rider and he poked around on my arm, doing who knows what. The pain started out dull, but as Rider worked on it, my arm began to throb. Soon, it turned in to one solid, angry pain.

Oddly enough, I was thankful. It gave me a distraction.

Did I want to be distracted?

Maybe not, but I needed to be.

"The bullet has torn through a muscle," Rider said in a steady voice. "I only know enough to add the stitches."

I nodded and grit my teeth.

"Do you want to talk about it?" Rider asked.

I shook my head, but still answered. "I killed her. There's nothing to say." Tears filled my eyes, but the pain was reason enough to have them.

"There's a lot that could be said," Renick said as he walked over.

"Go away," Rider said, stiffly.

"No offense, but you scare me less than the Walker right now," Renick said. "Boone's not in great shape, and aside from him, she's the only one of you who may not want to kill me right now."

"It's okay," I said to Rider, not wanting to look at Renick. What do you say to someone that saved your life by killing their friend? "If anyone should be here, he should."

Rider hesitated. "Do you want me to leave?"

"Bad wording," I said, trying to force a smile at my friend and failing miserably. "I really want you to stay."

He nodded and rummaged through the first-aid kit again. "Then I will stay."

"She would have killed you," Renick said, watching me. "She liked you, but she'd have killed you all the same."

"I thought you were okay with that," I said without any real rancor. "In the woods, it didn't seem to bother you."

"I thought I could talk her out of it," Renick said, leaning against a tree. "That's why we were arguing."

"Talk her out of killing me? Why?" I asked. "Why did you all even want to kill everyone?"

"I didn't want that," Renick said. "When you all started working with us, I wouldn't have cared much if it was just the Walker, but—"

Rider let out a low growl. The sound reached deep inside and gave me an understanding of why people were afraid of the dark. It broke through the pain and the numbness I felt inside.

"That was before we got to know each other," Renick said quickly. "Anyway, tonight after Davis picked you up, they started talking about killing Boone and I knew they'd gone off the deep end."

"You didn't realize that before then?" I asked dully. "I thought you all could read each other's minds or something."

"You know how you toe a line or go a smidge too far? Then

you do it again and again until too far is the new norm? That's what we were like."

"What changed?" I asked.

"I couldn't let them kill Boone. Before that, I was just along for the ride," Renick said.

"Because he's human?" I asked, feeling the need to probe his feelings on humans and Lost.

"Because he's Boone," Renick said. "He's saved my life more than once."

"So you're okay with this situation?" I asked, feeling angry that he was so calm with the bodies of his friends lying not far away.

Renick glared at me. It was the first time I'd seen him look truly angry.

"Don't think I wanted this for a minute, princess," Renick spat. "Tolman lost his head when we felt Davis go. Just because I didn't scream at you didn't mean I didn't feel it, too. And just because Tolman shot you didn't mean I wanted him dead."

Hearing Renick get worked up over the loss actually made me like him, even though he obviously didn't think much of me.

Rider put a hand on my shoulder. "How did Tolman die?"

"There was no stopping him once Davis was gone," Renick said, his temper waning. "She was the only one that held him in check. They were... close. He would have killed you all. Starting with the princess here, and then going for Boone."

"I'm sorry," I said softly. "I didn't mean to hurt her." I closed my eyes and took a few deep breaths, willing myself not to cry.

"It wasn't like you planned it out. I can see that," Renick said. "I don't know what happened to push her so far."

"There was something wrong with the cave," I said. "After the nightmare died, it twisted the Path of the cave somehow.

That might have done something to her. Even then, I never intended this to happen."

"I've never seen someone get so bent out of shape over someone that was trying to kill them. You must suck at your job."

I glared at him. "My job isn't to kill people."

Rider leaned down and whispered into my ear, "Vincent knows what you are feeling. He would like to come here."

"Go ahead and let him," Renick said, having heard Rider despite the whispering. Renick stalked away. "I'll check on Boone."

"Do you think he's telling the truth?" I asked.

"He killed his partner to save you," Rider said. "I think he is mostly telling you the truth."

"She was one of *our* partners a day ago," I said, watching Renick disappear into the basin that led to the cave.

"It sounds as though she had not been stable for quite some time," Rider said. "Boone knew something was wrong. That is why we were asked to join them. Do you want Vincent—"

"I'm not sure what to do about Renick," I said. "Thanking him for saving me sounds gruesome, since he killed his friend to do it, but I feel like I should say something."

"We will figure it out, but I think it will need time." Rider cleared his throat and lowered his voice. "Vincent is quite distressed. I thought you needed space. I did not think he would be upset since you are with me, or I would not have had him stay away. He might still be upset with me."

"I did need to be away from it. Even from Vincent. I still do. I don't know what to say to him. To anyone. I killed her and I'm the reason Tolman is dead."

"You do not need to say anything," Rider said. "Not unless you want to. And when you are ready to talk, we will be there."

I nodded glumly.

Rider got up and followed Renick. He met Vincent, and I saw them exchange a few words before Rider disappeared and Vincent joined me.

Vincent looked over the stitch work that Rider had done. He looked as though he was going to say something, and I realized Rider was right. I didn't have to say anything if I didn't want to. I knew, though, that if Vincent asked anything, I would probably answer him.

Instead, I didn't give him the chance to say anything before hugging him fiercely with one arm. The other screamed with pain when I tried to move it.

He was caught momentarily off guard, but then shifted a little and hugged me back, being as leery as I was about my arm.

Around us, noises of the forest began to grow louder and the woods seemed to lighten.

My grip loosened some, but only so that I could move to a slightly more comfortable position. Then I was able to hear voices. With the sound came thoughts that threatened to invade my peaceful moment with Vincent.

As the voices came closer, Vincent broke contact and sat back. He looked me over once again.

"The sun is coming up," I said, just for something to break the silence between us.

"You should get some sleep," Vincent said. "We all should."

"We were just talking about that," Logan said, walking up with the others. "I'm going to wrap up here with Boone and Renick. I think the rest of you should go set up camp."

"Aren't we calling for extraction?" Vincent asked.

"Not here," Logan said. "I don't want our signal to be anywhere near the nightmare. No one is getting their hands on it."

"Same with the rest of the team," Boone said. "We don't want anyone to find them."

My heart cringed at the word team.

Vincent put his hand on my shoulder, a small gesture of comfort.

"We'll stop for the day at least two miles out," Logan said. "Tomorrow, we hike farther before deciding on the next steps. How's the arm?"

"There's a hole in it," I said, feeling unamused with the question.

"Keep it clean and no lifting. Maybe we can make a sling for it or something," Logan said. "We'll catch up with you all later. I'll keep in touch."

When Rider, Vincent, and I were left alone, I managed to get to my feet. Anytime my arm moved or tensed, a lance of pain shot through me.

"How's Boone doing?" I asked as Rider chose our direction. "I know he was hurt."

"Concussion," Vincent said. "Apparently, he hit the cave wall pretty hard. I don't think anything is broken, but he's pretty bruised up. He won't be doing any heavy lifting for a while either."

"He is taking the deaths very hard," Rider said.

I nodded, not able to respond. It was possible that Boone wouldn't blame me for what happened, although I wouldn't hold it against him if he did. There are some things, though, that although are forgiven, can't be forgotten.

I knew I'd never forget.

"Let's go," Vincent said. "The sooner we find camp, the sooner we can get some rest."

Guilt about not being able to carry any gear rose up, but it didn't last long. We had barely gone anywhere before I started to wear down. Before long, it took all my concentration to stay on my feet.

It would be impossible for me to know how far we had walked—I suck at knowing distances—but I was pretty sure if Logan or Boone yelled, we'd still be able to hear them without an issue.

Even my full concentration on moving forward didn't help for long.

Just a moment's rest and I'll catch up. I leaned against a tree and closed my eyes. When I opened them again, which I swear was only a second later, Rider was standing directly in front of me, inches away from my face.

Even being startled didn't get my blood pumping any faster. "I just need a few minutes."

"Is this another one of those lies meant for you?" Rider asked.

I looked at him in confusion until my brain kicked into gear, remembering that I had told him some lies we tell ourselves to make things easier.

The thought made me smile weakly. "I can't be sure yet."

"I will carry you," Rider said.

"You will not."

Rider frowned at me and looked like he was going to pick me up anyway.

I raised an eyebrow at him, wondering if he would.

"Everything okay?" Vincent asked.

Rider grinned.

I worried for a moment that he might throw me over his shoulder or something.

"I have seen people carry others on their back," Rider said.

"Where have you seen that?" I asked.

"On the television."

Vincent joined us, looking concerned. "You're pale."

"Come on," Rider said, slinging the bags he was carrying off his back. "This will make it easier for everyone."

"Everyone?" I asked.

"We won't worry as much and we will get out of here faster," Rider said.

I sighed and nodded, though I was reluctant.

Rider squatted down. I carefully maneuvered myself so that my arm didn't get jostled too much. Rider stood up quickly and I squeaked, which was embarrassing, but the sound just popped out. The movement was so quick and I was so much higher than I normally stood. Higher than almost anyone stood.

"Are you comfortable?" Rider asked.

"As much as I can be," I said before lowering my voice. "Thank you."

It wasn't long before I leaned my head on Rider's shoulder and closed my eyes again. I was determined not to fall asleep. When they started talking in low voices, I was so deeply resting that the sound didn't startle me.

"How much blood did she lose?" Vincent asked.

"I have seen her lose more," Rider said.

"You've also seen her die. It doesn't mean it's okay."

Even though Vincent's voice wasn't accusatory or angry, I could feel Rider's body tense over the words. "Of course it is not okay. I do not know how much blood humans can lose before it becomes harmful." When Vincent said nothing, Rider continued, "Her body makes more blood, right?"

TWENTY-ONE

"It does," Vincent said.

"She has been given blood from me before."

"Your body probably restores blood faster than ours. Everything happens faster than ours."

"Does she need to be given blood now?" Rider asked.

"We would need a doctor to know for sure. Logan didn't seem too worried, though."

"He has a lot on his mind," Rider said.

"When we find a place to stop, she does nothing," Vincent said.

A part of me wanted to argue. I shifted slightly on Rider's back. The small part that disagreed was a stupid part. I was fit for nothing but bed. I just wished it were my own.

Whether because of my movement or the want to end the conversation, the two went silent for a while.

"Thanks for taking care of her back there," Vincent said, after what seemed like hours later.

"She took the accident very badly," Rider said. "By the time we arrived, I don't think she was paying attention to anything around her."

He wasn't wrong. I made a mental note to thank Rider and Vincent later for helping me and patching up my arm.

"Shock," Vincent said.

"She has seen dead people before," Rider said.

"Not like this. She feels responsible."

"For what Davis did?"

"For what she did to Davis."

Maybe sleep would be better, I thought. I didn't want to hear this. I certainly didn't want to be reminded about what I did to Davis.

"Is there something we can do to help?" Rider asked, lowering his voice a bit more.

"If she lets us. Cass avoids dealing with things like this. We just need to be there when she can't avoid it anymore."

"Is it a human thing? Do you avoid talking about those you have killed?"

Vincent didn't respond right away. "It might be a human thing. It's something most people don't have to deal with."

"What do you do?"

Vincent was silent once again.

"It might help me understand how to help Cassie," Rider insisted.

"It's not something I want to talk about. In the past, I mostly concentrated on the job. That's all. It helped me to be around my sister some. She doesn't do what I do."

"And now?"

"Now? With you all around, it's different. After I hurt Cass, well... things changed."

"How so?" Rider asked.

Vincent sighed. "This probably isn't the time or place to talk about it."

"Is there a time and place that will work?"

"Probably not."

"Then this will work as well as any other."

"I think it was Cassie. She got inside me and I felt lighter somehow. I think I have the opposite effect on her."

"I do not think so, except possibly when you do not stay in touch."

"It was hard to know what to say," Vincent said. "I left at a bad time. What I wanted to say, I couldn't, not over the phone. Then I was gone for so long, it only made things harder."

"Your sister needed you. We understand that."

"It wasn't just her. Recovering from traveling between the worlds isn't too bad. A couple of days and I'm back on my feet. When I come back after taking a soul or leaving someone to the void... I'm not the best person to be around. At least usually."

"We are your friends. We would understand."

"All the more reason to stay away. So we stay friends."

"I do not think I understand."

"I'm probably not saying it very well. This time, each day I stayed away made it more difficult to come back. But when Boone called... I knew I had to be here."

"We are glad you are here."

"It was the right thing to do. I couldn't risk losing her."

"She is safe now," Rider said.

"I've screwed a lot of things up. Staying away while you all went with Boone's team would have been a huge mistake, even if they hadn't gone crazy."

It was Rider's turn to sigh. "Another thing I do not understand."

He wasn't the only one, but I was more than glad that Vincent had come with us.

"You don't have to. In fact, it's probably better if you don't. Do you think we're far enough away?"

"It is possible. This does not look like the best area, however."

"A little farther, then."

"I hear running water in that direction."

"Let's head that way. We're definitely going to need fresh water. Cass and I still have that nightmare blood on us, and we need to keep her arm clean. How are things with Logan and the others?"

"They are digging holes."

I shifted uncomfortably, and they went silent once again. It was too much effort to talk. Too much effort for anything but rest. The idea that they were digging graves didn't make me more apt to open my eyes anyway.

"How do you think she's doing?" Vincent asked.

"She needs to get some real sleep. We may have a better idea after that."

I wanted to reassure them, but again, it was so hard. It was taking everything I had just to stay conscious.

Time was impossible to track. It could have been minutes or hours before they stopped.

"This place looks ideal," Rider said.

"Let me help you," Vincent said.

Soon, I was sliding off Rider's back. The brief panic sparked a tiny spike of adrenaline and I looked around, making sure I wasn't about to fall. Vincent had me.

"It's good to see your eyes open," Vincent said.

"I will set up a hammock," Rider said, getting to work.

I blinked at Vincent and smiled. He helped me to a seated position and I leaned against a tree.

His hands felt cool and clammy when he put them on my face. "How's the arm?"

I started to talk, but had to clear my throat twice. When did my throat get so dry?

"Sore," I managed.

"Are you feeling okay aside from your arm?" Vincent handed me an open bottle, putting it in my good hand and remaining ready to catch it if I dropped it.

I sucked down some water. "I just need some sleep." It was all I could do to keep the trace of a whine out of my voice.

"It's going to take more than a little sleep. Let's put some clean bandages on your arm," Vincent said.

I frowned, knowing it was going to sting like hell.

"Don't look at me like that," Vincent said, giving me a soft smile. A real one, open for the world to see. "If you don't like it, don't get shot. That's my advice."

My heart gave the faintest of flutters. "I'll try my best." Vincent doctored my arm and I remembered the promise I'd made myself. "Thank you for helping me out of the cave." I raised my voice, even though it was unnecessary. "And for cleaning up my arm and getting me here." I looked around for the first time, getting an idea of where 'here' was.

The place was beautiful. The water was running swiftly and it sounded as though there was a waterfall not far away. The trees looked a little more solid here and moss covered the rocks. It was vibrant—a green so jewel like, that it seemed amazing a plant could create it.

"Nice spot," Renick said.

I started at the sound, but my brain was already catching up to who it was. I closed my eyes as vertigo hit me.

Rider let out a low growl. Not true menace, but it held the promise of menace if things didn't go the way he liked.

"I thought I'd get a better reception this time," Renick said. "Saving the princess and all."

Vincent glared at the man, but didn't let his attention waver.

"It might help if you weren't such an ass," I said. "Where are Boone and Logan?"

"They had to go the slow way," Renick said. "The cat's out of the bag, but they didn't seem interested in catching up quickly. You all picked one hell of a spot." Renick wandered off in the direction of the river.

Vincent kept one hand on my arm as much as possible while he worked. The connection was warm, and my skin tingled as energy flowed back and forth between us. By the time he was done, I was feeling a little better.

"You're going to argue about going to sleep, aren't you?" Vincent asked while he was putting away the first-aid kit.

He felt... worried, as though afraid of what my answer would be. "I thought I could help—"

Vincent shook his head, but smiled and felt relieved. The feeling was so thick and heavy in the air that I stopped talking.

"Come on," Vincent said. "Rider's got you set up."

He helped me to my feet. For a moment, I think we both held our breaths as I swayed, hoping I wouldn't fall. With his help, I made it to the hammock.

"You'll be close by, right?" I asked, glancing at Renick, but looking away before he noticed.

"Very close," Vincent said.

It took me time to get situated in a spot that didn't put pressure on my arm. Sleeping on my side wasn't very comfortable in a hammock, but it was what I was stuck with. It didn't matter for long, though. I watched the sunlight drift in through the canopy and quickly fell into a dreamless sleep.

When I opened my eyes again, I only felt a little rested, and the sun was still filtering down. I started to stretch but remembered my arm when hot flames shot their way out of the wound.

"Cass?" Vincent said from somewhere nearby.

"Yes, I'm okay," I said.

"We were starting to worry," Vincent said.

I peeked over the side of my hammock and looked around. The entire camp had been set up. "How long was I asleep?"

"Never mind that," Vincent said. "Are you hungry?"

As soon as he said it, I realized that I was starving.

"How are you feeling?" Vincent asked.

"Worn, hungry, and desperately in need of getting clean. Some morphine wouldn't hurt either."

He gave me a wan smile. "We can do something about hungry and clean."

The meal he handed me was a power bar. You would think I'd have been tired of them, but at that moment, I'd have eaten almost anything put in front of me.

"Come with me," Vincent said. "You're going to love this."

We strolled over to the swift river and then started following it upstream.

"Where is everyone?" I asked.

"Boone's around here somewhere. Logan and Renick went to search out another spot for us. One far enough away that we can safely signal for extraction. And Rider is up this way."

"Where are we going?" The power bar left me even hungrier—if that was possible.

"Here," Vincent said, pushing into small clearing that opened out onto the base of a cliff, a waterfall, and crystal-clear pool of water.

"This is beautiful."

"The water is deeper than it looks. And cold. Really cold."

I sat down to unlace my boots. "I love it already."

"Here's the soap and a towel. I'll, um, I'll just wait for you back at the camp."

I stopped before pulling off the second boot. "You're leaving me out here?"

Vincent nodded up to the top of the small waterfall.

Rider stood there with a large grin on his face. "It is good to see you up. You will like this place. It is very alive."

"You'll stay close by, right?" Vincent asked.

"I will."

"I'm going to put a meal together for when you're done," Vincent said.

"That sounds good," I said, the enthusiasm coming straight from a place of hunger.

Rider scampered down the cliff face.

"I would like to visit this place again," Rider said after Vincent was gone. "Not for work, but to spend time in an area that is still wild."

I smiled at him and peeled off my socks. "I'm not sure we can come back to this exact place, but I know of a few others you might like."

"I would like to see them." After a while, he added, "I thought there was a clothes thing with friends."

"There is," I reassured him as I folded my pants and set them aside, "which is why I'm going to ask you to turn around for a minute."

Rider shrugged and sat on a rock with his back turned.

After changing my underclothes, I pulled my undershirt down. "You can turn around now." I stepped into the water. Goose pimples rose and only the gin-clear look of the water drove me forward.

Rider had already wandered into the woods, but I knew he'd be close by. When I was waist deep, I lowered myself down, and within a few minutes, I was dunking my head under the water. The bar of soap was put to good and thor-ough use on one half of my body. I kept an eye on Rider, noticing when he was in view and when he wasn't. Bit by bit, I started feeling more like a normal person once again. The cold was numbing the ache in my arm as well, which was an added bonus.

Frustrated that I couldn't clean one arm, I called for Rider and embarrassingly asked him to help.

Once I was clean, I floated for a minute.

"I figured I would find you here when you woke up," Boone said.

I grinned. "It's definitely colder than the last time we did this."

"How's the arm?"

My smile faded a little, but I was determined not to let it completely disappear yet. "The cold numbs it. Everything feels better now that I'm clean."

"Can I talk with you for a minute? Alone?"

That was enough to change my mood. Boone's face looked blank.

I hadn't been looking forward to this. "Rider," I called.

Rider stepped out of the woods. "You want me to go back to camp?"

"Boone and I need to talk for a bit," I said. "In private."

"I'll see her back to camp," Boone said. I raised an eyebrow at him, and he grinned and shook his head. "We'll get each other back to camp."

"I will see you back for dinner," Rider said.

"How long did I sleep?" I asked when Rider disappeared.

"A day," Boone said.

"The sad thing is, I still feel like I could curl up and go back to sleep."

"You should. After dinner, anyway. We probably have a long hike tomorrow."

I curled up my nose at the idea.

Boone was quiet for a while, so I made my way out of the water, feeling better about the idea of talking to him on dry land.

Boone tactfully looked away. "You saved my life in the cave."

My insides clenched and I toweled off quickly, already wanting the conversation to be out of the way. "I'm sorry for the way it happened." Even though they were the cleaner of the two pairs, my pants felt dirty when I put them on as though they were ruining all the work I'd just done to get clean. It was a good thing though, as it kept me distracted from the conversation at hand.

"I'm sorry for everything that happened as well," Boone said. "This didn't end like I expected."

"Me either," I admitted. I sat down trying to concentrate on putting on my socks and not the fact that I'd killed one of our teammates. "What do you think they'll do about the project?" A part of me was wondering what the office would do about me. Suspension? Termination? Would there be a trial? The thought was fleeting, though. I'd get whatever was in store for me and I'd deserve it.

"I'm requesting the project be put to an end."

"What will Renick do?"

"I'm going to push for him to join AIR, or liaise between the military and AIR. He's almost as adamant as Logan that this shouldn't happen again."

When I stood up, vertigo hit me. It felt like a storm had been released at camp, but the feeling went away so quickly that I wasn't sure it really even happened. "Let's head back." I kept my eyes peeled for anything in the direction we would be traveling.

Boone fell in line behind me.

"How are you feeling?" I asked. "How's your head?" I corrected quickly.

"I should be fit for the trek tomorrow. I didn't want to risk it today. Well, Logan didn't want to risk it today."

"It's probably for the best."

We walked in silence for a short while. When we reached the edge of the camp, I saw the storm that was Vincent. When he saw us, he only nodded, thin lipped.

"I shouldn't have brought you all out here," Boone said. "I'm sorry for all this."

"I think it's better that we found out about the experiment." I chose my words carefully. "I know Logan's upset about it, but he's also better off now that he knows."

"Maybe," Boone said as we went to join the others. "It's a moot point now, but I'm sorry you got hurt."

"I'll be okay with some rest."

"We made dinner," Vincent said as we approached.

This close, I noticed that Rider looked worried, but then, I was getting tired again. It was hard to say for sure.

"You look worn out," Vincent added.

"It was worth it," I said, smiling wearily. "I'll sleep well, though."

Vincent handed me a plate, and to my surprise sat down right next to me, close enough that our legs touched. The relationship and work was going to be tricky, but I thought he would put more space between us when someone like Boone was around.

I made it halfway through the meal before tiredness overtook hunger. I determinedly ate a little more before I gave up.

Since I was enjoying the closeness with Vincent, I didn't make a move to go to sleep.

"Done?" Vincent asked after a while.

I wanted so much to lean over and put my head on his shoulder, but I didn't want to make Vincent feel awkward with Boone being there.

"I am heading back to the cliff," Rider said.

"Not alone," Vincent said. "Wait for me; I can join you in a while."

"I'll go," Boone volunteered. He practically jumped to his feet.

The moment they disappeared, I wanted to lean over to Vincent, but he had other ideas.

"You should get some rest," Vincent said, taking my plate.

He set it aside, then took my hand and helped me to my feet. When he tried to let go, I pulled him into a hug.

His response was stiff at first, but soon he relaxed and held me. I wanted to kiss him, but I was already practically falling over from overexertion. So, I contented myself with the contact.

After a few moments, he pulled back, but only enough to look me in the face. I blinked tiredly at him while he inspected me for who knows what.

"Come on," he said at last, his voice softer than it had been. "Back to bed."

Reluctantly, I let him lead me over to my hammock. "I almost wish we had tents," I said. "Then I could keep you close by."

"I'll be close by," Vincent said.

"That's good. I feel better when you are."

He caught me by surprise by kissing me. It was quick, but it lit a fire in me and woke me up. "I'll stay close for as long as you want me to."

I sighed and opened my bug net. "I'm not sure that's possible."

"Why did you send Rider back?" The question shot from Vincent and caught me even more by surprise than the kiss.

"Boone wanted to talk," I said, sitting on the hammock, but not getting situated for sleep yet. "I wasn't sure what about, so I thought I'd get it over with."

"He had to talk while you were bathing?" Vincent asked. He didn't sound mad, but looked like he didn't believe it.

"It's not like I was naked."

"You weren't?"

"No, I'm in the middle of a jungle in water with who knows what in it. Knowing my luck, if I got naked, a giant snake would swim over to me. Besides, I wasn't alone, remember? Rider was there."

He grinned in a mischievous way, one that I hadn't seen before. "Had I known that, I would have stayed."

I shook my head. "That sounds like it could lead to fraternization."

"I'm game if you are."

My eyebrow raised. "I was under the impression it was the opposite."

"That was before."

"Before what?"

"Before you got shot."

I rolled my eyes and maneuvered around in the hammock to find a comfortable place to lay. "That's always a possibility. In fact," I stopped and looked at him. "I think out of the four of us, you're the only one that I haven't seen get shot."

"I try to avoid that. It's bad for your health."

"You're not lying. My arm feels like it's on fire again." I closed my eyes.

"I should have checked it," Vincent said.

My eyes felt heavy, so I didn't bother opening them. Or replying.

"Why don't you let me check your arm before you sleep," Vincent said.

I made a non-committal murmur.

"Cass?"

"Later," I mumbled, then fell asleep.

CHAPTER
TWENTY-TWO

The sun was barely up when I opened my eyes again. I laid still, trying to figure out what it was that had woken me. Then I heard a rustling noise.

Carefully, I pushed the edge of the hammock down and looked out. A small spider monkey sat on the ground next to me.

It was adorable, and I wanted to tell it so, but I also didn't want to wake anyone or scare it away.

A scrambling on the tree made me look around, and I spotted one on the tree. Another one jumped on the line that held my bug net. It immediately twisted and tumbled off performing some acrobatics that very few humans could ever pull off.

When I looked over the other side of the hammock a few more were there. One of them had a baby clutched to it.

The mama monkey took a few hopping steps back, then cocked its head. After that, she held up her baby for me to see.

I was amazed. Thrilled, even. For years, I had been treated as a second-rate human by most other people, although they could never articulate why. To the animal kingdom—and really really low-intelligence humans—I had been a target.

"You have quite the fan club," Vincent said, keeping his voice low. He was in a hammock not far away from my own.

"Aren't they cute?" I said, admiring the little monkeys.

"This is... different," Vincent said. "And not what I would have expected."

"A lot changed in the past month. You may have to run to catch up."

"I'll do my best. How's your arm?"

The monkeys had caused a distraction enough for me to ignore the worst of the pain. Vincent's reminder brought it back with interest.

"It could be better," I said. I leaned up and started to unzip my bug net.

"Are you sure you should do that?" Vincent asked.

I stopped, worried I was missing something. "Why not?"

"Because you're surrounded by wild animals."

"I think if they were going to attack, they already would have." I went ahead and left my hammock.

Vincent was scrambling to get out of his bed, so I took my time and looked around the camp.

The monkeys screeched at Vincent and backed away from him, leaving a Path for him and closing back in from behind.

"It's good you're awake," Logan said, exiting his own bed. He stretched and his ears, already unfolded, seemed to lengthen with him.

Rider, who had been on watch, stepped out from behind a tree as the camp came alive.

"Let's take care of your arm," Vincent said.

When he touched my hand, the familiar tingling sensation rose and the monkeys were drawn even closer to us. Then a headlamp landed on Vincent's head. He jumped and the animals scattered.

"What the—" Vincent looked up in time to snatch a large water bottle out of the air. A monkey, larger than the others, screeched and reached through the netting to grab something else from one of our bags.

It pulled out a pack of waterproof matches and threw it down. Whether it was aimed at someone or not, it was hard to tell.

"I've got it," Rider said.

Somehow, he managed to scamper up the tree as easily as he might have crawled across the floor. Looking closer, I saw marks in the tree where his nails had scored the trunk. When he untied the rope, and started lowering the bags, the trouble-maker screeched at him, ran up the rope, and swung off and over to another tree.

"That wasn't so bad," I said, trying not to laugh at the little thing.

"Not at all," Boone said, coming over to join us. "It could have been throwing something far worse than our stuff."

I had to stifle a laugh, and even Vincent looked like he was having a hard time keeping a straight face.

Once the gear was down, Vincent found a first-aid kit and started looking after my arm. While we did that, our camp sprang alive. Boone attempted to wake Renick up twice before the man actually got up. It seemed like he could sleep through anything. Breakfast was made—an actual meal, because lunch was apt to be a protein bar on the go, and bags were packed.

While the others worked, I started to take down my bed. The straps were easy enough to unhook one handed. I thought about the monkeys, then thought about Davis. She probably would have liked to have seen them.

Feeling melancholy, I concentrated on each step of taking

apart the hammock and bug net. One step at a time, trying not to let my heart get weighed down.

"Cass?" Vincent laid his hand on mine, and I jumped.

Somehow, I had missed him approach. He looked worried and the camp was still. Looking around, everyone was staring at me. Boone and Renick were just watching me as though I was about to do some trick. Rider looked agitated and Logan...

Logan looked upset. I've never seen the elf appear as though he might break into tears.

After a few moments, Logan was the one to break the silence. "We push out in five minutes." It was said as an order—a stark one, at that.

I looked up at Vincent, wondering what the hell had just happened. He hadn't let go of my hand.

"Come on," he said quietly, "I'll help."

"What just happened?" I asked.

"You were humming," he said.

"Oh..." I hadn't realized that I had been humming, but surely, it couldn't have been that bad.

He must have seen my puzzled look. "Humming like Logan would."

"Oh." Light dawned. That was the second time it happened on this trip. Memories of many souls had imprinted themselves on me, and every now and again one of them would sneak up and take me by surprise. I wondered if the jungle was what had brought out the elf. "I guess that could have been worse as well," I added, looking at Rider.

"I've got your hammock," Vincent said. "Boone had something for you, so why don't you talk with him for a while."

I raised an eyebrow, surprised that Vincent would send me to seek out Boone. Since I wasn't much help here, though, I went ahead and found Boone, who was arranging the last of the items in his pack.

"Hey," I said, walking up, "Vincent said you wanted to see me."

"Oh yeah," he replied while shifting a few items. "I made a sling for your arm. You're using it too much and I think you'll need it today." He held up a strip of cloth that had been sewn up in a few areas, and then slid it over my neck.

"Thank you," I said. "That was..." I sucked in a sharp breath when I tried to bend my arm.

"Don't use the muscle for anything if you can help it," Boone said. "You might damage it even more than it already is."

I gritted my teeth, breathing shallowly. "I'll keep that in mind."

"Anytime you need to move your arm, use your other arm to lift it. It sounds strange, and it takes some getting used to, but trust me, it'll help."

"You sound like you know from experience," I said.

"I was in the military in some pretty hostile situations. You're not the first of my teammates to get shot."

Hearing the words made me hold my breath and bite my lip. I waited to see if he'd realize what he'd just said.

It took him a moment, but I could see when his own words sunk in.

"Anyway," he said a little more formally, "I think Vincent's got the rest covered."

"Time to go," Logan called. "I'm going to scout ahead, and Rider can lead you in my direction."

With that, Logan was gone.

Was he mad? I wondered what it was I had been humming that could cause such an effect on my partner.

I wasn't allowed to carry so much as a water bottle. Once we had the first mile behind us, I realized it was for the best. It didn't take long before I realized I wasn't going to make it to where we were going. Not under my own steam.

That realization started a small fire in me, making me determined to move on, but I asked Boone how far we'd gone a little while later, and even thought it was around a mile and a half, I called for a break.

It sucked and I hated it, but the fact of the matter was that I was exhausted.

"How far are we going?" I asked, passing the water bottle after having my share.

"Only six miles or so," Boone said, casting Vincent a worried look.

"Only," I muttered.

No one said anything, so I rested while I could and made it another half mile.

Feeling dejected, I pushed on until someone else called for a stop.

"You look pale," Vincent said.

He looked pale as well, but I didn't say so.

"Come on," Rider said. "Same as the other day."

I made a face, but didn't argue when Rider kneeled down. My complaining would only slow everyone down more. Once my arm was situated, he rose far enough up, I was surprised not to get a nose bleed and we were off again.

It might not have been so bad, but I kept expecting Renick to say something inappropriate. To my surprise, he stayed quiet on the subject of princesses.

We made good time after that. Even with Rider doing the walking for me, I felt like crap when we finally caught up with Logan. He already had a cooking fire set up. After he checked in on me, he and Boone went off with the sat phone to a rocky clearing. By the time I had eaten something, they were back. Extraction was set for tomorrow morning.

I was too tired to feel thrilled about leaving, but it was the next best thing. Logan seemed happy about the outcome, but Boone looked bothered by it. Had I felt any better, I would have asked him why, but my bed was calling.

"How's the arm holding up?" Logan asked, walking with me over to my hammock.

"It could be better," I admitted. I bit my lip and plunged on with what was on my mind. "I'm sorry about earlier. With the humming, I mean. I didn't mean to upset anyone."

"Do you know the song?" Logan asked.

I shook my head.

"It was an elven song. Something my wife used to sing from time to time."

"Sorry," I said again. "I'll try not to do that again."

"No worries," Logan said. "It surprised me is all. You look tuckered out."

"Something like that."

"Get some rest." Logan tipped his hat and walked away.

I crawled into the hammock and went to sleep again.

What I needed, I thought as I drifted to sleep, was Dr. Yelton out here. He was all about rest when someone got hurt. Now, I could see why.

"Cass." Vincent's voice was low, but I could hear other movement in the camp. "It's time to get up. We need to head to the extraction point."

"Isn't that tomorrow?" I muttered, not wanting to open my eyes.

"It is tomorrow."

How was that even possible? With some effort, I managed to drag myself out of my bed.

"I've never done anything like this before," I admitted, looking around at the camp. Everyone was almost packed.

They had let me sleep for as long as they could. "How does extraction work?"

"There's a clearing of sorts that we marked yesterday. The military will send a helicopter to come and get us out of here. They know you're injured, so I think they'll have someone with emergency medical training with them."

"The emergency was days ago."

"I'm not certain that's the case." Vincent put the back of his hand to my forehead and then against my cheek.

For the first time that day, my lips curled up into an almost smile. "Give me a shower and a real bed and I'll be fine in no time."

Vincent didn't look convinced. "I'll pack. Rider," he called, "she's ready."

"For what?"

"He's going to help you get to the extraction point."

"I can walk on my own." I thought about yesterday and about how much faster we'd traveled once I'd relented and let Rider help me. "At least for a short way. I need to stretch my legs a little."

Vincent looked as though he wanted to argue, but at last turned and started pulling my bed apart. "A short way."

"You said the place is close. How far away is close?"

"A little over a mile," Vincent said.

My shoulders slumped at the thought of traveling that far. "Maybe I'll just walk around the camp a little to stretch my legs instead."

"Just a sec," Vincent said. "I'll walk with you."

He stowed the straps and started shoving my hammock into its little carry pouch.

I almost told him he didn't have to go with me—that there were others around—but I wanted him next to me. Not only did I feel better with him nearby, but also I wanted to spend more time with Vincent. I would have enjoyed it more if we didn't smell of sweat and the hell that this jungle brought with it, but I couldn't have everything.

"Let's grab something to eat before we head out," Vincent said, joining me.

My body was tired, worn, and hurting. The last thing I wanted was food. "I'm not hungry."

"I know you're not feeling well," Vincent said, "but it'll keep your strength up."

I shrugged noncommittally. He was probably right, but I still didn't want to eat anything.

"Over here," Boone called to us. He was packed and ready to go when we joined him. "How's the arm?"

"It'll be better after I get to sleep in a real bed," I said.

"Vincent mentioned you might not be feeling the best today. Looks like a lucky guess," Boone said. He handed me three pills. "Take these, they'll get you through the day."

I reached out automatically, but Vincent beat me to them.

"What are they?" Vincent asked.

"Two pain killers and an antibiotic," Boone said.

"Is the pain killer going to make me loopy?" I asked.

Boone grinned. "That's one way to put it."

"I'll pass," I said. "Save it until the helicopter gets close. I want to keep a clear head until we get out of this place."

"Suit yourself," Boone said. "Stick them in your pocket for later, just in case."

"I'll keep them for you," Vincent said. "Thanks."

"Yeah," I agreed, "thank you."

"Are you two ready to go?" Boone asked.

I looked to Vincent because the sad thing was, I didn't know. I had no idea where my stuff was or who was stuck carrying it. For all I knew, we were leaving it behind.

"Almost," Vincent said.

I stretched my legs a little more before Logan joined us. "Time to move out. You ready for the trip?"

I shook my head. "Only with Rider helping me out."

"I am ready," Rider said.

"Saddle up, partner," Logan said.

CHAPTER
TWENTY-THREE

Being towed around by Rider was embarrassing, but once again, no one said anything. The terrain was particularly rocky, but even with me on his back, Rider made his way silently across the landscape.

As we reached the clearing, grass and underbrush started to become a main feature. In the clearing itself, the grass was tall and hid who knows what.

There was a flash of an animal bounding up above the grass line. I perked up. A feeling of dread began to fill me.

There it was again. A flash of white. But the animal didn't disappear under tufts of grass or behind something. It just disappeared.

"Fenrir?" I sat up straighter. It looked like the others hadn't noticed. The flash was moving toward us, weaving its way in and out of this world as though it was hunting.

Was Fenrir the only creature that could walk from the Path and into the real world?

"Stop." I patted Rider on the shoulder. "Stop and put me down."

"What is the matter?" Rider asked. He stopped and tried to look up at me with some difficulty since I was behind him.

"I think..." The animal was visible a while longer this time. It was Fenrir or someone that looked very much like him. Why would he be here? How in the hell could he even get here? "I think something's wrong."

Rider whistled loudly, recalling the others.

"Rider, did you see Fenrir?" I asked quickly as the others showed up. "Did anyone see Fenrir?"

Vincent put a hand to my forehead, which aggravated me, but I was distracted and didn't bat his hand away as I should have.

"She's burning up," Vincent said.

"Did you see him?" I asked.

"I do not see him," Rider said, keeping an eye on the grassland.

"Who's Fenrir?" Boone asked.

"He's a wolf, sort of," I said.

"Think about it, Cass, how could he possibly be here?" Vincent said. "We have almost gotten to where we need to be."

"I think I hear the helicopter," Boone said.

"The only reason I can think of for Fenrir to be here is to get a message to us," I said.

"Who would give him a message?" Vincent asked. "Look, if he is here, he can meet us at the extraction point."

"The only one that can talk to him is Gran's crazy ex-boyfriend," I said.

Renick watched the sky looking tense. "I don't think that's a helicopter."

"You're feverish," Vincent said. "Are you sure you actually saw him?"

"I'm not crazy," I snapped. "He's out there." Or at least someone who looks damned close to Fenrir.

"We've never doubted her before," Rider said.

"And we won't now," Vincent said, still not looking convinced. "The helicopter will wait for us—it's not like they're going to leave us out here."

Renick shook his head. "That's not a helicopter. It's a plane, maybe a jet, and it's flying low." He gave Boone a meaningful look. However, whatever the meaning was, it was lost on me.

"Drug plane?" Vincent suggested.

Renick sighed. "Wait here. Don't move." He took a step and disappeared.

"How far away was Fenrir?" Rider asked. "Maybe we can meet him."

Renick appeared in the spot from where he'd vanished. "It's one of ours."

"Maybe they aren't able to find us," Rider said.

"We marked the spot," Boone said. "They'll find us."

All the words were flying around me and I didn't care about any of them. My head was starting to swim. Maybe Vincent was right to worry about what I might have seen.

Overhead, a fighter jet flew by going much slower than I would have expected.

"An escort," Boone said, sounding happy about the response.

"It's an older plane," Renick said, "and there are three of them."

There was a loud crack in the direction we were heading.

"Shit," Renick said under his breath.

"What?" I asked, seeing that he had grown pale.

"That sounded like—"

"No," Boone cut Renick off.

"We're not waiting around to find out," Renick said. "I'm getting you out of here."

"We stick together," Boone said.

"I smell something odd," Rider said.

We heard the approach of another jet. When it flew over and past us, I felt relieved, but I couldn't put my finger on why.

A crack that sounded as though thousands of guns were shot at once ripped through the air. Going by instinct, I jumped into the Path. A rush of air nearly bowled us over. Debris began to rain. Adrenaline coursed through me, giving me a boost.

"Move together," I yelled. I froze the Path above us. Looking up, time seemed to slow.

"Whatever you're doing, double it!" Renick yelled.

I glanced over at him. He was sweating buckets and focusing on an object above us.

"Are you done?" Renick yelled.

I grabbed the solid Path and saw what Renick had noticed. A missile. It was almost above us, ready to slam down and kill us all.

Renick was holding it back.

No, he was slowing time for the thing.

"Shit. Move close." It came out almost as a cry. Out of the corner of my eye, I saw Logan looking quickly from side to side. He was fully in his elf form.

The thin shell I had made wouldn't stand up to anything like a missile. Imagining a thick wall, I expanded the Path. Then, I brought it down to the ground for extra support and— like a dome—it rose over us.

What do the others see? It was a fleeting thought. A hand wrapped around my good arm and I could feel Vincent. My strength doubled and I poured it into our protections.

Beside me, Renick fell over. Moments later, as though on fast forward, time caught up.

The missile slammed into my shield and exploded. The force pushed the shield back while slamming it down. It knocked me to the ground. The moment I felt heat, I plunged more power into our protections, forcing the heat to go around us.

The force felt as though it passed through my creation and straight into me. Trees were blasted away beside us. I half expected fire to begin to crawl over my pathetic dome, but rock and the remains of trees hit our protection instead. I fed more of myself into the creation.

I put my hand out and it reached the shield about a foot over my head.

Did I get everyone in? I had to have done so, though.

The ground shook again.

Hold it back. Hold it.

Everyone had moved in close, right? I had asked them to.

Hold it.

Someone yelled something. I stared straight up. The Path had been ripped apart just like the trees. The flows were frantic. I fed some of the energetic streams into the dome and watched them freeze.

Hold it.

Keep them safe.

I put more in, watching the effect. My eyesight began to blur, but that didn't affect my views of the Path. Only our own world disappeared.

I could feel my nose running, but I couldn't move my arms. Hadn't I been holding my hand up? The pain was gone, though, that was the important thing.

No, that wasn't the important thing.

What was important?

Hold it.

That was it. I closed my eyes, intent on holding it and not letting go.

Then I fell, although I had been sure I had already been lying down.

The shield flickered and died. People started moving instantly.

Vincent was clutching his chest and he looked as though he were in pain. I could see some sort of battle going on inside his Path. Part of his Path was trying to escape, but he wasn't letting it go.

Rider lay on the ground several yards away. He tried to stand, but fell back down again. I could see blood pumping out from a gash in his head, though it was already starting to heal.

Already on his feet, Boone stomped out a small piece of burning debris. He checked on Renick, who lay on the ground not far from me. I could see the rise and fall of his chest.

Vincent pulled himself together, although I could see the war still raging inside him. He came to me.

My chest wasn't moving up and down.

No wonder I felt unaccountably good. As I stared down at myself, it was a stark thought with no real emotion behind it.

Vincent started CPR. Boone rushed over and helped, taking over chest compressions, trying to get my lungs working again.

A whine from nearby made me look around. Fenrir was standing at the edge of what could only be called the blast zone. A disheveled-looking Logan was standing next to him, pale and shaky. I'd never seen the elf look so out of sorts.

Fenrir came up to my body, crossing the scarred landscaping while fading in and out of our own world. Then he stopped and laid his head on my leg.

Awww, he's so cute. It was a good thing he couldn't hear me. I doubt he'd appreciate the sentiment. I tried not to look at myself. I got a queasy feeling when I did and I wondered how I could have vertigo when I had no body. It didn't help that I had blood coming out of my ears, nose, and eyes. I seriously looked like crap.

Boone gave the animal a sidelong look, trying to keep his

eye on Fenrir without losing his rhythm. After a few seconds, he let his hand stray to his holster. Fenrir didn't raise his head, but he growled.

"Leave him," Logan said, his voice every inch the leader I knew, even when he himself was still out of sorts.

Logan watched silently. It surprised me that he wasn't checking on Rider. I turned around and found Rider standing directly behind me. Not my body me, but the me that was floating out in the ether.

What was more surprising is that he was looking at me.

And he was pissed off.

Rider had his arms folded. Blood had stopped flowing down his face, although he hadn't wiped it clean. His glare added the finishing touches that made my friend look menacing—not at all like his normal self.

He looked me up and down, and then nodded toward my body. That's when I realized he wasn't looking at me, not directly. He was looking at air, but he must have sensed my presence.

He grit his teeth.

"Fine," I muttered, walking away from him. I sensed him following behind, but didn't look at him again. Instead, I focused on my body. "It's not like I even know how this works."

Vincent was stone faced and continuing to work with Boone to push my body back to life. I circled them, stopped, and was suddenly nervous. The one thing I knew, more clearly than anything else, was that this was going to hurt.

I glanced at Rider, and he didn't look angry this time. He looked concerned, but still nodded once again to my body.

Knowing it would suck, I closed my eyes and mentally felt for my body. I sensed it there, dimly connected to me. Much like I would tug on a Path, I pulled on the connection and let myself be drawn back into my body.

My eyes flew open and I coughed a few times. Everything was still a bit blurry, but I had a vague idea that there was blood that might be causing the issue. I was starting to tear up.

Vincent took a shuddering breath and leaned over me. He started wiping the blood off my face, but he wasn't talking. There was a bark from somewhere by my feet. For a moment, I worried about what Boone's reaction might be, but I could only see Vincent.

His face looked carved out of marble, but I could see a flurry of emotions trying to lay claim to him only having his eyes as access to show the rawness he felt.

Someone had my wrist in their hand.

"Cassie—"

In that one moment, my mind caught up with my body. Pain lanced through me and exhaustion clouded my thoughts. I took my good hand away from Boone. I was weak, but when I tugged, he let me go.

"—I need you to tell me your name," Boone continued.

I rolled my eyes and groped around until I found Vincent's hand. He wrapped his fingers in mine.

After that, exhaustion pulled me into sleep. I let my partners take over from there.

CHAPTER
TWENTY-FOUR

I smelled the smoke before I saw him. This time, though, Gran's crazy ex-boyfriend had another old man with him. Fenrir was there as well, wagging his tail. It took me a few moments to recognize the second old man. We had met in the park back home, what seemed like ages ago. He had stopped time, warning me about Einar, the crazed golem that had been killing people, although the old man hadn't actually said much.

I crouched down and held my hand out to Fenrir.

"How did you find me?" I asked when he licked my fingers. He let me run my hands through his silky coat, but I didn't push my luck.

"You were lost and then found," Gran's ex said. "Then lost and found again."

"Patterns," the other old man said. "The Patterns that cross through time and space. They found you."

"Hunh," I said, half laughing at them. "It was Gran, wasn't it?"

"She had a bee in her bonnet, make no mistake," Gran's ex said.

"I think I should be resting," I said. "I don't know if I'm doing that when I'm here. Wherever here is."

Gran's ex exhaled smoke, but I couldn't help but think that he hadn't yet puffed on his pipe.

"Who are you all?" I asked. "And what do you want."

"You may call me Chronos," the other old man said.

"Chronos? Wasn't he a Titan or something," I asked.

Fenrir barked sharply twice.

"The titan is Cronus. I am Chronos. Named after a god of time."

"Because you can stop time?" I asked. "I really never expected to see anyone else be able to do that. Although, I guess Renick didn't stop time, he really just slowed it down."

"We will be asking him to join us," Chronos said.

"Join you doing what?" I asked.

Gran's ex cackled and it felt like my skin crawled. I concentrated on Chronos, trying to ignore the crazier of the two.

"We are asking your human friend to join us as well," Chronos said.

"Join you in what?" I repeated.

"And it is time for you to join us," Chronos said.

"Ha," Gran's ex muttered.

I crossed my arms and glared at them. "If you're not going to answer me, I'm going back to sleep."

"You will heal. In a month's time we will return, and you will join us," Chronos said.

I turned my attention to Fenrir, ignoring the others. "I wanted to thank you for being there today. Or was it yesterday?" I looked at Fenrir, wishing there was actually a way for me to understand him.

"You may wish to warn your friends that we will be contacting them," Chronos said. "We have a job for them."

"What? Contacting them how—" I started, but when I looked up, Chronos was gone.

Gran's ex was still there.

"How's Gran?" I asked.

"Fired up. Trying to find a way to keep you safe."

"I'm just doing my job."

"Your government tried to kill you."

"That had to have been some sort of mistake," I said. It sounded hollow, even to me.

"Believe as you wish. One survived. They don't want to deal with that and they certainly don't want proof of their little experiment going wrong."

"How do you know?" I asked.

The old man cackled, but sounded a little less crazy this time. "Time rolls on and turns back in on itself. We want their experiment."

"What are you going to do with Renick?" I asked.

"He will be on our side now."

"And what is your side?"

The old man grinned and puffed on his pipe. Much too soon, he was obscured by smoke. I coughed and choked on the smoke. I couldn't see Fenrir anymore, but when I felt around, there was soft fur.

I'd been put in a similar position before. This time, I closed my eyes, took a few deep breaths, and willed myself to wake up.

I EXPECTED PAIN, but there was none. The heat was there. The blasted heat of the summer in the jungle.

But no, the air was dryer.

Fur rubbed against my hand, and when I opened my eyes, it was to find Fenrir curled up beside me, still in his dream—maybe still talking to the old men. Who knew?

More importantly, at the moment, we were in a bed. Not mine, and not a particularly comfortable one, but it was a real bed all the same.

I expected to see Vincent, but he wasn't there. One person I never would have thought to see at that moment, however, was Taylor.

"I think I'm still asleep," I murmured and closed my eyes again.

"No, no," Taylor said quickly. "I need you awake."

Reluctantly, I looked at him, trying to decide if I was awake or not. In the end, I decided I must be awake, because it was too unlikely for a dream.

"How are you here?" I asked.

"Hank got me here, and your grandmother," Taylor said. "She was adamant and she wasn't wrong."

I had been attacked by changelings in the past, so while I was pretty sure he was there, I wasn't as convinced that he was really Taylor. "There's no way Gran could have told you where I was, or even what happened."

"She didn't, but whatever she did see disturbed her enough to press down on Hank pretty hard."

That could be Gran. She was good at getting her way. "Where is everyone?" I looked around the room, which had a door and a little balcony outside. "Where am I?"

"Brazil," Taylor said. "Do you remember how you got here?"

"Where is everyone?" I insisted.

"Boone, Renick, and Logan are outside of town. We'll meet up with them shortly. Rider is outside the building and I told

Vincent to get some rest. He refused, but settled for taking a shower. He's down the hall. Now, do you remember how you got here?"

"The last thing I remember was waking up after the missile dropped."

"Good. That's good. Now, how are you feeling?"

"Tired, confused, and aggravated. How did I get here?"

"What's your level of discomfort?"

"It's growing," I snapped, then I moved and pain jolted my arm and radiated out. Looking at it, I saw that it was thickly wrapped in gauze. Even though I stopped moving, the pain remained in a dull form.

"Pain levels?"

"Bearable, but it sucks when I move my arm wrong." Or at all.

"I need the truth here," Taylor said. "No bravado or holding back."

"If the muscle gets clenched, it hurts," I said. "That's all I have."

There was a tap at the door and Vincent stepped in, not waiting for an answer. He was dressed in jeans and a t-shirt. When he saw me, his face remained stoic save for the tiniest unclenching of the jaw. His eyes lit up, though.

Some of the anxiety that I had begun to fade away.

"Let Rider know that we'll be leaving soon," Taylor said.

Vincent looked surprised, though it was possible I was the only one who would have noticed. "She just woke up," Vincent said. "Isn't that a bit soon?"

"We have to weigh the risks," Taylor said. "She'll be okay to travel as long as we keep her arm still."

"As long as I keep my arm still," I mumbled, not liking the sound of it being done for me.

"That, too," Taylor said. "I'll do one last exam to be certain."

I felt movement next to me and Fenrir laid a head on my stomach. It wasn't until now that I truly realized how large he was. Larger than any wolf I've ever seen outside of movies or TV.

Except maybe for Rider.

I patted his head, loving the feel of soft fur beneath my fingers.

Vincent seemed to ignore Taylor's haste and came over to see me. "How are you feeling?" Vincent squatted down next to the bed, not disturbing it, but he took my hand and looked me over. For the first time since waking up, I worried about how I looked. Was the blood gone? Were my clothes...?

Where were my clothes? The t-shirt certainly wasn't mine.

"Cass?"

"Confused," I admitted.

"Do you feel up for traveling?"

Taylor's distress hadn't had time to soak in fully, but I still sensed his urgency. "I can travel."

He rose, but didn't drop my hand. "Don't push yourself."

I grinned. "Who, me? Seriously, though, what's going on?"

He smiled. "We'll explain on the way."

Vincent went to the door, but then held it open and waited. Fenrir, got up, stretched, and jumped off the bed, following Vincent out.

"We asked him to leave during examinations," Taylor said in response to my quizzical look. "He seems to understand everything we say."

"He's a person. He knows our language, even if we don't know his," I said.

"Rider seems to understand him," Taylor said. "Mostly,

anyway. Now, let's take a look at that arm. I don't have much in the way of equipment here, but we'll do the best we can."

When I saw what was under the gauze I scrunched up my nose and looked away.

"It's not too bad," Taylor said. "The infection is almost gone. There's some muscle damage, but with a bit of physical therapy, you should be okay. It will leave a scar, though. I'm afraid I made things a bit worse there."

"What do you mean?" I asked while Taylor wrapped the arm back up."

"These weren't exactly ideal conditions for surgery."

"Surgery? You mean you took the bullet out here?"

"Not here, a small village near where I picked you up. If I'd left it in, there would have been a higher chance of more damage, or possibly losing your arm if the infection became any worse."

I shivered despite the heat. "I don't remember any of that."

"It's for the best."

Taylor performed all his doctorly duties which—even in the middle of nowhere—included trying to blind me.

"Tell me about your powers," Taylor said. "How are you getting along?"

"Some strange things happened out here. I don't know if they were because of the nightmare or because of the changes from re-breaking my soul. The headaches are almost gone, though. At least they were until I was drugged."

"Hopefully that's temporary. I can't exactly say you're fit, but I think you're in good enough condition to get out of here."

I could have done without the 'I think' part. "What's the hurry?"

"News and rumors spread fast, even out here. You're here without a passport, in odd circumstances. Once the local authorities or the military find us, there will be trouble. And that's saying nothing about the drug cartels. If someone thinks we're here to mess with their business, they'll do whatever they can to make sure we don't live long enough to leave."

"Why did we stop here, then?" I asked, throwing back the blankets with my good hand.

"It was a necessity. You and Vincent weren't in great shape."

"He's hurt?" I asked while sitting up, suddenly worried I had missed something. "I thought... I mean, I remember him being okay." But was he? What happens if one part of your soul starts raging against another half? At least that's what I thought was happening when I died.

"I won't know for sure until we are back in the states. Here, put this on." Taylor handed me some sort of long skirt that looked as though it had seen better days.

"You can't expect me to run around in a skirt if there are people after us." This should have been logical for anyone in their right mind.

"It's all we could get. You can't go around in fatigues out here."

"Fine," I muttered and slipped it on. It fit like a sack, but beggars can't be choosy. "How are we getting out of here?"

Someone rapped rapidly on the door and Vincent stepped in again. "We're ready."

"We'll explain on the way," Taylor said. "Let's get the others and get out of here."

A FEW MILES out of town, our van pulled to a stop and waited. It was an old van with bucket seats up front, one small bench seat, and a lot of floor space.

Fatigue was already starting to sneak in, but I was determined to stay awake until I found out what the heck was going on. Logan, Boone, and Renick came out of the forest a few minutes later. The three had all of our supplies between them, which they threw into the back of the van before crawling in themselves.

"You're looking better," Logan said to me, settling down. "We weren't expecting you back so soon, doc."

"We've still got a long way to go before we get home," Taylor said.

"How *are* we getting home?" I asked.

"MyTH and Hank are helping us out with that," Logan said. "Along with a big assist from Boone here."

"I'm still not sure going back is the best idea," Renick said. "The government tried to kill us, after all."

"Do they know they failed?" I asked.

Rider shifted uncomfortably and no one said anything.

"What's wrong?" I asked, getting a sinking feeling in my stomach.

"Only a few people at MyTH know we're alive, along with Hank," Logan said. "And it needs to stay that way until we know more about what's going on. It's possible they didn't try to actually kill us—"

Renick snorted.

Logan pretended not to notice. "But if they did and found out they failed, they'd try again."

"That's understandable, I guess," I said.

"That means no one else knows," Logan said after a few moments. "Hank is keeping it very low profile. It's important that everyone else thinks we're dead until we can be there in person."

No one said anything for a few moments again.

"What am I missing?" I asked.

"Your mother and grandmother are going to get someone

coming to their door," Vincent said. "They'll be told you're missing or dead."

"Oh no." I bit my lower lip and thought quickly. "Maybe Gran won't tell them otherwise. I'm not sure."

"I don't think she knows," Taylor said. "She didn't seem to know for sure when she sent me down here."

"She knows," I said. "She may be mad as hell about it, but she knows."

"You can't be sure—"

"Her boyfriend came to see me," I said.

Boone groaned.

I turned around and grinned at him. "It gets better. He and another guy, Chronos, said they'd be coming to see you and Renick a little later."

"There goes any chance of sleep," Boone muttered. Louder, he added, "Why do they want to see us?"

"They have a job for you, apparently," I said.

"I feel like I'm missing a lot here," Renick said.

"Did you say Chronos?" Taylor asked.

"Yeah, I met him once before," I said, "but I didn't have his name at the time."

"Is he any better than your grandmother's boyfriend?" Boone asked.

"From what I've seen, not even a little bit," I said.

"When you say Chronos, are you taking about the titan?" Taylor asked.

Fenrir growled and Taylor gave him a sideways glance. Fenrir was riding shotgun and had been thoroughly enjoying putting his head out the window. At the mention of the titan, however, he seemed to pay more attention.

"I don't know what he is, really. He says he's not a titan and he doesn't look like I would expect a titan to look. He's a little old man. He does something with time."

Logan whistled through his teeth.

"What?" I asked.

"Chronos is... not someone you want to be around," Taylor said.

We hit a big pothole and I winced when my arm brushed against the side of the van. I leaned into Vincent more, which besides the protection of being away from the door, had the added benefit of being closer to Vincent.

"You know the guy?" Logan asked. "I've only heard about him. Rumor, mostly. I wasn't even certain he was real."

"I met him once," Taylor said. He glanced at me through the rear-view mirror, but I wasn't sure if he was checking on me or if he was still worried that I might have told someone that he wasn't human.

I shook my head almost imperceptibly in case it was the latter.

"So, why are these people looking to hire Boone and me?" Renick asked.

"They said you're on their side now," I said. "They're trying to recruit me too."

Vincent stiffened, and from the corner of my eye, I saw him frown at me.

"Side of what?" Renick asked.

"No idea," I said.

"I think I'm starting to have an idea," Vincent said. "There's been a lot of indications over the past few months that humans and Lost have been having some trouble with each other."

"I'm not sure why they think I'd turn against humans because of the experiments, though," Boone said. "I'm not too keen on the military right now, but I don't want humans hurt any more than I want the Lost hurt."

"I think Vincent has a point, though," I said, yawning and

trying to shift to get comfortable. "In the past two months, we've had Lost try to kill us, saying they hated humans and those of us with powers. Then we have humans trying to cover up their experiment of turning humans into people that could take the Losts' place at work."

"Didn't Chronos send you after Einar?" Logan asked.

"Einar was made by the military," I said.

"By humans," Vincent said.

"Who's Einar?" Boone asked.

"A golem," I said before anyone else could answer. Einar had started out as a Walker and I didn't want Renick to gain a worse impression of Walkers. "He was built to kill humans and Lost, though."

The van lapsed into silence for a while. I used the opportunity to close my eyes and lean my head back.

"How are we going to get back into the country?" I asked, yawning again.

"I know a few people in South America," Taylor said. "There's an eccentric old ogre that lives another sixty or so miles away. He's meeting up with us and we're handing over the van in return for his help."

"What is he helping us do?" Rider asked.

I was glad he asked for me. Exhaustion was trying to pull me down again. My eyes were heavy, and my brain was getting foggy.

"He's helping us get to Columbia. That's where Hank steps in. He's helping us to Honduras and Boone is taking over from there, getting us into the United States."

"How?" I asked when no one else did.

"I have a friend that owes me a favor. We're leaving it at that until we get there."

I was vaguely aware that the conversation continued

around me. Potholes constantly tried to jolt me awake, but they didn't do anything more than make me stir.

When we stopped, I woke up long enough to move from the van to some sort of ATV on steroids. The man driving the ATV was indeed an ogre. While Taylor worked things out with him, I once again slept. When the new vehicle roared to life, however, there was no way to get any rest.

Wedged between Rider and Vincent, I was very uncomfortable. The road to the man's shed wasn't a smooth one. By the time we stopped again, I was in agony from bumping my arm repeatedly.

The pain was enough to take my mind off the fact that we were at someone's decrepit shed in the middle of nowhere. When the shed opened to show a small airplane, I was somewhat surprised.

"How are you holding up?" Vincent asked when we entered the plane.

I was too tired to lie. "Badly." Seeing the look on his face, I knew I should have at least made the effort. "I'll be okay when we stop moving."

Taylor hovered over me during the flight, but I only noticed the few times I woke up. It wasn't until we landed in Columbia that I was even aware we had stopped to refuel along the way.

When we stepped out of the plane, the air was hot and felt thick until a breeze picked up. Each time the wind stopped, it was as though a weight pressed down on me, making it hard to breath.

Taylor's friend didn't wait around and I couldn't say that I blamed him. This strip seemed to be in the middle of nowhere. A small building was there that looked as though it was falling apart, and we were surrounded by forest. It felt very isolated.

"Are you sure this is the spot?" Taylor asked, looking around nervously.

"These are the coordinates Hank gave us," Logan said.

"You're sure he isn't setting us up for another attempt to keep us quiet?" Renick asked. "No offense to Cassie, but she doesn't look up for helping us out like last time."

Renick pointed in my direction, and it was only then that I realized I was leaning heavily on Vincent. I stood up a little straighter, although there wasn't much point. He was right. I wasn't good for much of anything except maybe holding down a pillow.

Long after Taylor's friend disappeared, someone walked out of the forest.

"Keep on your toes," Logan said in a low voice. He stepped forward and waited for the approaching man.

The stranger stopped maybe five yards away, and it was evident that he was armed. He spoke in rapid-fire Spanish, practically barking out the words. He looked us over and started pointing at me and sneering. His voice grew louder.

"He does not sound happy," Rider said, slowly moving toward Vincent and me.

Taylor broke in in a rush, joining the conversation.

"He thinks you're sick," Vincent said. "He doesn't want to spread something contagious."

That made me actually feel better about the man.

Taylor came over and carefully rolled up my sleeve. He pulled back the bandages to show an angry red mass that seemed to throb worse in the heat.

"It's time to clean this again anyway," Taylor mumbled.

The man seemed satisfied and pulled out a long-range radio while Taylor cleaned and dressed the wound once more.

"When we get to Honduras," Taylor said, "we need to track down some antibiotics in a hurry."

"That won't be a problem," Boone said.

"A hospital would be even better," Taylor said. "We might need to go that route anyway."

"It's that bad?" Vincent asked, shifting his weight toward me, I could tell he was trying to hold me up.

I patted his arm reassuringly.

"She was shot in the jungle," Taylor said. "Since then, we haven't been in a clean environment, much less a sterile one. I can't keep the infection back without some much stronger antibiotics."

"You'll have everything you need," Boone said. To me, he added, "you'll be fine in no time."

The man started talking to Logan again and waved to the end of the airstrip. Another small plane waited for us. Inwardly, I was groaning.

We were stuffed into the little plane like sardines. Even with the discomfort, I fell asleep almost immediately once I was off my feet.

CHAPTER

TWENTY-FIVE

A beeping noise woke me up and I opened my eyes before I remembered I had no idea where I was. Had I remembered, I might have kept them closed longer until I got a better sense of my surroundings.

With the noise and the odd feeling of oxygen being pumped up my nose as I breathed, I had a good idea that I was at least being looked after, even if I didn't know where I was.

It was dark in the room and I had the feeling we were moving. The walls looked like... metal and cloth? It took me a minute to realize there was a curtain around my bed.

Vincent was also there. He was asleep on what looked like a very uncomfortable chair.

I stared at him and couldn't help but smile. We hadn't had time to talk yet, but it didn't matter much. It was more important that he be here now. It didn't matter that he had been gone before.

He must have felt my gaze on him, because he opened his eyes. He looked really cranky until he saw I was awake.

"You're up," he said, sounding almost surprised. He breathed deeply. "And feeling better."

I wrinkled my nose up at the reminder that he had a sense of what I was feeling.

"I mean, how are you feeling?" he asked, apparently noticing my expression.

I grinned at him. "Better. Where are we?"

"Almost to Texas, I think."

"What happened to Honduras?"

"We met up with Boone's friend there. He's a captain in the Coast Guard and he's getting us back in the country."

"That seems like a big thing for Boone to ask for," I said.

Vincent shrugged. "Boone said he called in a favor. The captain didn't even ask many questions." He hesitated. "I should go get Taylor." He stood to leave.

"Don't go yet." I patted the edge of the narrow bed. "How are you feeling? Taylor mentioned that you weren't well, but I haven't had a chance to ask you about it."

"I'm fine," he said.

I raised my eyebrow at him.

He sighed. "I'm not sure what happened. At one point, it felt like I was being torn in two, but I assure you, I'm fine now. One hundred percent."

"How is everyone else? I don't even know what happened."

"Rider had a pretty bad head injury, but he seems fine now. Logan was trying to find an enemy on the ground that he could fight, but Fenrir caught up with him. I'm not sure what happened there, but Logan was fine after a little while."

I wanted to ask more. Much, much more, but I didn't know where to start and I was starting to get worn down.

"You and I should talk sometime," Vincent said.

I blinked a few times, confused. "I thought we *were* talking."

"I missed a lot while I was away and it seems to be affecting things now. Rider told me to talk to you about it."

"We must have missed a lot from your end as well." I wasn't going to ask why he stayed away for so long.

"There is something," Vincent said, "but I never pictured asking you about it in a place like this. When we're home, maybe. When you're feeling better."

"Fair enough," I said, feeling intrigued.

✻

BY THE TIME the ship reached its destination, I was actually starting to feel like a real person again. Boone's friend dropped us off at a car rental place, where Hank had a large van with four rows of seating for us to stretch out in. Well, stretch out may have been an overstatement once we were all inside and our gear was stowed, but at least we weren't bumping up against one another.

Taylor drove, Vincent drove, and finally Logan drove until we arrived at my house.

My stomach churned with nervous energy, but I didn't know why. I was home, after all.

"I'm taking the van with me back to the city," Taylor said. "Let your grandmother know I'll talk with her later. Vincent, Cassie, I want you in the clinic or with Dr. Yelton tomorrow."

Once we had all of our supplies out of the van, we waved Taylor off. Our breath hung on the cold air.

"I want to go check on the kids," Logan said. "Renick, why don't you come with me? You can use Jonathan's old room until you decide what to do. Tell Margaret I'll be over—"

"You'll tell me yourself," Gran said, stepping outside the house.

Logan grinned. "It's good to see you, Margaret. You have no idea how good."

Gran gave him a quick hug before turning to me and wrapping her arms around me, careful not to touch my arm, even though she knew nothing about it yet.

By the time Gran pulled away, we were both teary eyed. I knew how close I came to missing all this and to never coming back.

Gran might have known as well.

"And you boys," Gran said, "why don't you grab those bags and come inside. I've got dinner waiting. Logan, you and your new friend can join us once you're settled in. Where's Fenrir?"

"How do you know Fenrir?" I asked as the wolf appeared from the Path next to Gran.

"I asked him to go with Taylor to find you," Gran said.

Rider picked up our bags and carried them to the door, following Gran. Boone picked up the remaining gear and did the same.

Vincent and I were left alone, standing in the cold evening air.

"So," I said, "I guess technically we're off work now."

"I think *technically* we've been off work since they tried to blow us up," Vincent said. "But I know what you mean. We'll have to sort out how this is going to work."

"We can talk inside," I said.

It wasn't until Vincent walked in that I remembered that this was the first time he'd visited since we'd adopted Molly.

With a screech, Molly thudded into the room. She ignored Boone and Rider—she'd met them before—and made a fast beeline straight for Vincent.

"Molly," I warned, but before I got anything else out, she skidded to a stop between Vincent and me, her claws etching grooves into the wood floor of the entryway, and bared her fangs.

Molly was an ichneu, kin to the ichneumon, which was a creature of legend that killed dragons. Molly still looked like a large house cat, although she might have been crossbred with a sabretooth at some point, because her fangs were indeed fangs.

"Brrrr?" Molly looked at Vincent and me.

That noise wasn't what I had expected from her. Hissing, hair standing on end, biting and clawing—those, I kind of expected. The confused purr was new.

"What is that?" Vincent asked, his voice monotone.

"This is Molly," I said.

Molly curled around my feet, watching Vincent intently as though unsure of what he was. Then she backed up a few steps, opened her wings and launched herself up to my shoulder. From there, she stretched out her nose toward Vincent.

"Molly, this is Vincent," I introduced him as though Molly understood every word I said. I was still unclear on whether she could or not.

Vincent blinked at Molly, then looked at me. I could tell he was trying to keep his stoic face blank, but it was a losing battle. Molly had that effect on people, although usually not until they had known her for a while.

"She never acts this way. Hold out your hand to let her smell you," I said.

Vincent did so, and Molly stretched out even farther, and then put her paw on his hand as well.

"Well, I'll be," Gran said, coming in from the kitchen. "I have never seen that creature take to someone she just met."

Molly tottered on my shoulder and Vincent's eyes danced.

"What are you amused with?" I asked.

"She's cute," Vincent said.

"She's supposed to be vicious." I reached up and scratched her behind the ears. She moved her head around and sniffed my hand, acting as though she and I had just met. "Some guard cat you are."

"It's good to see you, Vincent. And Molly already knows you're one of the family. Isn't that nice." Gran walked up and gave Vincent a hug, much to Vincent's surprise. "I'm glad you're back."

Molly, apparently bored now that she knew there was no threat in the house, leapt off my shoulder and bounded over to the couch, where she promptly curled up and went to sleep.

"Fenrir is around here somewhere," I said. "I'm not sure what Molly will think of him."

"He's met her," Gran said, to my surprise. "I can't say that they took to each other. Get on in here. Logan, Hank, and that other man are going to be back over here in ten minutes. With this many people, we'll have to eat in shifts." Gran laughed. "I'm sure we can make room in any case."

The smells in the kitchen were amazing. Gran had put together beef stroganoff, which was one of my favorites. There was also a layered cake that looked divine.

"Now, Mr. Boone, you can take the room upstairs," Gran said as we ate. "I already have it made up for you. Vincent, your room has fresh sheets, but I'm a little fuzzy on if you need them. Rider, you're welcome to stay as well."

"Thank you, Margaret, but I am looking forward to my own bed tonight," Rider said.

Since I wasn't sure if we could tell Gran where we had gone or anything that had happened, I asked her about her trip with Dee Dee.

She filled in the silence as we ate, telling us all about her trip and getting 'that nice young doctor' to go get us.

I skipped dessert for the time being and made my escape upstairs. There had been showers on the ship, but they were small and cramped. I was ready for a real shower or maybe even a bath.

I looked around my room, feeling lost. It was a shame I couldn't wash away some of the memories from our trip.

At the same time, though, I wanted to remember. I *needed* to remember. It couldn't happen again.

"Cass?" Vincent came up behind me. "What's wrong?"

I wiped away tears I hadn't realized had been running down my face. "Nothing. Just... remembering."

He nodded and looked unsure about what to say.

"You wanted to talk to me?" I asked, changing the subject. "On the ship you mentioned asking me something when we got back home."

"I thought I'd wait—"

"Who knows when you'll get another chance?"

He took my hand for a minute. "That's true."

I waited, not wanting to rush him, but in truth, I really wanted to know what he wanted to talk about.

Still, I held my tongue.

"Not a lot of people know much about Walkers," he started. "What they do know is enough to make everyone nervous and cause rumors to spread like fire."

He stopped again and my mind felt more awake. It buzzed with the anticipation of learning more. I sat on the bed and gestured to the chair next to it.

"I mentioned that my sister can walk in and out of this world easily. For me, it's a lot harder. The space between worlds doesn't run by normal rules. If I step out of this world and take two steps, I might end up being ten miles away when I come back, which is dangerous." He sat on the offered chair and took my hand again.

"What happens if you come back to this world so far away?"

"I could end up Walking straight into the center of a hill or in the middle of a wall or tree. It's not a nice way to go. My sister senses this world strongly. By feel, she can come back in just the place she wants to. Some of the stories about Walkers are about those with that ability."

He seemed to be talking around the subject, but I let him take his own path to his question.

"For me, I have to have an anchor in this world in order to come back. My sister ties me to this world."

Thoughts raced about what would occur if something happened to his sister while he was between the worlds.

"She's not the only one," he added when he saw the alarmed look on my face. "There are objects and landmarks that I know as well. Those are more dangerous, though. I can never be sure if it's been moved or shifted. When my sister senses me, however, she can make her surroundings safe enough for me to return without issue."

I'd had no idea it worked like that, but it seemed the wrong thing to say. Of course, I didn't know about it, not when so few knew about Walkers.

"You can sense her no matter how far away she is?"

"Yes, I can sense all the anchors."

"It seems like it would take you months to get to her if you went by foot." That was probably an exaggeration, but not much of one.

"Distance and space don't work the same way between the worlds. It's true that someone farther away is likely to take longer to get to, but if you know the right paths, you can shorten the space between you and the anchor."

"That's why it takes you so long to get back, though, isn't it?"

"It is, and I want to fix that."

"How?"

"I want you to be my anchor."

My eyes turned misty and I blinked rapidly. It felt like the sweetest thing anyone had ever asked me, and I didn't even really know what it meant. "How do I become your anchor?"

"It takes time, mostly. Time spent close together. But there are some other things to do when the time is right."

I smiled, liking the sound of that. "So if I'm your anchor, you'd get back to this world faster."

"Yes, but it still could take time. It won't be immediate."

"I'll do it," I said.

"I'm not the best person to be around when I come back," Vincent warned. "You may want to take some time—"

"I don't care," I said. "That doesn't matter. It's getting you back and that's what matters."

He smiled, which made my heart jump.

"I, um, should probably go," Vincent said, standing.

I stood and didn't let him let go of my hand. "Don't. Not tonight."

He kissed me. My toes curled and my insides quivered.

When he pulled away, there was no getting the smile off my face.

I put my good arm around him and he pulled me to close. "You said time close together, right?"

"I did."

"Let's get started on that."

Want to read further?
Krampus (AIR Series Book 9)

Writing the AIR series has been a fun and amazing experience. There's more planned for Cassie and her partners!

If you enjoyed this book, please leave a review on the site where you made the purchase. Leaving a review helps the reader and author in many ways. Your support is appreciated!

Thank you for reading!
Amanda Booloodian

COMPLETE WORKS

Complete works by Amanda Booloodian:

AIR Series (In Reading Order)
Stonecoat: Novella 0 (AIR Series Book 0)
Shattered Soul (AIR Series Book 1)
Redcap (AIR Series Book 2)
Broken Paths (AIR Series Book 3)
Stolen Sight (AIR Series Book 4)
Fenrisúlfr: Novella 3.5 (AIR Series 5)
Fractured Worlds (AIR Series Book 6)
Reliquary (AIR Series Book 7)
Never-Ending Nightmare (AIR Series Book 8)
Krampus (AIR Series Book 9)
Eclipsed Pathways (AIR Series Book 10)
Void (AIR Series Book 11)
Marked Soul (AIR Series Book 12)

AIR Series Box Set
AIR Series Books 0-4: Welcome to the Farm
AIR Series Books 5-8: Conspiracy Theory
AIR Series Books 9-12: Redacted

Spellbound Murder Series
Oath Bound (Spellbound Murder Series Book 1)
Grim Magic (Spellbound Murder Series Book 2)
Fallen Witch (Spellbound Murder Book 3)

Spellbound Murder Box Set
Spellbound Murder Complete Trilogy

AIR Series Audiobooks
Stonecoat: Novella 0.5 (AIR Series Book 0)
Shattered Soul (AIR Series Book 1)
Redcap (AIR Series Book 2)
Broken Paths (AIR Series Book 3)
Stolen Sight (AIR Series Book 4)
Fenrisúlfr: Novella 3.5 (AIR Series 5)
Fractured Worlds (AIR Series Book 6)
Reliquary (AIR Series Book 7)
Never-Ending Nightmare (AIR Series Book 8)
Krampus (AIR Series Book 9)
Eclipsed Pathways (AIR Series Book 10)
Void (AIR Series Book 11)
Marked Soul (AIR Series Book 12)

Spellbound Murder Series Audiobooks
Oath Bound (Spellbound Murder Series Book 1)
Grim Magic (Spellbound Murder Series Book 2)
Fallen Witch (Spellbound Murder Book 3)

ABOUT THE AUTHOR

Amanda Booloodian lives in Missouri with her loving, and often times peculiar, husband. She has been passionate about the written word throughout her life. Now, much of her spare time is spent at the computer, delving into worlds accessible only through vivid imagination. In warm weather, when she isn't pounding on the keyboard, she can often be found wandering through the wilderness. Occasionally she gets it into her head to SCUBA dive or to sit back at home and make wine, which can have interesting results and inspire her writing.

You can find out more about Amanda and her writing, including upcoming releases, on www.Booloodian.com. You can also find her on Facebook: Amanda Booloodian - Author and Instagram: AJBooloodian.

9 781947 382848